the GOOD AFGHAN

KEVIN MAURER

A PERMUTED PRESS BOOK
ISBN: 978-1-63758-426-2
ISBN (eBook): 978-1-63758-427-9

The Good Afghan

Permuted Press, LLC
New York • Nashville
permutedpress.com

Published in the United States of America
1 2 3 4 5 6 7 8 9 10

Anything worth fighting for is worth fighting dirty for.

—*Rusty Bradley*

AFGHANISTAN 2010

CHAPTER 1

It was exhausting living in fear of the sky.

Razaq gazed out of the window at the clouds above. He used to think as a child that Allah looked down through the holes on a cloudy day. Now, only the Americans did.

"Quiet," he hissed, trying to get the two men in the truck's front seat to stop talking about cricket. "Listen."

They had left Spin Boldak before dawn hoping to make it to their destination before the sun rose. But the rutted road was in disrepair, forcing them to drive slowly for fear of damaging a tire or axle. Now, the sun was over the horizon and they were late.

Razaq searched the sky.

He craned his neck hoping to pick up the faint sound of an engine, or worse, the boom of a Hellfire missile. His hands flicked prayer beads back and forth in an attempt to burn off nervous energy.

Then he saw it.

A glint of sunlight off something metallic. Razaq blinked his eyes. He slid forward in his seat and pressed his face against the dirt-streaked glass of the passenger window. Another flash of sunlight off metal.

"Pull over," he said, slapping the driver on the back of the head. "Pull over now."

The white 4x4 Toyota Hilux pickup truck slowed to a stop, and Razaq bolted from his seat. The skinny old man ran for a small cluster of trees at the speed of fright. His bodyguard climbed out of the truck, scanning the sky for the drone.

"Stay by the truck," he told the driver.

"But what if there is a drone?" the driver said, looking into the gray sky.

Zahir, Razaq's bodyguard, shrugged.

"Then we'll all meet Allah today."

Razaq watched as Zahir strolled over to his hiding place. The boy didn't understand what the drones could do, he thought. The boy had never seen the crater after a strike and the body parts of friends or family thrown like dice across the ground.

"Get down, fool," Razaq said as Zahir reached the trees.

"OK," Zahir said. "OK, I'm here."

Razaq looked back at the truck.

"Why did you leave the driver?"

Zahir squatted next to the elder. "Because if we have to leave, I want to be able to go quickly."

Razaq nodded. It was a good decision, even if it cost the driver his life.

"What did you see, Commander?" Zahir asked.

"A reflection. Some sunlight off a wing. It had to be a drone."

Zahir looked up.

"I don't see anything."

Razaq was still scanning the sky. He saw the gray bug-like aircraft in his nightmares.

"Do you hear it?" he said. "Do you hear the buzz of the engine?"

"I hear only the wind," Zahir said. "Come, we've got to go. I am sure the drone is after another target. No one knows our mission."

Razaq looked at his bodyguard and then at the truck.

"How can we be sure?"

"We can't," Zahir said. "But, *inshallah*, we make it to our meeting safely."

"And if Allah doesn't will it?" Razaq said.

"Then we will meet him and get paid for our years of jihad."

Zahir helped the old man up.

"I don't want to meet Allah today."

"I don't either," Zahir said as they walked back to the truck.

The dusty road took them to a highway near Kandahar City and eventually into the city proper. Razaq's anxiety waned as they fought the traffic on the outskirts of town. The Americans wouldn't shoot a missile if civilians were around. It was why he lived so close to a school in Spin Boldak. The best armor was the innocent.

At the eastern edge of the city, they caught the Kandahar-Ghazni highway north toward a small village near Jaldak in Ghazni Province. Abdullah, an old friend, wanted to meet. The village was a collection of biscuit-colored compounds with a dirt road down the middle. From the air, the compounds were arranged like the six on a dice cube. A little creek ran down the east side of the village, providing water to a few grape fields and a small pomegranate orchard.

The driver parked the truck outside Abdullah's walled compound, which sat at the end of a row. The gate's peephole opened, and a small child with a dirt-streaked face and a mop of curly hair peeked out. Zahir asked the boy to get his grandfather. A few minutes later, the gate creaked open. Zahir went first, keeping his AK-47 rifle aimed at the ground. Razaq followed. Abdullah met them in the courtyard with an embrace.

"Come, old friend," Abdullah said in Pashto, ushering him toward the house.

Razaq stopped.

"What's wrong, Razaq?" Abdullah asked, putting his arm around the elder.

Being in the house was too claustrophobic. Razaq didn't want to die in a mud box.

"Let's talk in the orchard," he said, nodding to the bodyguard to lead the way. "Safer to keep moving. Bring your grandsons."

Zahir led Razaq and Abdullah out of the gate and under the canopy of trees in the orchard. Razaq couldn't see the sky any longer.

"Zahir," he said. "Take Abdullah's grandsons and show them your rifle. We will talk here."

"It has been a long time," Abdullah said when the boys were out of earshot but close enough to protect him from a drone strike. "It is good to see you. You look strong."

Razaq knew Abdullah was lying.

"War is for the hearty," Razaq said. "Long are the days in the mountains, but that is why we call it jihad."

"I'm too old for that," Abdullah said. "I'd break an ankle up in those mountains."

"You have become soft like a woman," Razaq said. "But in your time, I'd have followed you to hell."

"I'm glad I led you better than that."

"I wouldn't have survived without you."

"Your brother deserves the credit," Abdullah said. "I still mourn his passing."

Razaq nodded and looked away.

"How is your family?" Razaq asked.

"Very good," he said. "Yours?"

Razaq didn't have any family left. At least, no family he claimed. Abdullah knew that, but it was impolite not to ask.

"I hear your nephew is doing well," Abdullah said. "I hear he is very rich."

Razaq had heard the same rumors.

"You raised him well," Abdullah said. "But he has a little of his father in him."

"Too much," Razaq said. "Headstrong."

Razaq didn't want to talk about his nephew or the past any longer. He hoped since they were old friends they could move past the pleasantries and get down to business.

"Why did you call me here? It wasn't to talk about past fights and dead friends."

"Some farmers found something," Abdullah said. "It was buried in a grape field."

"What is it?"

"I think it was left by the Russians. The writing doesn't look like the Americans'. Maybe it's a bomb?"

"What am I supposed to do with an old Russian bomb? Why didn't you get in touch with the local commander?"

"I trust you," Abdullah said. "If it is dangerous, I don't want it in my village."

"Show it to me."

Back at the truck, Abdullah gave the driver directions to a nearby hill.

"What are we doing, Commander?" Zahir asked.

"Abdullah says some farmers found an old Soviet bomb," Razaq said. "How is your Russian?"

"Passable," Zahir said. "It was my mother's native tongue, but I haven't spoken it since she died."

Zahir looked like a Westerner. His hair was fair and his eyes were blue, but he was an Afghan. His father was a communist and had gone to study in Moscow. He came home with a wife.

"But you can read?"

"Yes," Zahir said.

The truck bounced up the dirt track toward some grape mounds. A chest-high dirt wall separated the fields. The driver stopped near a gap in the wall.

Zahir led the way into the field, his AK-47 held close to his body as he followed the path along the perimeter. Grapes grew over dirt mounds, but it wasn't the season. Instead, the mounds looked like uncooked cookies on a tray waiting for a turn in the oven. Zahir stopped at the third row and walked to the middle of the field.

"It's buried at the bottom of one of the mounds," Razaq said.

Zahir saw the upturned dirt and some shovels and other tools. The hole was little more than a crevice at the bottom of the mound. Razaq peered into the darkness and then stepped back to inspect the opening.

"I'll get it," Zahir said.

He handed his rifle to Razaq.

"Be careful," Razaq said.

Zahir sucked in his breath and shimmied his way into the crevice headfirst. A few seconds later, Razaq saw Zahir's thighs, then his waist, and finally his chest. It looked like the Earth was giving birth. As more and more of Zahir appeared, Razaq heard something scraping against the rocks. Zahir was covered in dust as he slid from the mouth of the hole.

"It's too big to fit through the opening," he said.

Razaq peered into the hole.

"What is it?"

"I don't know," Zahir said, picking up a shovel. "But someone didn't want anyone to find it."

Zahir attacked the face of the hole, first widening it and then digging a trench so the box could slide out.

"Help me," Zahir said, reaching into the hole and dragging the box forward.

The box was breaching the hole.

"Use the shovel and see if you can make the hole a little wider."

Razaq lifted the shovel and knocked the loose rocks and sand away. Zahir pulled on the box with all his strength. The corners cracked and it slid free.

In the afternoon sun, the wooden box looked old and worn. It was no bigger than a footlocker. Razaq held his breath as Zahir opened a clasp on the lid. Inside was a polished metal cylinder embedded in one half of an old leather case. Some sort of component was in the opposite side of the case. Wires connected both sides, but the mechanism and wires looked old and neglected. A manual was wedged between the case and the box. The pages were torn and littered the box.

Zahir reached for the manual.

"Careful," Razaq said.

Zahir chuckled.

"If it was that fragile, don't you think it would have exploded when we dragged it out of the hole?"

Zahir found a small section near the back of the manual that was legible. He looked at the writing and then back at the box. Zahir didn't trust what he was reading. His Russian was rusty, but the cylinder was like nothing he'd seen before. If he was reading the warnings in the back of the manual correctly, they'd stumbled upon something a weapon could tip the scales in their favor.

"Well?" Razaq said. He was impatient and didn't want to be out in the open any longer. "What is it?"

"Commander," Zahir said. "I think this is a Soviet nuclear bomb."

CHAPTER 2

The wheels of the gray C-17 cargo plane screeched when they hit the tarmac. The engines revved as the plane slowed, finally stopping at the end of the runway. The plane taxied to the terminal, and the Air Force crew chiefs—dressed in heavy body armor—opened the gray hydraulic cargo ramp. The cool temperature enjoyed at altitude was replaced by the oppressive heat of late summer.

Welcome to Kandahar, Charlie thought as he pulled his ever-present tan Third Special Forces Group ball cap over his shaggy graying hair and soft hazel eyes and walked down the ramp with a smile.

He was home.

Charlie cleared the ramp just as tan trucks and forklifts arrived to remove the cargo. The crew chiefs snapped off the tie-down straps and rolled the pallets to the waiting forklifts. Cargo planes—both Air Force and commercial—were parked nearby. The other soldiers on the C-17 filed off toward a white bus, but Charlie spotted a bearded guy in shorts standing off to the side.

"Charlie? Blake," the guy said, shaking Charlie's hand. "Got any more gear?"

Charlie tossed his small brown backpack into the bed of the Hilux—the Afghan equivalent of a Toyota Tacoma compact pickup truck. He looked back at the C-17.

"My rucksack and two Tuff Boxes are on the baggage pallet."

"I'll send some guys over to the terminal to get them," Blake said.

Charlie climbed into the front seat as Blake started the engine.

"Good flight?" Blake asked.

"Yeah, one stop in Germany."

Blake smiled.

"Crew rest."

Charlie nodded.

"Beer fest," he said. "Two days. I watched the crew drink their faces off the first night. I love the Air Force."

Blake laughed.

"So much for being at war."

Blake flashed his flight-line badge at the gate and merged with the rest of the traffic on the road running parallel to the airfield.

"You been to KAF before?" Blake asked.

KAF was short for Kandahar Airfield.

"Yeah. A couple of times," Charlie replied. "This place has gotten big."

The road was clogged with military and civilian trucks. It was at the end of lunch, and soldiers stationed at the base from all over the world—America, New Zealand, Great Britain—were coming back from the chow hall.

"About thirty thousand troops and contractors," Blake said. "It's easy to forget guys are fighting less than twenty miles away. Been a while since you've been here?"

"Two years," Charlie said.

"Wait until you see the Boardwalk," Blake said. "You'll flip your wig. Fucking TGI Fridays and everything. It's like Disneyland."

"TGI Fridays, really?" Charlie said, shaking his head.

It was a short ride to Camp Brown, the Special Forces compound. Charlie scratched his gray whiskers and yawned as the guard waved the truck through the gate.

"Boss said to drop you off at overflow. You can crash and then catch up with him after the future ops meeting and before the BUB."

Battle update brief. Commanders usually held the meeting daily to offer guidance and stay up on the day's battle rhythm. It sounded important, but it was often boring.

"Sounds good," Charlie said.

Up ahead, he saw the tan headquarters building and the white latrine building. He was getting his bearings. Blake passed the latrine and made a right turn, parking along a series of wooden B-huts, squat wooden buildings used for offices and barracks. Charlie hopped out of the truck and grabbed his pack.

"Your room will be ready today," Blake said, then looked at his watch.

"If you hurry, you can just make lunch. You know where the DFAC is?"

Dining facility.

Charlie smiled. Blake climbed back into the truck.

"I'll get some of the boys to go over and get your stuff now."

Charlie waved as Blake put the truck in reverse and left. Charlie opened the wooden door and stepped into the dark B-hut. Made of plywood, it was about the size of a three-car garage. Metal bunks were set up along the walls, with a narrow path down the middle. A few soldiers were sleeping on bunks in the back corner. Charlie threw his pack onto a bunk near the door. It was a toss-up between hunger and sleep, but his bunk would be there after the chow hall closed. He held the door as he left so it wouldn't slam.

After a short walk, he arrived at the DFAC, a tan building near the front gate. Charlie washed his hands under the scalding water at the sink just inside the door and grabbed a brown tray. Lunch was pretty picked over. Meatloaf, some sort of canned vegetable medley, sandwich meat, and some dry hamburgers and soggy fries. Charlie opted for a sandwich, an apple, and water. Scanning the dining hall, he spotted Frank in the corner reading over some PowerPoint slides.

Frank's food sat untouched. He looked up as Charlie approached.

"Charlie!" Frank said. "What's up, man?"

Frank stood up and gave Charlie a half hug before sitting back down.

"Hey, Frankie, or should I say Major Spitz?"

"How about sir?"

Both men laughed. Frank was Charlie's former team leader. They'd deployed together on the same Special Forces team when Charlie was the senior engineer. Officers came and went every two years, but Frank was one of the good ones. Now, Charlie was a warrant officer and Frank oversaw operations for every Special Forces team in southern Afghanistan. Charlie nodded at the pile of slides next to Frank's tray.

"I see they let you animals out of the TOC."

The tactical operations center was where staff officers like Frank fought the war one PowerPoint slide at a time.

"Just barely," Frank said. "We've got a couple of ops tonight. More tomorrow. Takes forty slides to get out of the wire now. Death by PowerPoint."

"How's it going?"

"Like shit," Frank said. "Back when we were out there, the Taliban were in the villages. We usually ran into them on patrol but never in the city. Now, they're blowing up restaurants in Kabul. That's why I asked you to come out. I know you want a team, but I need you first."

"What do you need me to do?"

Frank gathered up his papers.

"You got time to walk with me? I've got a meeting."

Charlie picked up his tray. The two men walked silently through the chow hall's exit. Both paused to slide on their sunglasses before walking toward the headquarters building.

"I need you to get a handle on things," Frank said. "The other chief had to go back to Bragg on emergency leave. But in reality, we fired him."

Charlie shook his head and let out a little whistle.

"Pete was a good dude," Charlie said. "What happened?"

Frank grabbed the door to the headquarters and held it for Charlie.

"He didn't get it. Look around. Guys are tired. Every year, Washington and Big Army come up with a new mission."

"Mission creep," Charlie said.

"We're sending guys out to the villages now," Frank said. "I want to make sure we're putting teams in the right spot. That's where you come in."

Charlie followed Frank through the headquarters' lobby toward the hallway that led to the TOC. He glanced at the memorial wall. The list of names of his brothers who'd been killed since 2001 was a lot longer than he remembered. Frank stopped at the door of the TOC and punched in the access code on its digital keypad.

"That still doesn't explain why you called for me by name," Charlie said.

"We need a win," Frank said. "We're still looking for bin Laden. Fucker vanished nine years ago. Locally, we've had four suicide bombers in the last month. One hit an American convoy. Roadside bomb incidents are up too. It's getting like Iraq over here. I want to shut it down. Who's making them? Where are they? Where's that shipment of bomb-making materials? We need to know, now. I figured you were the man for the job."

Charlie smiled. What Frank was asking for was a miracle, but he was up for it. What did he have to lose? He was just happy to be back in the fight. It beat sweating his ass off in North Carolina training future Special Forces soldiers.

"Roger, Cap," Charlie said.

"Find me some targets, Charlie," Frank said. "Ones that move the needle. We need to show Washington that we can dig this one out. Otherwise, we'll leave here like Iraq, telling the world we won only to watch it all fall apart. Let's spike the football before we go."

CHAPTER 3

Charlie tried to sleep, but every time the door to the hut slammed, he woke up.

Pulling on his boots, Charlie walked back to the TOC and punched in the code. The red light signifying a TIC, or "troops in contact," was lit, which meant American forces were in a firefight.

Charlie slipped into the room and walked toward the back. The TOC was built on a half-circle platform that resembled an altar. A Predator feed—"Kill TV"—took up the main screen, showing a dusty road with a line of American trucks. A pilot's voice echoed through the speakers.

The JTAC—an Air Force sergeant tasked with calling in air strikes—was talking the Predator drone onto the target. Charlie heard gunfire each time the JTAC keyed the mic.

"Vengeance Four One, Roulette Three Three," the JTAC said. "We are taking small-arms fire from across the river. Unable to provide direction. Lead vehicle disabled and unable to move column at this time. No known friendlies across river. We see something south of the bridge, possible weapons fire. Scan and report. How copy?"

Charlie stood in the back watching the Predator feed. The drone's camera followed the road that paralleled the river. A truck was parked near the bridge. Seconds later, a staccato of flashes erupted. The hot gasses from the burning gunpowder appeared like deep black accents against the gray screen. The picture shifted as the Predator started its attack run.

"Vengeance in from the southwest," the Predator pilot said.

"Vengeance, Roulette Three Three, you're cleared hot," the JTAC said.

"Copy, cleared hot," the pilot said. "In three, two, one..."

A hush fell over the TOC as everyone waited. From out of the frame there was a flash. The missile hit the truck dead center. The engine flipped end over end as the truck's body was engulfed in a cloud of smoke. The missile detonated with such force the fighters were obliterated. Their bodies remained invisible in the sandy gloom.

The JTAC came back on the radio and thanked the Predator pilot. The tension of the fight quickly switched to the next problem. A team on patrol needed an emergency supply drop. The Predator strike was already forgotten.

With Kill TV done, Charlie headed for the intelligence office. It sat off the right side of the TOC. He punched in the code and entered the room. Maps and pictures of possible targets covered the wall. A large table cluttered with laptops and intelligence reports was situated in the middle of the room. Intelligence analysts sifted through radio intercepts, satellite pictures, and Afghan tips, trying to build a clear picture of what was going on in southern Afghanistan.

Blake met Charlie at the door.

"Hey, Chief," Blake said, his lip packed with snuff. "Thought you were racking out."

"Couldn't sleep," Charlie said. "Figured I'd send an email back to household six and the kids."

"Roger," he said. "I talked to the camp mayor. Your room is ready. Your stuff is there now."

"Sounds good," Charlie said. "I'll move in later."

"Let me show you your desk."

Blake walked him over to an empty desk at the far end of the room. Two laptops sat on the wooden desk. One had a red cord connecting it to the SIPR net (Classified/Secret internet)—evident by the stickers warning the user about illegal disclosure—and the second computer, with an "unclassified" sticker, was connected to the NIPR net (Public/Non-Secret internet) by a green cord.

"Let me introduce you to the crew," Blake said.

Two analysts—an African American female and a pudgy white kid with thick glasses—looked up at Charlie.

"Hey, this is Chief Book," Blake said. "He's taking over for Pete."

Charlie shook hands with the woman first.

"Specialist White," she said. "Nice to meet you, Chief Book."

"Charlie or Chief. You pick."

Specialist White smiled.

"Ebony."

The pudgy guy was next.

"Chris. Nice to meet you, Chief."

"Don't let me get in the way," Charlie said. "We'll officially meet tomorrow after I get read in."

Blake gathered up his notebook.

"I've got the future ops brief," Blake said. "You want to come?"

"No, unless you need me," Charlie said.

"I think we can manage, Chief. The war ain't going anywhere."

Charlie opened his unclassified computer and logged in to his AOL account. He typed a message to his wife, Cheryl.

Hey honey,

Made it. Still getting settled. Just got my room. Once I get settled, we can Skype. Miss you and the boys already. Give them a squeeze for me. Love you.

Cha

The words filled the screen, but his family already felt like a distant memory. His home life—wife, two kids, mortgage—fell away when he got on the flight to Afghanistan. Charlie never wanted to be a soldier. He wanted to attend North Carolina State Universtity to be a veterinarian. Even though he was a high school football hero, Charlie knew he wasn't good enough to play at N.C. State, and his grades weren't high enough to get him into a veteraniaran school.

When the Army recruiter came to school, he figured it was his best option. Charlie was just looking for a paycheck and a ticket out of the hills of Western North Carolina. He got both and found the infantry suited him. He liked being in the field. He liked shooting. The Ranger regiment gave him an opportunity to be a cool guy and the courage to go to Special Force selection.

That is where he found his true home in the Army.

He loved being in the team room at Fort Bragg. The guys on his ODA—Operational Detachment Alpha—were his family. He spent his junior team time working out in the morning, training all day, and drinking in the Fayetteville bars with the boys at night. That cycle continued until he met Cheryl and had kids. Even with his own family, his team often came first.

But after September 11, 2001, his fun job turned into a calling. His only focus was his war life. The message to Cheryl was a formality. It was a peace offering and a way to keep his home life in balance. Cheryl came to terms with his mistress long ago. When he got home, they'd pick up like nothing happened. Until then, his mind stayed overseas.

Frank popped his head in the office.

"Thought I saw you come in," he said. "Figured you'd be doing rack ops."

"Can't find you a win on my back," Charlie said.

"If you're up, we're headed over to Ahmed Wali Gul's place later," Frank said. "He throws a party every Thursday."

"Our Wali?" Charlie asked.

"Yeah," Frank said. "Our boy is now a contractor hauling supplies for us and the Canadians, I think."

"Man, I remember when he started that business," Charlie said.

"He's a baller now," Frank said. "Fucker makes more than we do put together times ten. And he throws a good party."

"No shit," Charlie said. "He learned from the best, right? Hell yeah, I'm in."

Charlie logged off and went to clean up. On the way out of the TOC, he stopped and looked at a map near the door showing all the main roads in southern Afghanistan. The colored lines cut through the countryside linking the bases and villages. Frank's words echoed in his head.

We need a win.

With teams in the villages, he knew what was going on there. He needed to know what was happening in between. The idea hit him like a Predator strike. He needed better eyes and ears. He needed to see in the cracks.

CHAPTER 4

Ahmed Wali Gul pulled his foot up onto his chair and started to pick his toes as he listened to his operations manager ramble on about some convoy headed to Herat, the major city in western Afghanistan.

The Thursday meeting was Denise McKenna's idea. They used to do it at the rental car place she managed in Toronto. Sihe did a good job keeping things organized, but today Wali was bored and couldn't stop thinking about the party in a couple of hours. He hosted it every Thursday. Wali glanced at Khalid, a school friend who ran the finance office and managed Wali's gas station in Kandahar City, and rolled his eyes.

"OK," Wali said, putting his leg down on the floor. "Just make it happen."

Denise stammered.

"But..."

Wali closed his laptop.

"Just get the trucks to Herat, OK?"

"But we were talking about maintenance," she said. "We've got a couple of trucks down, and we need money to buy parts."

Wali looked at Khalid.

"Make it happen," he said. "Now, we've got to get ready for the party. Go out there and make sure the motor pool is cleaned up. Then go over to the flight line and pick up the raisins."

Raisins was code for beer. Namely, Vietnamese beer smuggled in by contractors from Dubai. Just having it was against General

Order Number 1, which banned US soldiers from any and all fun in Afghanistan. Wali peeled off a couple of crisp one-hundred-dollar bills.

"Take my truck and flight-line badge," he said. "They won't fuck with you."

Back at his bedroom, Wali peeled off his shalwar kameez and slid on a pair of camouflage pants and hiking boots. He pulled on a *Straight Out of Kandahar* shirt that resembled the NWA stacked logo. He walked out of his bedroom toward the sound of Khalid playing PlayStation on the sixty-inch flat screen.

"Yo," he said as he entered the room. "I've got next."

Wali slumped down on the couch. Khalid was moving a SEAL down a hallway. A terrorist who looked like Wali and his friends raised an AK-47. Khalid opened fire. The terrorist exploded into digital blood and guts.

Khalid let out a whoop.

Wali snapped his fingers and motioned for the controller.

"I'm up," he said. "But you've got to be the terrorists."

Khalid paused the game and changed his avatar. Wali loaded his favorite look—M4, beard, badass—and entered the game.

"She get everything at the flight line?"

Khalid shrugged.

"What the fuck does that mean?"

Khalid shrugged again.

"Go make sure everything is ready."

Khalid got up and shuffled toward the door. Wali turned back to the game just in time to see his soldier get hit by an RPG. Khalid was at the door with his controller.

"Allah Akbar!" he said, putting the controller on the back of the couch.

Wali hit the PlayStation's reset button.

ꕥꕥꕥ

Wali's compound was in the gray area between Kandahar Airfield and Camp Hero, an Afghan Army base. It sat near a small market that hugged the dirt road between the compounds. It comprised three buildings and was surrounded by a tall rectangular mud wall. Wali's office, living room, and bedroom were in a small building near the front gate.

A massive warehouse served as the motor pool, where supplies and parts were stored. Near the back of the compound was a small village of trailers and shipping containers converted into rooms for his workers.

In front of the warehouse was a gravel staging ground. At any time, there were a dozen trucks parked there ready to take supplies and heavy equipment to the NATO bases scattered throughout southern Afghanistan.

In Afghanistan, Friday was the off day, so Wali hosted a party every Thursday for his friends. A life preserver in an ocean of war. The party started after dark. Christmas lights were strung up on the rafters of the warehouse. The far end was a dance floor with a karaoke machine. Two large speakers and lights sat on either side of a small stage built out of plywood and spray-painted black.

Wali hung near the door. He smiled as the cacophony of conversations and the clank of beer bottles hitting the bottom of the garbage cans washed over him. The room still smelled like rubber and motor oil, but no one noticed after a few beers.

Everyone was dressed in Afghanistan chic. Cargo pants. Ball caps. Hiking boots. There were few Afghans. This wasn't their party. This was for the legion of Westerners looking to make millions by saving Afghanistan's women, economy, arts, and environment. Wali spotted Denise trying to get the crowd to settle down so she could start karaoke.

Wali always went first. With the noise at a low murmur, she waved to Wali, who grabbed the mic just as the music started.

Jay-Z. "99 Problems."

"Let's get this party started!" Wali said.

The crowd cheered as he started to rap.

If you're having girl problems, I feel bad for you, son
I got 99 problems but a bitch ain't one...

Wali paced on the stage like a caged animal, switching up the lyrics to fit the audience.

I tried to ignore him and talk to Allah
Back through the system with the Taliban again
Karzai tried to give the Pashtun the shaft again
Half-a-mil for bail cause I'm with the Americans.

The crowd clapped when Wali was done. He never knew if they did it to be polite or if he was any good. Didn't matter. It was his party.

A pair of blonde contractors from Australia replaced him. They were at the beginning of a tortured rendition of "Shoop" by Salt-N-Pepa when Wali saw Charlie by the bar. As he moved through the crowd, he shook hands and said hello to his guests but kept his eyes focused on his old friend.

Charlie looked older. Sadder. His brown hair was graying and his beard had a lot more salt in it. But he looked fit—if not a little skinnier than when they used to patrol Kandahar Province years ago.

That's how Wali got his first job with the Americans. Charlie hired him as a fixer for the base. Wali made a living getting office supplies, local clothes, and cars for the American Special Forces. He graduated to interpreter and went on missions with the team before starting his own business. Teams rotated in and out of Afghanistan, and Wali had a lot of Special Forces friends, but Charlie was his best because he was the one who changed Wali's life. There was no business, no party without Charlie.

"What's up, pimp?" Charlie said.

Wali smiled as he unscrewed the top from a bottle of water.

"Cheers," Wali said and touched the bottle to Charlie's cup. "Welcome back, brother."

Charlie took a sip of his whiskey.

"Good to be back."

Wali cocked his head.

"Come on, brother."

"Somebody has to get the bad guys," Charlie said. "Ain't no wars in North Carolina."

Wali smiled.

"Why didn't you tell me you were coming?" Wali asked. "I got your Facebook message, but I didn't know when you were coming."

"Just got in," Charlie said. "I was about to check in with you on Facebook, but Frank mentioned the party. Figured I'd surprise you."

"I'm surprised," Wali said. "You with a team?"

Charlie took a drink.

"Working with Frank."

Charlie scanned the room.

"A lot has changed. You've been busy. Frank was telling me you're one of the top trucking contractors."

Wali looked away.

"I do all right."

"How many trucks do you have now?"

"Twenty on a good day running water, food, and ammo for the Canadians and some Big Army units," Wali said. "Renting a couple of trucks and some heavy equipment to some aid groups. Sometimes I do some jobs for you guys."

Wali signaled for more whiskey for Charlie.

"What are you doing at Brown?" Wali asked.

Last time Wali talked with Charlie, he was training Green Berets at Fort Bragg and waiting to join a team.

"Got a spot where we can talk?" Charlie said.

Wali nodded and headed for the door. He led Charlie out of the motor pool and across the gravel yard to the office building. They passed the flat screen in the meeting room and went into his small private office. Wali sat in his leather desk chair. Charlie took the couch opposite. Hanging above the couch were several posters—George Bush, Tupac, Kate Upton, Jay-Z. It looked like a dorm room shared by a hip-hop fan and a Republican.

"What I am about to tell you stays between us," Charlie said.

"Cool," Wali said, but his heart was racing.

"We're losing," Charlie said. "It's been what, a decade since we got here, and how close are we to winning?"

"I don't know."

"Yes, you do," Charlie said. "We had the Taliban on the ropes in 2004, but Washington snatched defeat from the jaws of victory with the Iraq War and now here we are."

"But the Taliban can't fight you guys," Wali said. "I saw it myself. They lose when the shooting starts."

Charlie sat back and spread his arm across the back of the couch.

"They don't have to win," he said. "They never win a battle and still beat us. That's why I need your help."

Wali shrugged.

"If you need trucks, I can help," he said. "I'll give you a good price."

Charlie shook his head.

"I don't do logistics," he said. "I need eyes and ears. You've got drivers and trucks going to villages all over the country. Your drivers know where the Taliban checkpoints are. They know the safe roads. They gossip with the locals. We need to know what they're hearing."

Wali smiled.

"I never thought of it that way," he said.

Charlie smiled.

"Your network is going to help us win the war."

CHAPTER 5

Neil Canterbury felt the barrel of his Beretta M9 digging into his hip.

His holster kept the gun high on his hip and it rubbed against his love handles. He'd bought the holster online before he left Seymour Johnson Air Force Base in North Carolina. The website said it was popular with special operations soldiers and federal agents. Maybe he'd put the holster on wrong, because it wasn't comfortable at all.

Canterbury took a sip of green tea and burned his tongue. He was having a hard time feeling cool. This wasn't how he envisioned his first meeting in Afghanistan with an Afghan general.

"Tech Sergeant Sweet was sorry he didn't have time to say goodbye," Canterbury said. "He asked me to thank you for all your work in helping to protect Kandahar Airfield."

General Mohammed Jan smiled.

"I understand, Sergeant Canterbury," Jan said. "Welcome. Welcome to my country."

They were meeting in the general's office. The room was big, with a large desk polished to a mirror finish. Behind the desk was a map of southern Afghanistan. On the shelves and walls of the office stood or hung plaques from American units. The men were sitting in a small lounge area with a pair of faux leather couches and two matching faux leather chairs all on top of an ornate rug. A coffee glass table was between the chairs and couch.

Mohammed Jan was the garrison commander for the Afghan soldiers who protected Kandahar Airfield. He was rail thin with a graying beard and wavy black hair. His hooded eyes had a constant look of skepticism. He spoke some English, but with a thick accent.

"I'm here to talk about security," Canterbury said. "I'm replacing Tech Sergeant Sweet. He had to go home early. His wife had a baby."

Canterbury took out a plaque from his backpack. Embossed with the Air Force insignia, it recognized Jan's work with Tech Sergeant Sweet. Jan accepted it with a little bow, placing his right hand over his heart.

"Thank you," Jan said. "I'm sure you and I will do good work as well. Do you speak Pashto?"

Canterbury shook his head no.

"But I hope to learn while I am here," he said.

Jan smiled.

"Basir," Jan said.

The general motioned to a stocky Pashtun with jet-black hair and a long beard. Jan traded the plaque for some papers.

"Every couple of months they send me a new guy and a new plaque," Jan said to Basir in Pashto. "My walls are covered in words I can't read."

Basir laughed. Canterbury took a sip of tea. It was finally cool.

"Now, do you need anything from us?" Canterbury asked Jan.

Jan shuffled the papers from Basir.

"Yes. My men need a new building at Checkpoint Two," Jan said. "They have to stand out in the cold."

Canterbury took the papers. It was a project proposal and a bid by Jan's construction company to do the work. Total cost was about half a million dollars for a one-room guard shack.

"I will pass this along to my captain," Canterbury said.

"Please," Jan said. "Tech Sergeant Sweet said you guys would build it. He said the project was approved."

"I will get you an update immediately," Canterbury said. "Now, what are you hearing about the enemy? Any reports of Taliban activity near the base? Any threats of an attack?"

Jan shook his head.

"No," he said. "But my men did recover a mortar tube and some rounds. The Taliban were taking them into the mountains to shoot at the airport."

Mortars, Canterbury thought. *Shit yeah. Now that is something.*

"Where did your men get them?" he asked, leaning forward, his forearms resting on his knees. "Did you arrest the men?"

"At the checkpoint on the highway," Jan said. "It was a day ago. The Taliban were driving in a car. The mortar tube was in the back under some blankets."

Canterbury was taking notes as Jan spoke.

"And the Taliban?"

"In jail," Jan said. "We took them to Kandahar City."

Canterbury looked up from his notebook.

"How many?" he asked. "What were their names?"

Jan shook his head.

"I don't know," he said. "But I will have Basir find out for you."

Basir smiled at Canterbury.

"I have the mortar tube," Jan said. "Do you want it?"

Canterbury stood up.

"Yes, sir," he said.

"Excellent," Jan said. "Come with me."

Canterbury was happy to be standing. The pistol barrel no longer dug into his hip.

One of Jan's men—dressed in an Afghan Army uniform—was standing next to a shed near the back of the compound. He had the three-foot smoothbore metal tube in his arms. In a box at his feet were about a half dozen shells.

"We also have some rockets," Jan said.

Canterbury's focus was on the mortar until he heard rockets.

"You've got rockets too?"

Jan ordered his men to put the mortar tube in Canterbury's truck.

"I'll show you," Jan said, waving for Canterbury to follow.

Jan guided Canterbury along the compound's back wall. A dozen shipping containers were lined up. Some of the containers still had the customs paperwork stuck to the door.

"The Taliban appear to be the threat," Jan said. "But you have enemies coming and going through the gates every day."

"What do you mean?" he said. "Your men control the outer perimeter."

Jan nodded like a patient parent trying to explain something to a small child.

"You Americans only care about the Taliban," Jan said. "How many fighters do they have? Where are they hiding? Who is giving them money? But the real enemy was always much closer. My men do stop the Taliban. But your men allow people like Ahmed Wali to threaten the mission."

"Who is Wali?" Canterbury asked.

"He owns a trucking company," Jan said. "But he is really working with the Taliban."

"He must be vetted, right?"

"Wali is a thief. He is stealing from you with his high prices. He is bribing Taliban to leave his trucks alone and giving the soldiers who award the contracts gifts at his parties."

Canterbury looked up from his notebook.

"You have proof that Wali is paying the Taliban?"

Jan nodded.

"And you have proof that he is bribing soldiers?"

Jan nodded again.

"You've seen him do it?"

"No," Jan said. "But others have."

Canterbury jotted down Wali's name so he could follow up.

"Will these others talk to me?"

"I can convince them," Jan said.

"Who else knows about Wali?"

Jan shook his head in disgust.

"I've reported him in the past," he said. "But no one has stopped him."

"What did Sweet say?"

"That he'd investigate," Jan said. "But Wali wasn't arrested."

Canterbury tapped his pen against his notebook. Why didn't Sweet tell him about Wali? Jan was a trusted source.

"When I get back to the office, I'll check the files," Canterbury said. "If Sweet started an investigation, I will continue it. But if he didn't, I will start one. I know he was in a hurry to leave because of his wife. Thank you, General, for bringing this to my attention. If Wali is a bad guy, I'll make sure he goes to jail."

Jan smiled and put his hand over his heart.

"Thank you, Sergeant Canterbury," Jan said.

"You can call me Neil, sir."

Two of Jan's soldiers stood by a pallet covered by a tarp. They pulled off the plastic to reveal eight gray rockets lined up like cigarettes in a pack.

"We found them yesterday in a house outside of the city," Jan said. "The house is near a site where the Taliban like to shoot rockets."

Canterbury squatted down to get a closer look. The rockets were in good condition.

"Was anyone at the house?" he asked.

"No," Jan said. "The house was empty."

Jan's mood changed. He looked at the rockets and scowled at his men.

"Next time don't bring out the good ones for the new guy," he said in Pashto. "If you damage them, we won't be able to sell them."

Canterbury stood up and tried to subtlety adjust his pistol. Squatting aggravated the spot on his hip.

"I'm sorry, sir," Canterbury said. "I don't understand Pashto."

Jan's scowl turned into a smile.

"I was just commending my men for getting the rockets."

Canterbury shook the Afghan soldier's hand. They looked at him with a bewildered look.

"That is eight less rockets that can be shot at us," Canterbury said as he shook their hands. "Good work. One team, one fight."

Jan and Canterbury headed back to his 4x4 pickup truck.

"I'll get an EOD team down here to get the rockets," Canter bury said.

"No need," Jan said. "I've already called the army. I just wanted you to see them. I wanted to show you we are brothers. That we are all trying to win the war."

"Thank you, sir," Canterbury said.

Canterbury got behind the wheel and drove off. He honked and waved as he cleared the gate. The truck's cab barely contained Canterbury's excitement. Not bad for his first real day on the job.

CHAPTER 6

Wali had trouble sleeping after Charlie left.

The prospect of helping his American brothers win the war stirred something. Wali was bored with his life. His shipping business was pulling in more money than he could spend. But he missed going on missions like he had as an interpreter with the Special Forces.

But first his old life was calling as he fought traffic in Kandahar City. He had a meeting with a man he wished he could forget. A man that put his business and his relationship with the Americans in jeopardy. But he was the only man Wali knew who might be able to help the Americans win the war.

Wali parked near a radio tower on the outskirts of the city and walked down a dusty road toward a small mosque. Halfway down the road, he stopped at a rusted gate in a wall. Peering inside, Wali saw a courtyard littered with debris.

A random sandal.

Tattered blankets.

Shredded newspapers.

It looked like the family that lived there had left in a hurry, which was true. This was Wali's uncle's house. Memories of growing up there flooded into Wali's head as he walked through the gate and into the one-story house. The kitchen was small and dusty. One of the walls was scorched from a fire, likely lit by squatters.

Wali stopped at his room. It was empty except for the remnants of some pillows and blankets. The room smelled of piss.

Wali walked back to the courtyard to wait. Being in his old house, his mind drifted to his childhood, or at least what he remembered about it. His mother had died when he was born. They were in the refugee camp in Pakistan. His uncle rarely talked about her. He only talked about Yusuf, his brother and Wali's father. Both Yusuf and Wali's uncle joined the mujahedeen when the Soviets invaded. The Soviets took his father's leg, but not his will to fight. He made it through the war, rising to commander and making Wali's uncle his second in command. Their unit was one of the first to enter Kandahar City when the Soviets left.

After the war, Yusuf settled back in Kandahar City with his infant son. He opened a small store and hobbled around on crutches. Yusuf tried to put down his gun but was drawn into the bitter civil war that followed the Soviet withdrawal. He was killed by his own countrymen when a rocket hit the house his unit was using as a command post. Wali was still a toddler. He didn't remember the funeral, only that his uncle helped him pack his things.

Wali learned English at school and spent time playing soccer and watching American action movies when he wasn't working in his father's store, which his uncle ran. His favorite movie was *Rambo III*. He always wanted to be Hamid and help Rambo free Colonel Trautman. From that moment, the Americans were the good guys. He saw it in every Hollywood action movie he bought in the market.

Wali was fourteen when the Taliban's Arab allies put Afghanistan in the crosshairs of the Americans. He was at the mosque when he heard America's towers had been destroyed. The rumor was the Arabs had done it. Wali didn't understand what was happening until a few weeks later when he heard jets overhead and then the faint rumble of a bomb strike. A loud explosion near Mullah Omar's compound on the outskirts of the city followed.

A few weeks later, after the BBC said the Americans were headed for Kandahar, Wali watched as his uncle packed up the house. He loaded it all into a 4x4 truck. His uncle's fighters—mostly young men—waited in trucks in front of the house.

"Get your blanket and clothes," his uncle told him. "We have to leave."

"I'm going to wait for the Americans," Wali said.

His uncle grabbed him by his arm, jerking him up off his feet.

"The Americans will kill you when they find you," he said. "I've seen what foreign invaders do. Your father fought the Soviets so you could be free. Now it is your turn to fight the invaders."

Wali pulled away from his uncle and dashed out of the gate. He didn't know where he was running, but he wasn't going with his uncle.

The Americans were heroes like his father.

The sound of a truck's engine shook Wali from his memories. Two men—long beards, dusty shalwar kameez, and AK-47s—appeared at the gate. Wali recognized one. It was Zahir. They had played soccer together before the war.

"Hello, my friend," Wali said, hugging Zahir.

"You look well," Zahir said, pinching Wali's stomach. "Your American friends have made you fat."

Wali pushed his friend's hand away.

"I can still beat you, brother."

Wali grabbed Zahir by his shoulders and started to wrestle him to the ground. The creak of the gate stopped the match. Razaq walked into the courtyard and hissed at the two young men.

"Sorry, Uncle," Wali said, kissing his uncle on the cheeks.

Zahir picked up his rifle and walked back toward the truck. Wali followed Razaq into the house. His uncle, once a large man with a thick chest and arms, looked frail.

"How are you feeling, Uncle?" Wali asked.

Razaq shooed away the question with his hand.

While most of the house was in disrepair, a small meeting room was clean. Razaq sat on the rug in the corner of the room and crossed his legs. Zahir poured green tea from a thermos and then went back to the courtyard. Wali sat near his uncle and sipped his tea. These meetings were tedious. Usually they ended with a lecture about the evil of the Americans. The first couple of times Wali tried to defend himself. Now, out of respect for his elder and really the last member of his family, he kept silent.

"Why aren't you married yet?" Razaq asked.

This was Razaq's new gripe. It didn't matter that Wali tried to explain how busy he was or how he wanted to get his visa and marry an American woman.

"We've talked about this," Wali said. "You know why."

Razaq sipped his tea. He stared past Wali.

"Your business. Is it OK?" Razaq asked.

Wali nodded.

"I'm very busy," he said. "Is there anything I can do for you?"

The question was just a formality. Razaq never asked for anything but these meetings.

"Yes, nephew," he said. "There is something you can do."

"What do you need?" Wali asked, shocked by his uncle's request.

Razaq flicked his prayer beads and paused. Wali saw his uncle struggling with something. It was the same look his uncle had had when he told Wali about his father's death.

"Do you know about the drones?" Razaq said. "These planes without pilots the Americans use?"

Wali nodded.

"I've seen them at the airfield. They look like insects."

Razaq shook his head.

"Yes," he said. "But their sting is much worse. These insects hunt me and the brothers at all hours. We can't move. We can't sleep. It is cowardly to fight this way."

Wali heard the same kind of complaint from the Americans. It was cowardly to use roadside bombs. Everyone wanted a fair fight until they had to walk into one, Wali thought. What they really wanted was an advantage, because the fighter with the upper hand usually went home at night.

"Do you still have contacts with the bearded ones?" Razaq asked.

The "bearded ones" were the Special Forces or special operations units like the SEALs. They were the only American soldiers with facial hair.

"Yes," Wali said. "They are my friends."

"I have something for them," Razaq said. "But before I can give it to them, I need assurances."

"What kind of assurances?"

"I want to go to America," Razaq said. "I can't live like this any longer."

Wali almost spit out his tea.

"You want to go to America?" Wali said, exasperated. "You're serious?"

Razaq nodded.

"What do you know about America?" Wali said.

"I knew a man who moved to Virginia," Razaq said. "I want to go there."

Wali had spent the last two years trying to get a visa. Now his Taliban uncle wanted to go too.

"You've spent the last nine years trying to kill the Americans. Now you want to go home with them?"

"I have something they will want," Razaq said.

Wali scoffed. Razaq glared at him. It was the look a father gives a son. Disagree, but do it with some respect. Wali looked down at his feet.

"And what do you want me to tell my friends you have?" he said.

"I can't tell you," Razaq said. "Tell them it is something they will want. But they can't have it until I have assurances."

"Anything else?" Wali said.

"I want them to call off the drones."

Wali nodded. But there was nothing he could do about that.

"Say nothing to anyone else," Razaq said. "Nothing to Zahir. Nothing to anyone but your American friends."

"Of course, Uncle."

Razaq's shoulders relaxed. They sat in silence sipping tea. After a while, Razaq got up and left without a word.

Wali waited for the sound of Razaq's truck engine to fade before calling Charlie.

CHAPTER 7

Charlie had a couple of hours before the future operations brief. Lunch, then maybe a workout? He'd slacked off since arriving. Charlie closed his computer just as Woody poked his head into the intelligence cell.

"Hey, Chief, you wanted to see me?"

Woody was in charge of logistics. He kept the boys fed and stocked with bullets.

"Sure," Charlie said, grabbing an empty water bottle off his desk. "Your place or mine?"

"How about the conference room?"

Charlie followed Woody outside the TOC. The room was empty except for a massive table and a hodgepodge of chairs liberated from nearby offices. Charlie picked out a padded office chair and spit a stream of tobacco juice into his empty water bottle.

Woody sat at the end of the table and pulled out his green notebook. If an infantryman's main tool was a rifle, a staff officer's was the military-issue green notebook. Bound like a hardcover book with wide-ruled paper, every staff officer had one. Some even decorated the cover with elaborate drawings of unit crests or photos. Woody's notebook was worn, with pages folded for reference. He stored his pen inside a hole in the spine, ensuring that he would always be able to take notes.

"You wanted to talk about Ahmed Wali?" Woody asked.

"Yup," Charlie said. "He was my terp for a while. Now he does logistics for us, right?"

Woody checked his notebook.

"He does a lot of logistics," Woody said. "Between our runs and his runs for the Canadians, he's making well over a million a month. Not to mention all the vehicles he rents to everybody."

"I was hoping we could use him more," Charlie said. "His trucks go everywhere, and he agreed to let us talk with his drivers. Imagine having eyes and ears on the road all day, every day."

"You've got some good timing," Woody said. "I'm looking for a sole source, and it's between Wali and Gul Mohammed Jan. We're pushing teams into the villages. I can't keep them stocked without a dedicated transport contract. We've been using Jan a lot lately, but his trucks are a mess. Tires are flat. Some of his trucks don't even have gas."

Charlie spit into his bottle and rested his arms on the table.

"And Wali?"

"His shit is squared away. How do you know him?" Woody asked.

"How much time do you have?"

"Give me the *CliffsNotes* version," Woody said.

Charlie fished the wad of tobacco from his lip. He took a swig of water and spit the remaining flakes into the bottle.

"OK," he said. "He worked for us and some other teams for a few rotations starting in '04. Besides being a terp, he also used to get us stuff. Energy drinks, phone cards, shit like that. It was a good side business. He even bought a car and rented it back to us for like eight hundred dollars a month, so we were really paying him double his salary."

Charlie sat back in his chair and threw his hiking boots up on the table as he reached back in his memory.

"It was my fourth or fifth rotation," he said. "We were out in Panjwai in a new firebase. By now, Wali was done with being a terp. He was fixing a clinic or something for the Canadians."

As Charlie talked, he saw Wali in his mind—a lot thinner and with little facial hair—bombing down the dirt roads of the valley in his blue 4x4 truck.

"He used to stop by and check on us," Charlie said. "I was having a bitch of a time getting supplies. We needed gravel, water, food, you name it. And it cost too much to helicopter out. We used military trucks. They got hit."

Woody was jotting down notes as Charlie talked.

"I know the feeling," Woody said. "We're running into the same shit."

"I bet," Charlie said. "So Wali knew some local drivers and arranged the trucks. We started getting supplies. He even smuggled some four-wheelers out to us buried under a pile of pomegranates."

"So that's how he got into business?"

Charlie smiled at the memory.

"Yeah, it was all unofficial at first. I finally took him over to the contracting office. We were back getting something from Camp Brown and I walked him over. He was dressed in his best shalwar kameez. He had this folder with letters of introduction and recommendations from me and my team sergeant and team leader."

Woody started to close his notebook and then stopped.

"Why did you do it?"

Charlie wasn't tracking.

"Do what?"

"Why did you help him?" Woody asked. "I get it. He was a good terp. But you made this guy into a millionaire. Guy has made ten million dollars this year. Why did you pick him?"

Charlie stared past Woody at a map of Afghanistan. His eyes tracked from Kandahar to a small area west of the city the soldiers nicknamed "the Belly Button" because of how it looked on the map.

"He saved my ass," Charlie said.

Woody nodded.

"We got caught in an ambush. He was still a terp. I took a round in the front plate. Knocked the hell out of me. He dragged me behind the truck."

Charlie rubbed his chest where the ceramic plate stopped the round.

"Thanks, Charlie," Woody said. "That's what I needed."

"Happy to help."

"You know this, but just so we're clear in case some JAG starts asking questions, you can't be part of this," Woody said. "I'm not going to hire him because of your relationship or because you're going to use him as a source. Don't call Wali about this meeting or even tell him we talked."

"Roger," he said. "All bullshit aside, Wali is a good dude."

Charlie's Afghan phone buzzed in his pocket. He looked at the number and smirked.

"Speak of the devil," Charlie said.

He ducked out of the conference room, leaving Woody to his notes.

"Yo, brother," Wali said. "Let's rap. Got something for you. Meet me at my store on the Boardwalk. Legend Apparel next to the House of Knowledge."

Charlie checked his watch. He had time.

"See you in ten?"

Kandahar Airfield's Boardwalk was a wooden walkway shaped like a quadrangle boasting three dozen glass-door shops stocked with Cuban cigars, condoms, and souvenirs. Charlie spotted the flashing neon sign and red-and-white tablecloths inside Mamma Mia's Pizzeria. Two soldiers pushed past on their way to TGI Fridays.

Charlie hated the Boardwalk.

It was everything that was wrong with the war. Fat staff officers and support soldiers sucking down milkshakes and pizza while he and his teammates ate dust. Charlie started to curse them but stopped. He was one of them now.

Shoot me if I ever crave TGI Fridays, he thought.

Legend Apparel was wedged into a white trailer next to Green Beans coffee. Charlie walked past the long line of soldiers and contractors waiting for frozen lattes and cinnamon buns.

It took a second for Charlie's eyes to adjust inside Wali's store. Racks of knockoff North Face gear hung along the perimeter. Hats, gloves, and other accessories took up a fixture in the middle. A pretty Filipino girl was behind the counter talking to Wali.

"Hey, brother," Wali said. "Almost done here. Pick something out and then we'll find a place to talk."

Charlie browsed the jackets for a bit. He heard Wali talking to the clerk—Anabel—about a shipment of shirts coming from Pakistan. The jackets were pretty good. Not obvious knockoffs. Toward the back corner of the store Charlie found a black ThermoBall Eco Snow Triclimate parka, or at least a well-made replica of one. He'd wanted one before he left but balked at the nearly $400 price tag back home.

"Grab it," Wali said.

Charlie turned to see his friend watching him admire the jacket. Charlie looked at the price tag. Wali wanted $200 for the jacket. A good deal.

"Sure," Charlie said, fishing his wallet out of his pocket on the way to the register. "Thanks, Wali."

Anabel took the jacket and folded it into a plastic bag.

"We'll come back and get it after our meeting," Wali said.

Charlie was holding his credit card.

"Let me pay first."

Wali guided his friend toward the door.

"Your money is no good here."

Charlie smiled, thanked Anabel, and followed Wali out into the afternoon sun. They sat down at a picnic table.

"I have a Talib who wants to talk," Wali said.

"That was fast," Charlie said.

"He's a commander," Wali said. "He knows things, but he also wants to go to America. That is why he wants to talk."

"Go to America?" Charlie asked.

"That is what he wants," Wali said. "He has good information. He knows a lot."

Charlie was starting to work out the math. He would need a lot before he entertained bringing someone to the United States. Charlie doubted the source would be alive by the time he earned the one-way ticket.

"First things first," Charlie said. "Who is he?"

Wali looked away.

"Do you remember a couple years back when I went home for Ramadan? The time I broke my ankle?" Wali asked.

"Yeah," Charlie said.

"I never told you the whole story."

"What do you mean?"

"My taxi got stopped at the Taliban checkpoint just off the highway. Four Taliban fighters. One had an RPG. We were a few cars back."

Charlie knew the story, or at least he thought he did.

"The driver started to go around. I grabbed the wheel and told him to just go through. But this farmer in the back kept screaming at him to go. The kids were crying. It was a mess. I took out the pistol you gave me and put it in my lap. I told the driver to chill. But the farmer wouldn't shut up."

Wali paused and looked around the Boardwalk. Charlie knew he didn't want to tell the story.

"We were almost at the checkpoint. I had money out to pay them when the driver gunned it. I screamed at him to stop, but it was too late."

Wali closed his eyes.

"He ran down the guy with the RPG. I can still hear the crunch. The windshield turned into a spider's web of cracked glass. I crouched down as gunfire tore through the doors. I wanted to fire back. It's what I would have done if you were there. But I couldn't. The kids were screaming. There was blood all over the car."

"I remember your call," Charlie said.

Wali nodded.

"We smashed into a ditch. I jammed the pistol under the front seat and called you."

"We spun up and left before I hung up," Charlie said. "All we found was the wrecked taxi."

"The driver was alive. I told him he'd killed us both. I should have shot him. The Taliban were angry. They dragged us out and beat us. I don't remember anything until the compound."

Wali looked down at the dirt.

"They held us in a storeroom. Dirt floor. A mullah with gray eyes came in to question us. I'll never forget those eyes. He looked at me for a second before he took out a long knife with a serrated edge and started to saw the driver's neck. The driver was kicking and trying to yell. The guards just dug their knees into his back. Blood gushed into the dirt and the driver stopped kicking. Then the mullah wiped the knife on the driver's clothes and kicked the head away from the body."

Charlie looked at Wali's hands. They were shaking.

"I pissed myself," Wali said. "I told myself I wanted to die with dignity. In defiance of this evil. But I really just wanted to die quickly. Painless. The mullah just walked out instead. He left the driver's head. It felt like forever until they came for me. They put a bag on my head and dragged me out. My ankle was swollen. I couldn't put any weight on it. One of the fighters helped me walk. When I couldn't go another step, they pulled off the hood and pushed me onto a rug underneath a tree."

Charlie was confused.

"That's where we found you," he said. "You told us you escaped."

"My uncle saved me."

Charlie cocked his head.

"Your uncle?"

"He was sitting on the rug. He told me I was lucky his men found me."

"What the fuck are you talking about?" Charlie said. "What uncle? His men?"

Wali stared at his feet.

"My uncle is a Taliban commander," Wali said. "He saved me. I asked why me and not the driver. The driver was unwise, my uncle said. The driver should have just paid the toll, but instead he killed one of my uncle's men. He took his chances and paid the price."

"Stop," Charlie said. "Your uncle was a Taliban commander at the same time you were helping us. You told me you escaped. We put you in for an award. But it was all bullshit."

"You guys were so excited that I was alive," Wali said. "That I escaped. I just went with it."

"Tell me the truth now," Charlie said. "What happened before we arrived?"

"My uncle asked me if my American friends were going to save me. I lied and said I didn't have American friends. But my uncle knew better. He wasn't surprised I went to work with you guys. Then he warned me. He told me you would leave. My American friends were just one of a long list of invaders."

"Then what?" Charlie said, a little harsher than he intended. "You called me for help. How did you get your phone back?"

Charlie was mad. If Wali lied about this, what else was he lying about?

"My uncle gave it to me," Wali said. "But only after I stopped working with you. He told me he couldn't protect me if I was riding in the infidels' truck."

Charlie just stared at Wali.

"You stopped being a terp right after that," Charlie said. "Because of your uncle?"

Wali looked away. He didn't have to answer. Charlie knew.

"You're still talking to him?"

Wali turned to face the American.

"Sometimes," Wali said. "He is my only family."

"What does he want now?"

"Out," Wali said. "But first, he needs assurances that you guys won't kill him."

"I don't know who he is. So I can assure you I won't kill him."

Wali smiled.

"Drones. He wants you to call off the drones."

"I can't do anything about that," Charlie said. "That's the Air Force."

He was mad at Wali, but deep down he understood. Survival makes men do bad things. But this was Charlie's chance to get a source inside the Taliban leadership. Could he trust Wali? Logic said no, but his gut told him otherwise. One meeting. Get a look at this uncle and then make the call.

"But tell your uncle if I'm with him, the drones can't attack."

CHAPTER 8

Razaq slammed the door of the truck and slumped into the back seat. Zahir climbed behind the wheel.

"Back to Spin Boldak?"

Razaq didn't say anything. He just looked out the window and let out a long sigh. Zahir put the truck into gear and slowly drove out of the gate. He picked his way through the crowded market of Quetta heading west toward the Afghan border.

"Can you turn up the air?" Razaq said.

Zahir juiced the air conditioning. For several minutes, the only sound in the cab was the whoosh of cold air.

"Donkeys," Razaq said. "They sit here safe from the drones and the foreign troops while we have to risk everything. They are fat and happy watching their brothers fight and die every year while they argue about where to build their compounds in Kandahar when we win."

"What did they say about the package?"

Razaq's tone went from anger to exasperation.

"They want us to wait," he said.

"You showed them the pictures?" Zahir said. "You told them we could win the war with it?"

Razaq shrugged.

"I told them everything. But they said bringing it over the border was too dangerous and would upset our hosts."

"Fuck the Pakistanis!" Zahir said. "They already have their own bombs."

Razaq fished his prayer beads from his pocket.

"They want more proof," he said. "They sent the pictures and the manual to the Arabs."

"What are the Arabs going to do?"

"Verify that it is a bomb," Razaq said. "And buy it."

Zahir almost hit a boy pushing a cart across the road. He blasted the horn before gunning the engine and racing around the offending cart, almost clipping it with his fender.

"We're just going to give it away?" Zahir said. "Why not keep it? Tell Kabul they have a day to surrender or we level the city."

Razaq was exhausted.

"After we level Kabul, what do we do? The bomb gives us leverage, but it also means the Americans will only send more troops. They will hunt us and kill us for using it. I want nothing to do with the bomb."

Zahir shrugged.

"But just having the bomb will end the war," Zahir said.

"Our war will end when all foreign invaders pull out of Afghanistan and a holy Islamic and independent regime reigns," Razaq said. "Blowing up what we hope to rule won't bring us victory."

They rode in silence for a while. Razaq didn't care about the bomb as a weapon. He was thinking about Wali and a deal with the Americans. The bomb was his way out. It was his path to peace, if he trusted them.

"We should take the bomb and hide it," Zahir said, breaking the near hour-long silence. "Then contact Kabul. When we've won the war, the Shura would have to accept the decision."

"Shut up," Razaq said. "We wait for word from the Shura."

Zahir turned on the radio. Razaq hated the Indian pop music but accepted it. At least with the radio on he didn't have to talk any longer with Zahir. He admired the boy's fight. It reminded him of himself before years of war. But now he was tired of watching young men die. He didn't want to die. He knew all about the rewards granted a martyr, but that was no longer enough. He wanted some of those rewards now, before he became too old to enjoy them. War was for those willing to die based on promises made by old men.

It was late afternoon when they reached the border. The Pakistani guards just waved them through, happy to have two fewer Afghans in their country. Razaq stared at the Afghan border checkpoint. It used to be a small mud building, but the Americans had turned it into a fortress. Concrete barriers funneled the cars into line. Massive walls shielded the guards from car bombs.

Approaching the border always made Razaq nervous. Zahir noticed an American Humvee parked near the guard compound. A soldier in the turret had a .50-cal machine gun trained on the border crossing.

The Afghan guards were lazy, more concerned with getting a little money to supplement their meager income. But American soldiers changed the equation.

An Afghan guard signaled for them to stop. He was little more than a teenager. His uniform hung off his thin frame, and the AK-47 at his side looked like a heavy machine gun. Razaq sat up a little straighter. Just as they stopped, an American soldier walked up to the guard. Next to the Afghan, the American with a thick chest and big hands looked massive. His black rifle was held at the ready. His eyes were covered by clear glasses, and his gloves had thick plastic protecting the knuckles. The only exposed skin was his fleshy cheeks.

"Evening," the American said. "You speak English?"

Zahir nodded.

"Yes."

The American smiled. His teeth were white and big. Americans seemed dangerous from a distance, but up close they were cartoonish, Razaq thought.

"We're going to inspect your truck," the American said. "I need you to pull over there."

He pointed to an area walled off by concrete barriers just past the checkpoint. Zahir drove the truck there as the American soldier and Afghan guard walked nearby. While Afghan soldiers opened the back and looked under the truck, the American soldier motioned for Razaq and Zahir to get out.

"What were y'all doing in Pakistan?" the American asked.

Razaq stayed silent. He just hunched down and coughed gently into his sleeve.

"My father is sick," Zahir said. "I took him to a doctor."

The American looked at Razaq.

"Sorry to hear it," he said. "How often do you take him over to the doctor?"

"Once a month," Zahir said.

Razaq shuffled over to one of the barriers and used it to steady himself. He let out another cough.

"He OK?" the American inquired. "We've got a medic if you want us to take a look at him."

"He'll be fine," Zahir said. "Thank you. I just want to get him home."

"Yeah," the American said. "Of course. Almost done."

The American watched the border guards finish the search.

"Good to go?" the American said, holding a thumb up.

The Afghan border guards nodded.

"Have a safe trip home," the American said to Zahir before walking back toward the checkpoint. "Tell your father to get better."

Razaq and Zahir climbed back into the truck and continued toward Spin Boldak. A mile down the road, Razaq finally spoke.

"Do you think they would have let us pass with the bomb?"

CHAPTER 9

Basir was waiting when Wali got back to his compound.

"The general wants to see you," he said.

"About what?" Wali asked.

"Contracts," Basir said and walked back to his truck.

Wali was pretty sure the general wanted to talk about the Special Forces contract. Wali had met with Woody that afternoon to go over the details. He was excited to work closely with the Special Forces again.

Basir showed Wali into the general's office. Wali sat on the couch in the small lounge area and waited. He heard Jan outside the door. The general was angry and barking at Basir and his men to bring tea. When the door opened, Wali stood at attention with his hands clasped behind his back. Jan threw a folder onto his desk and turned his attention to Wali.

"How are you are doing this big business?" Jan asked.

Wali stayed silent.

"I spoke with the Special Forces," Jan said, sitting down in one of the leather chairs. "They told me my services were no longer required. Captain Woody said he selected another contractor."

Jan paused as Basir and a young beardless soldier carrying a tray came into the room. The soldier's uniform was spotless and he kept his eyes down, careful to not look at Wali or Jan. Jan picked up a glass of tea and took a sip as he got up to pace.

"I called around to the others," he said, not offering Wali any tea. "No one else got the job. So it had to be you. Did you get the contract?"

Wali nodded.

"I have a lot of army," Jan said, turning to look at the map of southern Afghanistan behind his desk. "I have a lot of security. But I cannot take supplies to the locations the Special Forces want at your prices. How are you doing it?"

Wali started to talk, but Jan cut him off as he sat down behind his desk.

"You are paying bribes to the Taliban."

"No," Wali said, his stare burning into Jan's chest.

The accusation hung between them until Jan took a sip of tea. He leaned forward in his chair.

"So this is my proposal," the general said. "Whenever you get missions, we split them. And my men will protect your trucks."

Wali shook his head slowly, making sure Jan saw it before he spoke.

"I can't do that," Wali said. "This is my contract. It is my job to go and find the business. You pay your representative to do your business for you. Why is Basir not able to go to Kandahar Airfield and get business? I can show him where the business contract office is."

Jan started to respond but stopped when Wali took a glass off the tray on the coffee table and poured himself some tea.

"Let's start with our fate," Wali said, settling into the couch opposite Jan's desk. "Allah is making the decision. Who gets, how he gets, how much he gets. You are also getting the same business. Does that mean you have bribed somebody? And when it comes to security, you are the one who is illegally using the Afghan Army to escort your convoys. And then charging the Americans for security. So you are double-charging the Americans."

Jan slammed his glass on his desk.

"I am defending our country!" he said.

Wali started to talk, but Jan glared at him.

"Shut up, boy," Jan said. "I asked you to join us. We all signed the contract promising to charge the same, except you. I offered you the car rental business."

"While you took all the fuel deliveries," Wali said.

"Yes," Jan said. "I am a general. I am an elder. You are an orphan. I know where you came from. You're lucky I allow you to stay in business at all."

Jan pulled a pistol from the holster on his belt and put it on the table between them. The pistol landed on the table with a thunk with the barrel pointed at Wali's chest.

"I could send my men to Kandahar City to find you and kill you."

Wali looked at Basir, who had slipped into the room and was parked in a chair near the door.

"General, your representative is sitting here," Wali said. "He is our witness. My compound is just a few hundred meters from here. I have spent nights and days in that compound. You can kill me there or here."

Wali glanced at Basir. The general's lieutenant diverted his eyes.

Coward.

"I came here with my head and my eyes up," Wali said. "If I am leaving, I want to leave the way I came in."

Wali waited for a second, but Jan sat stone-faced. Wali put his glass on the desk, rose from the couch, and turned toward the door.

"I guess we'll have to see what happens," Jan said.

Wali stuffed his hand into his pocket as he left. He felt it shaking against his leg. At his truck, he pulled out his phone to call Charlie but stopped. This was his fight. He didn't back down in the office. He wasn't going to back down now.

Back at his compound, Wali found his Beretta M9 and slid it under his pillow. He didn't sleep that night, but the lump under his head made him feel safe.

ꝏꝏꝏ

The next morning, Woody came by Wali's compound with a contract. The first convoy was to leave that night, and Woody and Wali stood near the gate and watched as the jingle trucks rumbled out and turned toward the staging area—a massive gravel lot—where they'd be loaded. There were more than twenty trucks slated to leave at dusk.

"I'll see you tomorrow," Woody said as the trucks drove past.

Wali went back to his compound and the rest of the day's work keeping his business empire running. At dusk, his cell phone rang. It was one of his drivers.

"They won't let us pass."

"Who?" Wali asked.

"The general," the driver said. "His men are at the gate. They said we don't have adequate security. He is insisting that we take his men."

"I'm coming," Wali said as he ran out to his truck.

Wali dialed Basir.

"I want to speak to the general," Wali said.

"He is at the main gate," Basir said. "There was a security matter."

Wali slammed his fist against the steering wheel.

"I know," he shouted. "You're holding up my trucks."

As he approached the main gate, Wali saw his trucks surrounded by Jan's soldiers. He parked near a massive concrete barrier that protected the gate and walked over to Jan. The general was smiling.

"What is the problem, General?" Wali asked.

"You need more security," Jan said. "I brought some of my men. They can escort your trucks tonight."

"You're holding up the Special Forces cargo," Wali said. "What do you think they are going to say?"

"That you need more security," Jan said. "And that your company isn't able to meet the contract."

Wali closed his eyes in frustration.

"What do you want?" Wali said.

Jan nodded to a spot out of earshot of his men.

"I'll take fifty thousand tonight to pay for my escort," Jan said. "And I'll take half of every run."

Wali did the math. He would be paying twice what he normally would for security, and the deal would cost him his profits on the whole contract. But what was he going to do? He couldn't call Woody. The contract was supposed to make things easier for the Special Forces to get supplies to the new bases. Just as he was about to agree, his phone rang.

It was Charlie.

"What's up, brother?" Charlie said. "Any news on that meeting?"

"I'm working on it," Wali said.

"You OK?" Charlie asked, noticing the shortness of Wali's answer.

"Just dealing with a problem."

"Can I help?"

Wali was about to say no when he paused. He was in trouble, but Jan would listen to the Americans.

"Maybe," Wali said. "Can you come up to the main gate?"

Wali ended the call and walked back to Jan.

"I've got someone coming to the gate," he said.

The general smiled, but only Wali knew the "someone" wasn't bringing the bribe. Jan and Wali were standing near an Afghan Army truck when Charlie arrived.

"Hello, General," Charlie said, shooting a reassuring look at Wali. "What seems to be the problem?"

Jan scowled. He'd been outflanked by Wali.

"He's running a convoy," Jan said. "He doesn't have adequate security. My soldiers need to go with him."

Wali looked at Jan's men. They were barely in uniform. Their weapons were dirty. Their trucks were beat up. They didn't look like an army unit.

"These are Afghan soldiers," Charlie said. "They are not supposed to be escorting convoys."

"We have to make sure that there's proper security because people can be ambushed," Jan said.

Charlie smirked.

"Yeah, Afghanistan is a very dangerous place," he said. "People can be killed at any time."

Both men stared at one another. Wali wasn't sure what to do.

"Get your people in their trucks and get the convoy out of here," Charlie said to Wali, never taking his eyes off of Jan.

Wali signaled to his drivers. They climbed back into the trucks. Jan started waving his arms.

"No, no, no!" the general shouted.

"Let me explain something to you," Charlie said. "These convoys work for the US Special Forces. My soldiers need this equipment, and they're going to get it on time."

"No. I am a general," Jan seethed. "This is Afghanistan. You don't tell us what to do."

Jan wagged his finger in Charlie's face until he was coffee-breath close. Wali was about to step in and pay Jan when Charlie smiled.

"Let's talk about a way that we can work this out to make sure you're happy," he said.

Charlie motioned for Wali and the general to follow. He led them behind the concrete barriers so no one else could see them. When Jan was out of sight of his men, Charlie took off his ball cap and slapped him across the chin with it as hard as he could.

Jan was stunned.

"You don't threaten me," Charlie growled. "You don't threaten our organization. You don't stop what we're doing. You'll do exactly what you're told, when you're told to do it. I've respectfully asked you not to disrupt our operations, but I won't ask you again."

Jan opened his mouth to talk. Charlie hit him again, hard, with his hat.

"Shut up," Charlie said. "Get in your truck and leave now."

Wali stood in shocked silence. Jan waited but Charlie didn't back down. After a minute, the general got back into his truck and left. His eyes never left Wali.

"Thank you," Wali said.

Charlie just patted him on the shoulder.

"I didn't do it for you," he said. "Set up that meeting."

CHAPTER 10

Basir led Canterbury into the general's office.

Jan smiled at Canterbury and waved him to the couch in front of his desk. The general got up and walked around to sit on the couch opposite him.

Canterbury settled into his seat. This time he'd put his pistol in a shoulder holster. Jan slid a bowl of sweets in front of him.

"I know how you like the caramels," he said. "My men are bringing tea and some lunch. You can stay?"

Canterbury nodded. Jan had called him the night before, irate. He demanded they meet.

"But first, we need to talk about a grave danger facing the base," Jan said.

Canterbury sat up straighter and fished out his green notebook.

"What kind of danger, sir?"

Canterbury noticed how Jan puffed up when he said "sir" or "general."

"You researched Wali?" Jan asked.

"I called around," Canterbury replied. "Not much there. The Green Berets like him. We rent a truck from him. That was about it. I guess he was an interpreter, so everyone I talked to said he was vetted."

Jan shifted in his seat and folded his hands.

"He is working with the Taliban," the general said.

"You said that at our last meeting," Canterbury said, fishing another caramel out of the dish. "You also said he was taking bribes, but I can't act without proof, sir."

"I have a name," Jan said. "His contact is a Taliban commander named Razaq."

Canterbury jotted down the name.

"I'll check the name," he said. "But I need more. When do they meet? Where do they meet?"

"In the city," Jan said. "They meet at Wali's old home. Razaq comes to pick up his money. He protects Wali's trucks from Taliban attack and uses the money to buy rockets."

"You have witnesses?" Canterbury asked. "Photos? Anything that I can show my captain?"

Jan shook his head no.

"I will check the name," Canterbury said. "And you will continue to find proof, right, sir?"

"My men are watching Wali," Jan said. "He is a threat to my country first, but like you, we can't arrest him without proof. We are a civilized country. We have rules. But we can't watch him when he goes to the Special Forces compound or to his store on the Boardwalk. We need your help."

Canterbury shut his notebook.

"How did he become so close to the Special Forces guys?"

"He pays them too," Jan said. "He gives them gifts from his store and bags of cash."

Jan took out a few sheets of paper from a file on the table. Canterbury scanned the pages. It was a memo granting Wali a sole-source contract to transport supplies for the Special Forces.

"Do you see this?" Jan said, pointing to the memo. "Wali bought this from his friends. A small bribe guarantees him millions in profits."

The document was signed by the lieutenant colonel in charge of the special operations task force. It looked legit.

"This means Wali is going to transport all of the supplies for the Special Forces and use the money to pay the Taliban."

Canterbury looked at the memo again.

"But sir, the task force commander signed it. I'm not sure..."

Jan signaled to Basir. He opened the door to the office, and the clean-shaven soldier brought in a silver tray piled high with grilled lamb, rice with raisins, and fresh-cut cucumbers and green onions.

"Ah," Jan said. "Lunch is here. I beg you to check on Wali, but enough talk of business. Let's talk about something else."

❦❦❦

After lunch, Canterbury drove back to his office. On the way, he passed in front of the Special Forces camp. Canterbury parked his truck and walked up to the gate.

"Hey," Canterbury said to the gate guard. "I need to talk with your logistics guys."

"Roger," the soldier said. "Got a pass?"

Canterbury showed him his badge.

"Oh, OK," the soldier said. "Sit tight, my man. Let me make a call."

The soldier dialed a few numbers on the guard shack phone.

"Hey," he said. "Can you get Woody or one of his guys and send 'em out here? Some Air Force guy wants to talk with them."

A few minutes later, Canterbury was escorted to the conference room just outside the TOC. Woody was sitting at the table.

"You need a water?" Woody asked.

"Yes, sir," Canterbury said. "If you don't mind."

Woody asked the soldier who had escorted him to the room to snatch two waters out of the office refrigerator.

"Sure, Woody," the soldier said, using the captain's first name or nickname.

Canterbury looked at the soldier and then back at Woody, a captain. Everything was so informal. Chummy even.

"What can I do for you?" Woody asked.

Canterbury's mind went blank. He never thought they'd let him into the compound, let alone be so friendly. No need to hide anything.

"I'm here to talk about your sole source," Canterbury said. "I just wanted to know about Ahmed Wali."

"What do you want to know?" Woody asked.

"First," Canterbury said. "Let me get your name, sir. Woody?"

"Captain Woodrow Coyle. I'm in charge of the service detachment. We keep the greenie beanies fueled, fed, and stocked with ammo."

Canterbury took out a card and slid it over to Woody. The card had an embossed Air Force Office of Special Investigations badge and his name and rank—Technical Sergeant Neil Canterbury—printed in black. Woody picked up the card and examined it as Canterbury introduced himself.

"I'm Special Agent Neil Canterbury," he said. "I wanted to stop by and ask if you've heard anything suspicious about Wali."

Woody scratched his head and leaned back in the chair.

"Well," Woody said. "I'd say no. He was an interpreter for us for years and still works closely with us."

Canterbury rested his green book on the table and flipped to his notes from the Jan meeting.

"Can you tell me how he got the contract?" Canterbury asked. "At this point, I'm just asking questions. My office isn't investigating or anything..."

He paused for a second.

"Yet."

Woody was no longer leaning back.

"Look, Sergeant," he said. "Our sole source is permitted under regulations. There is no way my command would approve such a thing if it violated the law."

Canterbury quickly scanned his notes searching for a counterpoint.

"As for the allegations about Wali doing anything suspicious," Woody said, "let me get someone who knows."

The soldier came back with two waters and put them on the table.

"Hey," Woody said. "Go get Charlie and ask him to come here."

The soldier left and Woody opened his water and took a sip.

"Like I said, we're not investigating," Canterbury said. "I just wanted to make you guys aware…"

Woody just crossed his arms.

"Roger," he said. "I heard you the first time, Sergeant. Charlie will be here in a moment."

Charlie was tall with a bushy brown beard and a dirty Third Special Forces cap over shaggy brown hair. He was dressed in a T-shirt and brown cargo pants. His lip was plump with a wad of tobacco.

"What's up?" Charlie asked, looking first at Woody and then at Canterbury.

Woody started to collect his stuff.

"This is Technical Sergeant Neil Canterbury," he said, standing up. "He has some questions about Wali."

"What?" Charlie said.

"Yeah, there is something suspicious about him," Woody said.

Charlie looked at Canterbury and then back at Woody.

"Suspicious? Like he's Taliban or something?"

Woody just smirked.

"I'd love to keep chatting, Sergeant, but I've got a war to fight," Woody said. "If you decide to investigate, call JAG next time."

Canterbury stiffened.

"Charlie, can I get your full name and rank?" Canterbury said, opening his notebook to a fresh page.

"No," Charlie said. "I don't know what the fuck you think you know."

"First, I need to get your name and rank," Canterbury said.

"Look, unless you have pictures of Wali sitting next to Mullah Omar and Osama bin Laden, I don't have much more to tell you."

Canterbury closed his notebook and took a few breaths.

"OK, Charlie," Canterbury said. "I get it. Wali helps you do your job, but I'm trying to do my job too, and that means keeping you and this base safe."

Charlie smirked. Canterbury knew the look. The Army thought the Air Force were wimps until they needed an air strike. Then it was one team, one fight. Canterbury wanted to punch out Charlie's teeth.

"You don't know my job," Charlie said. "But I'll tell you this. If I ever had a doubt about Wali, I would put a bullet in him myself, period. End of story."

Charlie picked up Canterbury's card from the table.

"So, Sergeant...Canterbury," Charlie said. "Be careful. Wali is an important part of our operations. That is all you need to know."

Charlie turned and stuck his head out in the hall.

"Hey, get me someone to take this guy back to the gate," he said before turning back to Canterbury.

"And next time you come, make an appointment."

CHAPTER 11

Lieutenant Colonel William Kyle flipped through the PowerPoint slides. When he was done, he picked up the whole pile and tossed them down on his desk.

Charlie looked at Frank and shrugged. This was Charlie's first meeting with the commander of the special operations task force, and he wasn't sure how to read him.

"I don't like it, Chief," Kyle said, knocking his West Point class ring against his desk for emphasis. "It is an awfully big risk. This Wali kid. I know he was your terp and I know Woody has a deal with him to move some beans and bullets, but taking you to a meeting with the Taliban is another story."

Kyle was lean with a tight haircut and piercing blue eyes. He graduated top of his class and was an armor officer before earning his Special Forces tab. But he should have stayed with the Big Army, because he didn't get the culture of Special Forces. After his team leader tour—the highlights being two deployments to train in Thailand—he moved up to a staff job. That was when his special operations career took off. He did some time with the First Special Forces Group staff before going to Joint Special Operations Command at Fort Bragg, where he worked in the planning cell. Some soldiers are good in the field. Kyle found his groove in the office working future plans. He had a knack for keeping all the balls in the air, no small feat when you have soldiers in over forty countries worldwide. By the time he was up for command, he was a rising star well regarded in command circles.

Now he was in charge of all special operations in southern Afghanistan.

"Roger, sir," Frank said. "But we'll have guys less than five mikes from the meeting area."

"Five minutes," Kyle said, getting up to get a Red Bull out of his office refrigerator. "Charlie will be dead in less than two."

"You underestimate me, sir," Charlie said. "I'm pretty stubborn."

Kyle smiled. He popped open the can and took a long pull.

"Sir," Frank said, "this is the kind of win we've been looking for since we took over."

"Maybe," Kyle said. "But I don't like this Wali kid. I got pinged by higher about some information linking him to the Taliban. You know anything about that?"

Frank sat back in his chair and let out a long sigh.

"Sir," he said but stopped when Charlie shot him a glance.

This kind of hand-wringing was why America was losing. Charlie had lost too many friends to watch a commander with less combat experience lecture him about risk and the enemy.

"Hey, sir," Charlie said, "Wali is talking with the Taliban. He is setting up this meeting."

Kyle was silent, and Charlie didn't fill the void. He wanted the logic of what he'd said to sink in with his commander.

"That makes sense," Kyle said. "But how can we be sure?"

"We can't," Charlie said. "I understand that you have concerns. But what you need to realize is either we are dealing with the greatest double agent in the history of the Afghan War or all this is just bullshit slander by his competitors. I know the guy, and I'm betting against him being the war's greatest spy."

Kyle nodded and took another sip of his Red Bull.

"I can't approve your plan on a hunch," he said. "Come back to me with a plan with less John Wayne, and tell Woody to come see me about this contract."

Kyle turned back to his computer and didn't look up as Frank and Charlie cleaned up the PowerPoint slides. Back in Frank's office, Charlie balled up the pile of paper and tossed it into the burn barrel.

"Before this deployment, the only enemy he fought was the clap in some whorehouse in Thailand," Frank said. "This is Third Group. Shit is a whole lot riskier here."

"I've heard shit can get risky in a Thai whorehouse," Charlie said.

Frank laughed, but only for a second.

"Now what?" he said.

"How about a beer?"

❦❦❦

Unlike the European compounds, the American camps were dry and drinking alcohol was banned. But that didn't stop the special operations task force from building and stocking a bar at Camp Brown.

Tucked into a wooden hut near the back of the camp, the bar took up one wall and a collection of chairs and tables salvaged from other camps made up the seating. It looked like the display floor for a used office furniture outlet. An American flag and a Special Forces flag hung on the wall.

It was the best dive bar in Afghanistan.

Charlie went to get a pair of cold beers from the refrigerators that lined the wall behind the bar. When he got back, Frank was talking to a civilian with long surfer hair and a mustache that would make Sam Elliott blush. The surfer looked like Jeff Spicoli from *Fast Times at Ridgemont High* if he had been from Texas instead of California. He was dressed in jeans, a Guns N' Roses T-shirt, and camouflage Vans. No gun. He was chatting up one of the FBI agents assigned to the special operations task force.

"What's up, Frank?" Spicoli said. "You know Alice, right?"

Frank gave Alice—the FBI agent—a little bow.

"Oh yes," Frank said. "She's another casualty of the daily staff meeting."

"Glad I'm exempt from death by PowerPoint," Spicoli said as Charlie arrived with a beer for Frank.

"Charlie, you remember Felix Van Owen from Asadabad?" Frank said. "He's come a long way."

"What's up?" Felix said, shaking Charlie's hand. "What's happening?"

"Been too long," Charlie said. "Last time I saw you, you didn't shave. What happened?"

Felix ran his hands over his mustache.

"You guys have the beard market cornered, plus it pisses off the station chief in Kabul."

"I'll let you catch up with your old friends," Alice said. She joined a group of soldiers around a table. Frank followed.

Charlie turned his attention to Felix.

He liked Felix because he wasn't the typical CIA case officer. He didn't come from the Ivy League or have a bunch of advanced degrees. He went to a state school on the East Coast—Virginia or North Carolina—and did the job with pragmatism absent in many of his collegues.

"Last time I saw you, man, you were, what, the junior engineer sergeant, right?" Van Owen said.

Charlie nodded.

"And you were a polo-shirt, chino-wearing, fresh-out-of-grad-school CIA case officer," Charlie said. "Another guy with big ideas and dubious information."

Felix laughed.

"The CIA is the premier intelligence-gathering outfit in the world," Felix said, using his best briefing voice. "At least that's what we tell people. But lately all I've been doing is chasing cell phones and shooting Hellfire missiles at them. What are you doing now?"

"Intelligence," Charlie said with a sheepish grin. "Working with Blake."

"Welcome to the dark arts," Felix said.

The two sat quietly for a second, neither wanting to volunteer more than he should.

"Another beer?" Charlie asked.

Felix drained his last swallow and followed Charlie to the bar.

"What do you think of our war now that you're back?" Felix asked, his empty replaced by a full cold bottle.

"Slow," Charlie said. "Risk-averse. I miss the old days of running and gunning. We just got an op shut down because the colonel isn't comfortable with risk."

Felix smiled.

"Well, Rambo," he said, "sometimes it's better not to give a fuck. On to the next operation."

"Yeah," Charlie replied. "But this one could be big. The info we could get is worth the risk. We don't have a lot of sources in the enemy's decision chain."

Charlie was chumming the water. He had Felix's interest. Felix lowered his voice.

"You don't have to tell me shit, but if there is something we could do, let me know," he said.

Charlie nodded and took a drink. He was standing on the proverbial diving board. Jump off and dive into the pool with the CIA, or turn around and climb back down the ladder. If he brought Felix into it, there was a chance the agency would snatch the operation away and maybe get Wali killed. But he also couldn't go back to the office and pretend they didn't have a chance of turning one of the Taliban's local commanders. Did he really have a choice? Could he really return to Fort Bragg knowing he'd had a chance to do something important but didn't?

"Yeah, I think you might be able to help," Charlie said. "But with a few conditions."

Felix put his beer on the bar.

"Of course," he said.

ꟾꟾꟾ

Charlie was in the office a few days later preparing for the daily update when Frank stopped by to see him.

"Boss wants us," he said, a sheepish grin on his face.

Felix was waiting outside Kyle's office.

"Keep your head down," he said as Charlie passed. "Let's talk when you're done."

Kyle had his reading glasses off and was rubbing the bridge of his nose. In front of him was a memo with the CIA crest in one corner.

"So what the fuck is this shit?" Kyle said, not looking up from the memo. "I told you to get me a new plan, not go crying to OGA."

Other government agency, which almost exclusively meant the Central Intelligence Agency.

"Well, sir," Frank said, but Kyle shut him down with just a glance.

"This is a CIA op now, which doesn't mitigate the risks that caused me to can it in the first place," Kyle said. "I don't care how much you trust Wali or how close our guys will be to the meeting. Going out solo is not how we do things."

Kyle slid the memo over to Charlie. It was from the CIA, authorizing him to recruit Razaq on the agency's behalf.

"Don't get yourself killed."

"Roger, sir," Charlie said.

Outside the door, Felix was waiting.

"Not bad," Charlie said. "I'm impressed."

"I hope I didn't get you into too much trouble," Felix said. "But the bosses in Kabul jumped at the idea. When can you set up the meet? I don't want Kyle calling the station chief and everyone getting cold feet."

Charlie fished out his phone to call Wali.

CHAPTER 12

Razaq walked fifty steps to reach the end of the thicket. Then fifteen steps to the right before returning to his starting point. He counted each lap. It calmed him to keep track. He tried to put his sandals in his old footprints as he walked.

The sound of his phone shook him from his stupor.

"Hello," Razaq said after fishing it out of his pocket. "I thought you were going to call me earlier."

Wali was on the other end of the line.

"Sorry, Uncle," Wali said. "My meeting ran long."

Razaq pressed the phone against his ear.

"What?" he said. "Turn down that television."

Razaq heard the background noise fade.

"Can you hear me now?" Wali asked.

Razaq made his fiftieth step and turned right. *One, two, three...*

"Yes," he said. "Now, when am I meeting your friends? How much longer do I have to wait?"

"Tomorrow," Wali said. "Our friends want to talk with you."

Five, six, seven...

"They are not my friends," Razaq said.

"I know," Wali said. "But they will be."

Eight, nine, ten...

"Tell your friends I will only meet them in Spin Boldak," Razaq said. "You know the place. Where I found you after the taxi accident.

You come with your friend. No one else. Tell them I have something much bigger, but first I need to know they can get me to safety."

"I told you, Uncle, that they aren't going to send you to Virginia right away," Wali said. "It doesn't work that way. You are too valuable here. But I am sure they will help you when the time is right."

Twenty, twenty-one, twenty-two...

Razaq understood patience. He was still waiting for the invaders to leave.

"When you talk to your friends, tell them time is running out," Razaq said.

"How is it running out?" Wali asked. "We've been at war for decades and the Americans aren't leaving. You should see all the food and ammunition I'm transporting to their bases."

Thirty-five, thirty-six, thirty-seven...

"I'm not talking about the Americans leaving," Razaq said.

"Then what are you talking about?"

Razaq didn't answer. He wanted to tell his nephew about the bomb. He wanted to tell him that if the Taliban sells it there is no way of knowing what will happen. If Osama bin Laden brought the Americans here after crashing planes into their buildings, what will they do when al-Qaeda blows up a nuclear bomb in Washington?

Forty-eight, forty-nine, fifty. Right turn...

"Uncle?"

"Just set the meeting. Hurry."

Razaq closed his flip phone and slid it back into his pocket. As he walked, he looked over to a field near his compound. He could just made out the mound of dirt where Zahir had buried the bomb.

"*Inshallah*, I'll be rid of you soon."

CHAPTER 13

The next morning, Charlie flew out to the firebase at Spin Boldak with Felix.

From the open door of the Black Hawk helicopter, Charlie watched Afghanistan pass underneath him like a filmstrip. Small mud villages intercut with fields and irrigation ditches. In the distance, rust-colored mountains. It was one of the most beautiful countries he'd ever seen from the air. Seeing Afghanistan from that perspective gave him hope. Maybe once the fighting was over, the Afghans could turn their country's physical beauty into a destination for tourists.

But first, Charlie had a war to win.

They had a meeting scheduled with the local Special Forces team operating in the area. The town was the last stop before the border with Pakistan. Charlie made out the tan buildings from the helicopter's window as it circled the landing pad. Next to him, Felix slept. He dozed as soon as the helicopter's engines started and woke when the helicopter's wheels hit the dirt.

The firebase was small. Surrounded by Hesco barriers—large wire-mesh baskets filled with dirt to create a wall—and guard towers, it looked like a small fort from a western. Fort Apache. Charlie felt at home when he saw it. He was built for the field. That is where he wanted to be. But right now, they needed him near the flagpole. Right now, they needed him to dig out a win so the guys at the firebase could do some good.

One of the Black Hawk gunners pulled the door open, and Charlie grabbed his backpack and trotted toward a waiting pickup truck that took him and Felix to the Special Forces team's operations center.

"You guys have a map?" Charlie asked upon entering.

The team leader, a young captain on his first deployment to Afghanistan, walked Charlie over to a map spread out on a table while Felix introduced himself to the rest of the soldiers in the operations center.

"Here you go, Chief," the team leader said.

"Thanks," Charlie said. "But you can call me Charlie."

"Marc," the team leader said, shaking Charlie's hand.

Marc was dressed in a T-shirt and shorts. A VMI trucker hat was pulled over his blond hair. He introduced the team's sergeant—Dave—and the team's intelligence sergeant—Bryan.

Charlie spent the next hour walking the team through the mission. Everyone agreed the Special Forces team should get in position to watch the house before Wali picked up Charlie at the base.

When Charlie was done, Marc started giving out orders.

"We've got a lot of work to do," he said. "You guys are welcome to hang in here. If you need to rack out, we have a spare room."

The rest of the day, the Special Forces team loaded their trucks and got ready to leave. Felix found a spot in the corner and worked on his laptop. Charlie didn't even want to know what kind of OGA shit he was doing.

Bored, Charlie took a walk around the compound. It was just like the bases he'd built and operated in on previous deployments. The only difference was the amenities were better. The firebase's gym looked like the fitness centers back in Kandahar. The team room had internet and both an Xbox and PlayStation. Even three thousand miles from home, it was good living.

He started to complain to himself, ranting about how when he was on his first team, he didn't have anything. He lived out of a rucksack. But before he gave in to his inner grumpy old man, he remembered that his first deployments were to train foreign soldiers. Diarrhea was his only enemy.

Wali arrived around sunset in a beat-up station wagon. Charlie, dressed in the baggy pants and shirt of the region, met him just inside the gate. When Wali got out of the vehicle, he helped Charlie tie his headscarf.

"Wali," Charlie said, "this is..."

Charlie paused for a second, unsure if Felix was going to use his true name. OGA guys always went with John or something, and it always came off as fake.

"Felix," Felix said, filling in the blank. "It's great to finally meet you. Charlie and his green hat–wearing friends speak very highly of you."

Wali shook Felix's hand.

"It is my honor to help you."

Charlie slid a Glock pistol into a concealable holster on his hip and grabbed his "go" bag packed with survival gear. He handed Wali a radio.

"Felix is going to wait here while we meet with your uncle," Charlie said. "This is your radio in case we get split up. I've got a radio and a GPS tracker. We'll also have ISR overhead."

Intelligence, Surveillance, and Reconnaissance, usually conducted by a drone.

"No drones," Wali said. "It will spook my uncle. He is terrified of the things."

Felix and Charlie exchanged a surprised glance.

"I can't do this mission without it," Charlie said. "It was the only way we could get authorization. He won't even know the drone is in the area."

Wali started to protest but stopped.

"One final thing," Felix said.

He pulled out a small point-and-shoot camera.

"Mind if I get a mug shot?" he asked. "If this thing goes south and we have to bail you guys out, I want to make sure they know you're a good guy."

Wali smiled and Felix took his photo.

"Ready?" Charlie said.

Wali turned to leave. Felix and Charlie shook hands.

"Be safe," Felix said.

Wali drove the beat-up station wagon out of the gate. The streets were deserted as they drove around for a while making sure no one was tailing them.

"Who was Felix?"

Charlie slid his pistol under his leg.

"OGA."

Wali let out a little whistle.

"A real CIA spy."

Charlie smiled.

"Something like that."

Wali nodded.

"I guess I thought they'd be cooler."

Charlie laughed.

"Me too," he said.

Charlie watched as the sun set, turning the high desert a Mars red. Soon it was almost pitch-black except for a blanket of stars that seemed to stretch from horizon to horizon. Charlie could barely see Wali in the seat next to him, leaving both men with nothing but their thoughts.

Charlie finally broke the silence.

"What is your uncle offering?"

"I don't know," Wali said. "But it must be big. He is risking his life to talk with you."

The car bounced along the dirt road, jostling the two men.

"Where are we headed?"

"Out of town," Wali said. "Too many eyes."

Charlie laughed.

"I got that part."

"We're going to a house near Mulla Wali Waleh."

Charlie took out a folded map and turned on his red-light flashlight.

"How close are we getting to the border?"

"Not too close," Wali said. "My uncle is convinced you have drones watching it at all times."

The ride took about thirty minutes. They followed the highway for a while and then turned onto a dirt road that led toward a small cluster of compounds. Charlie spotted a young fighter cradling an AK-47 near the gate of one of the mud compounds in the headlights as Wali parked the car.

"That's Zahir," Wali said. "He's my uncle's bodyguard. Surrogate son, really. We played soccer together."

Zahir came up to the driver's-side window. They spoke for a second in Pashto.

"No weapons," Wali said to Charlie in English.

Charlie shook his head.

"No way," Charlie said. "He has a rifle. I'm keeping my pistol."

Wali shrugged and translated Charlie's answer. Zahir looked at his rifle and then at Charlie and Wali.

"Go," Zahir said in halting English.

Wali looked at Charlie.

"Zahir says if I trust you, he'll trust you," he said. "My uncle speaks pretty good English. I can stay here with the car and you can go in. Does that work? Do you need me?"

Charlie had his Winkler knife. He'd be able to defend himself in a pinch. But he hated to give up the pistol.

"OK," Charlie said. "I'll keep the radio."

Wali walked Charlie to the door. They were just out of earshot of Zahir.

"Keep your eyes open," Charlie said. "If shit goes down, key the radio and then run like hell. We'll link up at the rendezvous. Roger?"

Wali nodded.

"Roger."

Charlie pulled open the wooden door and entered the house. It was abandoned, and no one had lived there in a long time. Thick dust caked the wooden furniture. A small lantern lit up the room. Razaq sat in a corner on a clean rug. A teapot and two glasses were arranged on a tray in front of him. He was a small man with a massive tangled gray beard. A scarf was tied around his head, shielding his eyes. Charlie removed his boots and took a seat on the rug.

"*Assalamu' alaikum*" [Peace to you], Charlie said.

"*Aya ta pa pakhto khabarey kawalai shey*?" [Do you speak Pashto?] Razaq asked.

"Only a little," Charlie said. "But I was told you speak English."

"One language is never enough," Razaq said.

Razaq poured two glasses of tea.

"Why did you come here?" he said in accented English.

Charlie looked a little confused.

"To meet you," Charlie said. "Wali said you wanted to speak to me. You want to come to the United States. I'm here to help you."

Razaq paused to find the words.

"Do you know why your country came to Afghanistan?"

"You attacked us on 9/11," Charlie said.

"Those were the camels," Razaq said.

Charlie knew "camels" was a derogatory term for Arabs used by the Afghans.

"They brought us face-to-face with disaster and then you attacked us in revenge," Razaq said.

"We didn't ask to be attacked," Charlie said. "And you had your chance to turn over the camels. But your country chose to defend them."

Razaq pulled out his beads. He took a sip of his tea and changed the subject.

"When the bombing began, I was commanding some four hundred fighters. Then you came and slaughtered us. The bombs cut down our men like a reaper harvesting wheat," Razaq said. "After the bombing, I put on an old brown shalwar kameez and headed for Pakistan. I walked for days as the Americans chased me. We were like wild animals. They were shooting at us from the hills as we ran."

Charlie took a sip of his tea. He'd sat with Taliban in the past, but only after he'd captured them. This was different. Razaq was sharing his version of the war. Charlie had never considered what it was like to face the Americans.

"I hid my weapon in a wadi and walked to a village, saying I was a lost traveler and asking for food. The villagers fed me, but I had lost touch with my comrades. I got my rifle and walked on until a minibus came along. I aimed my gun at the driver and forced him to stop. The van was full of Taliban. They said they had no room for me, but I threatened to shoot out their tires unless they took me. I had to lie on the floor with their feet on my body."

"What about Wali?"

Razaq shook his head.

"He refused to leave. He wanted to see Rambo."

"So, how did you get to Pakistan? I mean, that's where you were headed, right?"

Razaq paused to sip his tea and then nodded.

"Yes. I opened a business and fixed washing machines until one day my old commander stopped at my house. He was traveling around Pakistan to rally our forces. When did you come to Afghanistan?"

"My first deployment was in 2004," Charlie said.

Razaq smiled.

"I returned at the same time," he said. "Did you fight in Iraq?"

Charlie shook his head no.

"Only Afghanistan," he said. "We had enough to do here."

"The American invasion of Iraq was very positive for us," Razaq said. "Arab and Iraqi mujahedeen began visiting us. They brought suicide bombers and tactics for roadside bombings."

"What can you tell me about IEDs and suicide attacks?" Charlie said.

If this was going to work, he needed information. Charlie was about to speak again when Razaq cleared his throat.

"Our men are watching American bases twenty-four hours a day. They inform us of American movements. We now have more destructive bombs. Ammonium-nitrate bombs with aluminum shards. We get regular deliveries of these fertilizers, explosives, fuses, detonators, and remote controls. One heavy shipment is on its way right now. I think we are better at making IEDs now than the Arabs who first taught us."

Charlie leaned forward.

"Where is this shipment?"

Razaq rolled the beads through his fingers.

"Do you know Gul Mohammed Jan?" Razaq said. "He's an ANA general and a contractor?"

"I know of him," Charlie said.

"Do you know about the rockets he provides to you?" Razaq said.

"No. He doesn't give us anything. Maybe he peddles the rockets to the Air Force guys, but we don't mess around with that."

Razaq chuckled.

"I sell him the rockets," Razaq said. "They come from my caches and are mostly defective. He pays me in dollars to make himself important in your eyes."

"He isn't important in my eyes," Charlie said.

"Jan also pays me every month to not attack his trucks," Razaq said.

Charlie just shook his head.

"What about suicide bombers? We've had four in the last month. One hit an American convoy. IED incidents are up. What do you have on the bombers? Where is that shipment of bomb-making materials? Who is making them? Where are they?"

Razaq looked up from his beads.

"He is in Pakistan," Razaq said. "Unless you guys can suddenly cross the border and raid Wana, he is safe."

Charlie was getting frustrated with Razaq. The old man was acting like a child. He wanted all the rewards but didn't want to do any of the work.

"Let me worry about that," Charlie said. "Give me a name. Give me a phone number."

Razaq started to work his beads again.

"Not until you promise me safe haven," Razaq said.

"A suicide bomber doesn't even buy you an economy ticket to Peshawar," Charlie said. "Give me bin Laden and I'll put you on the next flight to the Bahamas, first class."

Razaq worked his beads and didn't respond. Charlie looked at his watch. He had only a few minutes before he needed to head back to the base.

"Well, Razaq, I'd suggest you find me something worth trading or this is a one-time thing," Charlie said.

Charlie started to get up when Razaq motioned for him to sit down again.

"The shipment is in Spin Boldak," he said. "The bomber is coming to train some of my men. I will know more details soon. Is that enough?"

Charlie was happy.

"No, it's not enough," he said. "But it's a start. We get a good op out of it and you'll be on your way to paying for that ticket."

Charlie stood up this time.

"Help me with something," he said. "Wali says you don't want money. Just a ticket to my country, a nation you've been fighting for years now. Why?"

Razaq stroked his beard.

"Being Taliban is like wearing a jacket of fire," he said. "I've fought long enough."

CHAPTER 14

The Romanian guard approached Wali's window and stuck out his hand.

The war in Afghanistan was an international effort on paper, but on the ground it was a different story. Some countries, like the United States, did more of the heavy lifting, while others took care of more mundane but still critical missions, like security. That was Romania's contribution to the war effort. Guarding the gate.

The guards had more muscle than brains. When they weren't working standing at the gate, they were at the gym or chasing the women who worked at the stores on the Boardwalk.

"What's up, buddy?" the guard said.

All of them spoke some English and had a vocabulary straight from Hollywood action movies.

"Not much, brother," Wali said, climbing out of the truck so the guards could search it.

Denise was on the passenger side talking to another guard. The guard stuck his head in the truck and glanced around. He then turned to face Wali.

"Can I hold it?"

Wali smiled and fished out his bankroll. This started after the guards found cash in his truck on a previous visit. At first they were suspicious, but then he let them each hold it and fan it out so they could take pictures.

Now, if the right shift was at the gate, he got asked. Wali handed it to the guard, who palmed it.

"It's heavy," the guard said. "How much is it?"

Wali eyed his bankroll.

"Maybe twenty K," he said.

"I've never held this much money," the guard said.

Wali took the roll back and pulled off the thick rubber band, letting the bills unfold. He fanned them out with his thumb. The guard stood there dumbfounded.

"Hey," the guard said, waving over his partner talking to Denise. "Look at this."

The second guard came around the truck and let out a long whistle when he saw the cash.

"Just hit me with it," the second guard said. "I've never seen so much money."

Wali smacked the guard around the shoulders and face with the fan of bills as his unit mates laughed.

"You like that," Wali said, waving the fanned-out bills around.

"We've got to go," Denise said, ending the fun.

Wali climbed into the truck and the guards waved him through the gate. Denise waited until they cleared the checkpoint before she turned toward Wali.

"You don't worry about flashing your cash around like that? You know Jan is waiting for you to make a mistake."

Wali shook his head.

"Worry about what?" he said. "Who is going to touch me? I'm running all of the supplies for the Special Forces. They love me. Fuck Jan. That old man talks like a man but acts like a woman. He won't kill me. He can't."

"Why can't he?"

"Because my friends will kill him. You heard what Charlie did to him for just stopping my trucks. What do you think he'll do if he hurts me or my business?"

Wali pulled up to the parking lot in front of the Chapel—which was made of wood and resembled something from a Hollywood western—next to the Boardwalk. Denise climbed out and opened the back door to get out a box of supplies for the store. She also reached for a couple of iPads on the seat.

"Leave the iPads," Wali said. "They're not for the store."

Denise was confused.

"What are they for?"

"Charlie," Wali said.

"What does he need them for?"

Wali put the truck in gear.

"Work."

At Camp Brown, Woody brought Wali over to meet Charlie outside the TOC. Charlie and Wali walked around the back of the headquarters building and sat on the porch in front of Charlie's room.

Camp Brown was a mix of concrete buildings, modular trailers, and wooden B-huts. Charlie—because he knew the camp mayor—got a room in one of the concrete buildings. After more than a decade of war, some of the rooms had amenities like a front porch like Charlie's, with a wooden table and two camp chairs.

Wali put an iPad on the table between them.

"I know you put in a good word for me," he said. "Thank you."

Charlie picked up the iPad and inspected it for a second before returning it to the table.

"Thanks, man," he said, "but I can't take this. I recommended you because you can do the job, not so that I'd get a gift."

The iPad sat between them.

"It's yours," Wali said. "I am sure you can find other uses for it. Maybe for work?"

Charlie knew he could use the iPad as a gift for sources. It would be a nice tool in his tool box to use later.

"Thank you," Charlie said. "But you didn't come here to give me Apple products. What's up?"

Wali looked around to make sure no one was near and then leaned closer to Charlie.

"I heard from Razaq," Wali said.

Wali opened one of the iPad boxes and powered up the tablet.

"I loaded all the details here," he said. "Make, model, even pictures of the truck and the bomber."

Charlie took the iPad and swiped his finger across the screen as he looked at the pictures.

"When does he move?" he asked.

"Tonight," Wali said. "He'll leave Wana this afternoon and cross the border after midnight."

Charlie stood up and picked up both iPads.

"Hate to cut this short, but I've got a lot of work to do," he said.

"What should I tell my uncle?" Wali asked.

Charlie was already heading toward the TOC.

"Nothing," he said. "Better he has no idea. I'll link up with you tomorrow."

Wali watched Charlie as he disappeared into the headquarters building. It felt good to be doing his part.

CHAPTER 15

Canterbury sipped his iced coffee and watched the door to Legend Apparel. A bodybuilding magazine was spread out on his lap. He planned on hitting the gym hard while deployed. His goal was to come back ripped. So far he'd been a couple of times but found it easier to hit the rack in his room and watch a DVD after working long hours in the office. He was there for six months. He needed to pace himself. He still had time, he told himself.

The sun was starting to set, and it would be dinner soon. Canterbury was debating whether to eat on the Boardwalk or go to the DFAC when he saw her.

She was straightening some merchandise hanging near the door of the store. The girl had short-cropped black hair and olive skin. She was wearing tight khaki pants and a black polo shirt. When she leaned over to arrange something, he just caught a glimpse of the small of her back. Just seeing her bare skin gave him chills. She wasn't like the girls back home. Maybe Asian, Canterbury thought, but it didn't matter to him. She was intoxicating.

Closing the magazine, he walked into the store. She was getting her stuff from behind the register. Another girl, who was not so pretty, was standing behind the counter. They were talking but stopped when Canterbury walked in the door.

"Hello," the not-so-pretty girl said. "Let me know if we can help you."

Canterbury nodded and smiled. He pretended to look at some jackets but never took his eyes off the pretty girl. When she left, he followed.

"Excuse me," Canterbury said as the pretty girl walked down the Boardwalk. "Miss, do you have a second?"

The pretty girl turned around, and Canterbury got lost in her brown eyes.

"I was wondering if you'd like to get a coffee?"

The pretty girl looked at the cup in Canterbury's hand.

"Looks like you already have one," she said.

Canterbury tossed the cup into a nearby trash can. The pretty girl started to walk away, and for a second Canterbury almost let her go. He didn't know what to do or say.

"Stop," he said, the word coming out like an order more than a request. "Please stop for second."

The pretty girl turned, more confused than scared.

"I don't even know your name," Canterbury said.

"Anabel," she said. "Can I go now?"

Canterbury looked away, not sure what to do. Something told him that if she walked away now, he'd never get the nerve to talk to her again.

"No," he said. "You can't leave until you at least agree to have dinner with me."

Anabel paused.

"No," she said. "Not until you tell me your name."

"Canterbury," he said, pointing to the name strip on his uniform. "I mean Neil. Neil Canterbury."

"OK, Neil," she said, walking back toward the store with a little smirk on her face. "You got your chance. I need to let my coworker know I'm not going back to my room on the shuttle until later. Wait here."

Canterbury waited by the door. A few minutes later, Anabel came out. She'd put on some makeup and looked even more beautiful. They walked down the Boardwalk toward TGI Fridays.

"Is this OK?" Canterbury asked, holding the door for her as they entered.

"Sure," she said. "I've heard good things."

A Filipino waitress dressed in a red-and-white uniform shirt with the necessary pieces of flair took them to a booth. The restaurant looked like any of the franchises in the United States. A life-size Yoda holding a lightsaber sat near the bar.

Canterbury watched her as she scanned the menu. From the minute he walked through the door, he forgot he was in Afghanistan. This was a date, and he was going to do everything possible to keep it that way.

The waitress came over to take their order.

"I'll have the chicken and shrimp Cajun pasta, with a Blue Hawaiian slushy," Anabel said.

The waitress turned her attention to Canterbury.

"I'll take a burger and a vanilla milkshake," he said.

When the waitress left, Canterbury turned to find Anabel staring at him. He smiled and looked away for a second. He had no idea how he got here.

"I'd love to get a beer with my burger," Canterbury said.

"I know some guys if you need some beer or liquor," Anabel said.

Canterbury frowned. *I wish she hadn't said that*, he thought.

"I'm sure you do," he said. "But if you show it to me, I'm going to have to arrest you."

Anabel's face went white, and fear flashed in her eyes.

"Kidding," Canterbury said. "Well, kind of. I work for the Air Force Office of Special Investigations, so it is my job to keep this place safe."

Anabel relaxed, a little.

"And beer is a threat?"

Canterbury shrugged.

"No," he said. "But it's against General Order Number One. How would it look if I drank beer when my job is to enforce the rules?"

The beverages arrived before she answered. Canterbury took a sip of his milkshake and then folded his hands on the table.

"Where are you from?"

Anabel put her drink on the table.

"Oakland," she said.

Canterbury cocked his head.

"I figured you were from the Philippines or something," he said.

"I'm Afghan," Anabel said. "Well, Afghan-American. I was born in California. My parents fled there after the Soviet invasion."

"What are you doing here?" Canterbury asked.

"I wanted to see my parents' country," she said. "I kind of thought this was my chance to understand my parents better. My father isn't well, so the pay also helps."

"Have you been able to get out?" Canterbury said. "See the country?"

"Once," Anabel said. "Wali took me downtown and showed me around Kandahar. I saw where my father grew up. That is how I got the job. Some of his family knew people who knew Wali. He offered to give me a job managing his store. I figured I'd take a year, see Afghanistan, and then come home and go to college."

Anabel took a sip of her blue drink.

"What about you?"

"I'm from Boston," Canterbury said. "Grew up in Dorchester. Youngest of five. Joined the Air Force after high school. Wanted to be a pilot but didn't have any money for college, plus I didn't want to miss the war."

"You just wanted to scratch your Captain America itch?"

Canterbury shifted in his seat. She was probably right, even if he didn't want to admit it.

"Well, I did want to serve my country," Canterbury said. "And the college money isn't bad. But I'm no hero. Just a guy trying to do his part."

"And what is your part?"

"I make sure Taliban spies don't attack the flight line, and I investigate crimes."

"Like a cop?" Anabel said.

"Right," he said. "A special agent."

Anabel smiled.

"When I get out, I want to get into federal law enforcement," Canterbury said.

"Like the FBI?"

Canterbury smirked.

"Nah," he said. "I want to join the DEA. Keep drugs off the street. I saw what they can do back home."

Anabel took a sip of her drink. The blue liquid stained her teeth and lips so it looked like she'd eaten a Smurf.

"You're really set on saving the world," she said.

"Someone has to," Canterbury said.

The waitress arrived with their food. It looked edible, but just barely. The sauce on Anabel's pasta was paste. But Canterbury really wasn't there to eat. He just wanted to be around Anabel.

"What about you?" he asked.

Anabel let out a giggle.

"Nothing exciting, like you," she said. "I was thinking about getting into fashion. Move to New York."

"The Yankees suck," Canterbury said.

He was a Red Sox fan. It was his involuntary reaction to any New York reference.

"What?" Anabel asked.

"Sorry," he said. "It's a Red Sox thing. Can't help it. So why New York?"

Anabel took a bite of her pasta and put her fork down.

"I don't know," she said. "It really just might be a change of scenery. I don't want to be in Oakland. I want to have my own thing, you know?"

Canterbury did.

"Part of the reason I joined the Air Force," he said. "I tell people it was because I wanted to serve. But I really wanted to get the hell out of Boston and the neighborhood. I wanted something more."

Anabel smiled.

"And by 'something more' you meant a chain restaurant in Kandahar."

Canterbury laughed.

"Beats Applebee's," he said.

For the next half hour, they talked. The conversation came naturally and without pause. Later, Canterbury couldn't remember what he'd told her or vice versa. The only thing he could remember was how he found her intoxicating sitting across from him picking at her pasta.

The waitress was back and clearing their plates. Canterbury had barely touched his burger, but he wasn't hungry.

"Dessert?" he asked.

"Sure," Anabel said. "Maybe we can share one?"

Canterbury heard the wail of a siren off in the distance. He knew what that meant. The siren was a warning. Take cover. A rocket was inbound. Fired by the guys he chased on a daily basis. It had terrified him the first time it went off. But he'd grown used to it. Now, however, even with the threat of imminent death, all he wanted to do was order dessert.

The restaurant froze. The waitress placed her tray on the table, laid down on the floor, and covered her head. People at the tables around them did the same. Anabel stifled a nervous laugh as she slid off her chair and crawled under the table where Canterbury was also taking shelter.

Huddled there, Canterbury felt her fingers intertwined with his own. They were holding hands. At that moment, he was content to have a rocket end his life in a fast-casual American chain restaurant in Kandahar.

CHAPTER 16

Charlie flipped through a packet of laminated pictures of the bomb maker—code-named Pacman—his shop had put together for the mission. There was a map of the compound and several shots of the bomb maker's truck. Charlie took one more look at the map and slid the flip book into the shoulder pocket of his shirt.

It was just after midnight, and Charlie was itching to go. The hurry-up-and-wait mentality of the Army—regardless of the unit—grated on him. Afghan commandos milled around. They were wiry men dressed in green camouflage uniforms. Most had a few days of scruff on their cheeks. These soldiers were the best of the Afghan Army, trained by American Special Forces at a base just north of Kabul. But all of their gear still looked secondhand.

Charlie was just a "strap hanger" on this one. Another gun for the ground force commander—a Third Group team leader whose Special Forces team was tasked with advising the commandos. Besides the Afghan commandos and their Special Forces advisers, an Air Force JTAC, or Joint Tactical Aircraft Controller, was also on the mission. Embedded with the Special Forces team, it was his job to call in airstrikes. He was an essential tool in the American way of war. Find the enemy, fix his position, and then pound the shit out of him from the air.

This was an Afghan-led operation, but that was in name only. Charlie teed up the operation based on information provided by

Razaq, and the American team was in the lead. The Afghans were a tool to be aimed at the target and sent forth.

"Loading up in five mikes," Jerry—the team leader—said.

Charlie didn't know Jerry personally. Only by reputation. He was one of the rising stars in the regiment. A head shorter than Charlie, he had a barrel chest and a beard that would make a Viking jealous. A former Ranger, he was compact and stocky but moved with the economy of an athlete. There was something dangerous about him. He was like a predator perpetually coiled to strike. Prone to direct action—military jargon for shooting bad guys in the face—Jerry was a hammer in a world of nails.

His team reflected their commander's sensibility. Special Forces made its money working with the locals, the soft power of rapport building and medical clinics. But to "free the oppressed" sometimes meant killing the oppressor. That was Jerry and his team's specialty.

The mission was pretty straightforward. They'd land three kilometers from the target and patrol to the compound. Once the assault team led by Jerry's team sergeant—Red, a muscular man with thick arms and a curly mess of red hair—secured the compound, Charlie and his team of four Afghan commandos would collapse on the target and identify the bomb maker.

But right now, they were all sitting around the helipad as the crews made final checks on the two CH-47 Chinook helicopters slated to deliver them to the target. The Chinooks had two massive rotors and were the fastest ships in the Army's helicopter fleet. The engines started to whine and then the massive rotors started to churn. Soon the roar of the engine made it impossible to talk or even think. Charlie watched as the crew chiefs signaled for them to start loading.

Charlie nodded to his four commandos and followed them into the helicopter. His job on the mission was to set a blocking position with his team to the right of the target area. The Afghan sergeant spoke English, but the rest didn't.

Hours before, Charlie had watched as a drone filmed Pacman's truck crossing the border and parking at a compound near Spin Boldak. Once inside the wall, some fighters covered the truck with a tarp. Pacman and another man went inside the house. The drone operator counted ten pax—shorthand for people—on the target: one woman, two children, and seven military-age males, including Pacman and his driver. The Americans were coming with thirty men—ten Special Forces and twenty commandos.

It wasn't going to be a fair fight.

The whine of the engine changed, and the Chinook lifted into the night. Charlie dozed in the dark belly of the helicopter as it thundered its way toward the compound. Someone tapped him, and he saw the soldier hold up five fingers.

Five minutes.

Charlie looked at his commandos and flashed five fingers. Each one nodded. The pitch of the engine changed again, and Charlie felt the aircraft hover a second before descending. The rear ramp dropped, and he followed the crowd into a maelstrom of dust. Once Charlie made it to the edge of the cloud, he took a knee. The helicopter lifted off moments later. Everyone waited on a knee until the echo of the engines faded, and then got into formation and headed toward the target.

The compound was three kilometers away. Charlie heard Red in his Peltor headphones coordinating the movement to the target. Occasionally, Jerry offered an update from the drone watching the compound. So far everything was quiet.

The valley was narrow and sat just off the main artery between Kandahar and Spin Boldak. The recon element headed for a small hill near the compound. Charlie was near the front. As they patrolled, he spotted shell casings on the ground. A burnt tractor sat neglected outside the village. It was unclear if it had been damaged in a firefight.

Before they reached the target, Charlie and his team broke off from the main body. He and his four Afghan commandos set up on a hill north of the compound.

The radio crackled to life as Jerry and the rest of the team got close to the target. Charlie watched through his night-vision goggles as Red's assault team surrounded the compound. An Afghan commando blew a hole in the wall near the gate, and the soldiers behind him flowed into the compound with their rifles at the ready.

On the radio, Jerry provided a steady play-by-play of the search until a burst from an AK-47 shattered the silence after the explosion. The burst was answered by an M4 fired by either a Green Beret or a commando.

"We've got eight squirters," said the pilot of the drone watching from above, referring to the fighters fleeing the scene. "Four are headed east. Four are headed north."

It was Charlie's job to head off the squirters to the north. He signaled his Afghans to follow and led them down the side of the hill. They ran to a clearing at the bottom of the hill near a dirt road. The plan was to intercept the squirters just outside the village.

"Charlie, Jerry. ISR says your squirters are on motorcycles now. Heading down the road north of the village."

Charlie swore under his breath.

"Roger," he said into his radio. "We're in position."

His team set up in a ditch with clear sightlines into what looked like an abandoned campsite. There was a chest rack with several pouches filled with AK-47 magazines. Glasses of tea were left untouched. A scarf, likely discarded where a fighter had rested, was crumpled on the ground next to empty water bottles and stray AK-47 rounds. The fighters must have used the area as a bed-down or training site.

Up ahead, Charlie saw the squirters on a pair of motorcycles coming down the road. Two men were on each one. The men on the back were facing the rear, each with an AK-47 on his lap.

"When they get close, we'll take them," Charlie said. "Follow my lead."

The commandos' sergeant nodded and passed the word to the other three. The motorcycles were getting closer but seemed to be slowing down. Charlie looked back over his shoulder at the campsite.

Were they going to stop?

The commandos were getting antsy. Charlie was confident they didn't wait to shoot very often. The moments before a firefight were always the hardest. It was like being behind the wheel watching a car crash in slow motion and knowing that as soon as the shooting started, everything would be moving at a hundred miles per hour.

The motorcycles turned off the road. They were following a trail toward the campsite.

"Wait until they get off the bikes and then follow me," Charlie told the sergeant.

The fighters rode into the campsite and parked their bikes on the far side. Three of them dismounted and headed for the center of the camp where their discarded gear waited.

A lone man waited by the motorcycles.

"Wait," Charlie whispered to himself. "Wait..."

One fighter grabbed the chest rack with several magazines. Another packed up the scarf and some personal items. The third fighter uncovered the cache of weapons. Charlie moved his laser sight over so it hovered center mass on the man at the cache.

When the fighter pulled out a rocket-propelled grenade launcher, Charlie fired.

The bullets smashed into the fighter and he dropped the launcher. His body shuddered as each round hit and he crumpled to the ground. The whole campsite exploded with gunfire as the commandos and Taliban fighters opened up. The fighter with the scraf went down, cluthing his leg.

Charlie hesitated.

It had been more than a year since he'd fired a shot in combat. Everything sounded louder. Brighter. Then Charlie felt the rush. He took two short breaths to center himself and then scanned the campsite for a new target. It felt like adrenaline was coming out of his ears, and it took every ounce of his training to stay centered.

Charlie tracked to his left and spotted the Taliban fighter who had picked up the chest rack. The fighter started to spray and pray toward the commandos' muzzle flashes. The AK-47 in his hands kicked up and down as he raked it back and forth in a 180-degree arc. Most of the rounds flew harmlessly over the commandos' heads, but that was enough to make them stop firing.

Things were slowing down again. Charlie's old instincts were coming back. He put his laser on the fighter's chest and squeezed the trigger. The fighter spun around and then disappeared from his sight.

To his left, the commandos opened fire again, sending the last Taliban fighter scrambling away from the motorcycles. The commandos chased him. Charlie heard a burst from an M4 when they caught up to him.

Charlie pivoted back toward the camp. The fighter with the scarf was lying on the ground grabbing at his leg. Every few seconds he let out a muffled cry. Charlie started toward him as the commandos made sure the other fighters were down. The man at the cache was dead. So was the one clutching the chest rack.

Charlie moved slowly toward the prone fighter with the scarf.

"Let me see your hands," he said in Pashto. "Hands."

The fighter ignored Charlie's order. He was howling in pain and clutching his calf. Charlie took one hand off his rifle and grabbed the fighter's injured leg and dragged him toward the motorcycles.

The man howled.

The Afghan sergeant joined Charlie there.

"All clear," the sergeant said.

"Search him," Charlie said, covering the sergeant as he patted the man down looking for weapons.

While the sergeant searched, Charlie studied the man's face. There was something about him.

"Nothing," the sergeant said.

Charlie fished out a pressure bandage from his first aid kit.

"Cover me," he said.

Charlie forced the fighter's hands away from his calf. Cutting the man's pants open, he looked at the wound. Shrapnel or a ricochet must have hit the fighter in the calf. There was a small entry wound on one side and a larger exit wound on the other. Charlie put the dressing on the wound to stop the bleeding. *He'll live*, Charlie thought.

"The other fighters," Charlie said, standing up and looking back toward the campsite.

"Dead," the sergeant said. "The one who ran is dead."

"OK," Charlie said. "Let me call it in."

"Jerry, Charlie."

"Go ahead," Jerry said.

"We've got three EKIA," Charlie said. "One wounded. We're going to need a medic."

"Roger," Jerry said. "ISR says we've got enemy pax moving toward our locations. I've got CAS inbound with our exfil. We'll patrol to your location in five mikes."

Charlie had five minutes to get ready before the helicopters returned with fighter jets—combat air support—ready to bomb the Taliban reinforcements the drone pilot was tracking from above.

The surviving fighter was still moaning on the ground.

"Tell him to settle down," Charlie said to the sergeant as he fished out his mission packet.

Charlie flipped to the picture of Pacman and held it up next to the wounded fighter's face. A perfect match. Charlie knew he recognized him.

"Jerry, Charlie."

"Send it," Jerry said.

"We have Pacman," Charlie said. "He's our wounded fighter."

"How serious?"

"He'll live."

"Roger," Jerry said. "We're inbound."

Charlie turned to the sergeant.

"They're coming here. Have your guys pull security. I've got him."

The sergeant nodded and headed over to his men and set them up to watch all the approaches to the camp. Charlie took a zip tie from his kit and rolled Pacman over on his stomach. The Afghan bomb maker groaned as Charlie cinched his hands behind his back.

"You speak English?" Charlie asked after propping Pacman up against one of the motorcycles.

Pacman just stared at Charlie.

"OK," Charlie said. "Water?"

Pacman shook his head yes. Charlie had an old Army-green plastic canteen. He unscrewed the cap and gave Pacman a drink.

"I knew you spoke English, dickhead."

Pacman looked away. He was busted.

"I know who you are and why you're here," Charlie said. "Might as well talk to me. We've got nothing to do but wait."

Pacman looked down at his lap.

"Fine," Charlie said.

He put the canteen away.

Jerry and the others arrived a few minutes later. The other blocking positions reported two Hilux trucks coming toward the village.

"Hey," Jerry said. "Not sure how long we're going to stick around. We stirred up some shit."

"We get any bomb-making materials?" Charlie asked.

"Negative," Jerry said. "There was nothing in the truck. See if he'll tell you. I don't want to leave that stuff here."

Charlie turned back to Pacman. He took out a bottle of water and took a long pull before squatting down so he was face-to-face with the bomb maker. Charlie grabbed Pacman's calf and pressed hard on the pressure bandage. Pacman yelled in pain. Charlie shoved him onto his back and stood over him.

"We're leaving in a minute," Charlie said. "Either you can come and get that wound looked at or your friends will find your body here."

Charlie slid his rifle in front of him and snapped off the safety. Pacman's eyes never left Charlie or his weapon.

"No explosives," Pacman said.

Charlie raised his rifle into a low ready position.

"Just documents. Instructions. They were bringing explosives in a few days. After training."

"Where are the documents?" Charlie said.

"The truck," Pacman said. "Hidden underneath."

Charlie placed blacked-out goggles over Pacman's eyes and joined Jerry at the center of the camp. All around them, Afghan commandos and Special Forces soldiers were set up in a defensive perimeter.

Jerry was talking on the radio with the operations center back at Camp Brown. Nearby, the Air Force JTAC was talking to fighter jets circling above.

"I've got two Hornets waiting for a Nine Line," the JTAC said.

A 9 Line is a standard message used to pass information for a strike.

Jerry looked at the JTAC, who resembled the other Green Berets with a black beard.

"Tell them to stand by," he said.

The JTAC shot Jerry a thumbs-up.

Jerry looked at Charlie.

"Pacman says no explosives," Charlie said. "Just documents hidden on the truck."

"OK," Jerry said. "Well, this just got too hot to go back to the village. At least we got him. Make sure he's ready to move while I manufacture a firefight. Can't leave that truck here."

Because of the rules of engagement, there was no way to call in an airstrike unless they were under fire.

"Desert Eagle Main, Skull One Six," Jerry said. "We are troops in contact. Requesting ECAS."

Jerry fired off a few rounds as he spoke.

"Roger, Skull One Six. You've got two fast movers overhead. You're cleared hot."

Jerry looked at Charlie.

"Once they hit those trucks, we're moving."

Charlie went back to Pacman and checked his bandage. It was stained dark red, but the bleeding had slowed. Charlie hoisted Pacman to his feet. The bomb maker tried to walk but collapsed in the dirt.

"Get the litter," Charlie called to the commando sergeant.

One of the commandos arrived with the sergeant, holding a collapsible olive-green stretcher. They snapped it open and rolled Pacman onto it. Charlie secured Pacman's hands to the litter so he couldn't reach any weapons.

Overhead, Charlie heard the fighters getting into attack position as the JTAC talked them onto the target. Using the same grid as in the laminated mission packet, the Hornets zeroed in on the compound, where the Taliban fighters were now trying to locate the Americans.

"CAS is inbound," Jerry said.

Charlie took a knee and looked back toward the village. The F-18s thundered above. It was pitch-black and Charlie squinted through his night-vision goggles trying to pick up the jet aircraft above.

"Six seconds" the JTAC said.

Charlie counted off in his head. He saw the flash first. The farmland around them suddenly was in silhouette as a mushroom cloud of dust and fire erupted where the bombs hit. Seconds later, the roar of the blast washed over the team like a wave. Charlie heard Red laughing as the bombs impacted and fire shot high into the sky.

"I've got an Armageddon hard-on after that," the JTAC said. "The explosion just sat there and I am like whacking off to it. Yeah. Yeah."

Charlie knew a lot of JTACs, and every one of them was weird. Something to do with having the power to rain hell down on the enemy from above.

Then out of the darkness Charlie heard the whistling of a piece of shrapnel. It landed with a sickening thunk against the ground.

"That was close as fuck," Jerry said.

The team retreated a couple of hundred meters farther and waited for the next strike—this time a two-thousand-pound bomb. The flash again came first, but the boom was different. This one seemed to rumble from the core of the Earth. It reminded Charlie of the aftershocks from an earthquake. It was spectacular in a very scary way. Charlie couldn't imagine being the target of the US aircraft.

"They're going to think the end of the world just came," the JTAC said.

"And next time we go down south, it will be, 'Hey, they got a new lake,'" Jerry said. "OK, let's take it back to the house."

Charlie looked back toward the village as he stood up to leave. A small fire burned near the smoldering ruins of the compound. Just as he turned to head out, an explosion shattered the silence. Rock and gravel rained down on the waiting patrol.

Charlie looked over at Jerry.

"That was explosives," he said. "This fucker said there were no explosives."

Jerry turned to see Pacman on the litter by two commandos waiting to carry him to the helicopter, his eyes covered by the blacked-out goggles. In one swift motion, Jerry kicked Pacman in the face, sending the bomb maker and litter tumbling over.

"Let's go," Jerry said. "He's lucky no one got hurt."

CHAPTER 17

Basir watched as Wali left the airfield's main gate and turned toward Kandahar City. He started his motorcycle and fell in behind Wali's truck.

Jan wanted to kill Wali, but that would bring the wrath of the Special Forces. His only choice was Canterbury. But the Air Force investigator needed evidence.

That was Basir's job. Find evidence.

Wali picked his way through the city traffic before breaking out on the west side toward Panjwai. This wasn't a normal meeting. Usually, Wali stopped at his gas station on the outskirts of the city or at a soccer field near his old school. Routine stuff, but this trip was different. He was traveling alone and didn't even stop in the city.

The highway out of the Kandahar City was paved and smooth. Wali raced down the asphalt with Basir a few cars behind. Just past Sperwan Ghar, a man-made mountain that was once held by the Taliban until the Special Forces took it over, Wali turned off the main road and bounced along a dirt track toward a small village.

Instead of following Wali down the road, Basir passed the turn-off and went down another half mile before turning off the highway and going cross-country. The terrain was brown and dusty. The mountains looked like broken teeth sticking out of a sandbox. Basir cut through the grape mounds until he got to the outskirts of the village. Most of the houses had been destroyed. Mud walls were crumbling. Gates hung open. Trash littered the courtyards.

Basir saw Wali's truck parked in one of the compounds next to another 4x4 truck.

He left his motorcycle and walked around the perimeter of the village until he got to the back of the compound. There was a window, and he heard the murmur of voices coming from inside. It was difficult to make out what was being said, so Basir snuck closer to the window until he was squatting just outside it.

"But first, your friends have to promise to send me away," one voice said. "I promise you it is very important that this happens."

Basir thought he recognized the voice but couldn't place it. The other voice was Wali for sure.

"They will do it," Wali said. "But first I need to know what it is you know that is so important."

Basir heard the men moving about inside the room. It was getting cold, and Basir's teeth were chattering. He wished he'd taken the blanket from his motorcycle.

"Close that window," the unidentified voice said. "It is cold."

Basir held his breath and clamped his hands over his mouth to keep his teeth from knocking together. He closed his eyes and waited. The wooden shutter creaked and popped as someone closed it. Now Basir couldn't hear anything. Instead of waiting, he worked his way back to his motorcycle and set up across from the compound.

Huddled under the blanket, Basir watched for an hour before Wali left the compound. Fifteen minutes later, the unidentified man left. He was old with a thick gray beard, but he moved gingerly as he climbed into the back of the 4x4, which quickly exited the gate.

It was dark, but Basir took pictures with his phone anyway. He hoped Jan would be able to identify the man in the photos.

CHAPTER 18

Canterbury parked in front of the TWOFOR offices. The Eastern European company managed all the subcontrac tors moving supplies by jingle trucks. He was late for a meeting with Susie Baron, the manager of the jingle truck contract.

Just inside the door, he was greeted by a secretary who spoke with an Eastern European accent.

"I'm here to see Susie," Canterbury said, sliding his Oakley sunglasses on top of his head. He was dressed in civilian clothes—5.11 pants, a North Face button-down shirt, and hiking boots. His pistol was strapped to his thigh.

"Who should I say is here?"

"Special Agent Canterbury."

The secretary paused for a second and then walked back to the office to get Susie. Canterbury liked the reaction he got when he dropped "Special Agent." Baron came out almost immediately. She was short—no more than five feet tall—with graying hair and reading glasses around her neck. She wore Walmart khaki pants and a royal-blue short-sleeve blouse. She looked like an accountant or a grandma or both.

"Special Agent," Baron said. "Can I get you a water?"

Canterbury held up the water bottle in his hand.

"I'm good," he said.

"Then come on back," Baron said, doing a quick about-face and shuffling back to her office.

Canterbury walked into the stuffy room and took a seat opposite the desk. Baron eased herself into the chair behind the desk and closed the laptop on the desktop, which was covered with papers—spreadsheets, contracts, and memos.

"How can I help you, young man?" Baron asked.

Canterbury took out his badge and flashed it. Baron took a cursory glance at the badge and then looked at Canterbury.

"I'm looking into a contractor," Canterbury said. "It's part of an ongoing AFOSI investigation."

Baron nodded.

"So who is this contractor?"

"Ahmed Wali," Canterbury said, taking out his notebook and pen. "I was hoping you could pull together anything you have on him. I understand he has a sole source with the Special Forces?"

Baron shook her head yes. She knew Wali.

"We got some complaints about the sole-source agreement," Baron said. "But I understand why the Special Forces wanted it. Frankly, their concerns are understandable since Afghanistan is a combat zone and many Afghan contractors, apart from Wali, are unreliable, or worse, working for the insurgents."

"Maybe so," Canterbury said. "But it really isn't the Special Forces' job to pick contractors."

Baron shrugged.

"I had a meeting to discuss the contract with the movement control team and the NATO Maintenance and Supply Agency," Baron said. "They pay for the supply runs. I asked how the Special Forces could bypass procedure and use Wali exclusively. I was told Wali was vetted because he worked as an interpreter. I don't know the history of it. I don't know what agreement he has with Special Forces. I addressed my complaint and was told 'SF gets what they want,' so I just left it alone. I've got enough to worry about, you know what I mean?"

Canterbury was taking notes. He looked up when Baron finished.

"Who else has one?"

Baron looked at Canterbury funny.

"Has what?" she asked.

"A sole-source contract," Canterbury said. "How many other units have one?"

Baron shook her head.

"Only the SF guys. I think other units talked about it, but except for Wali, there are no other contractors that are dependable enough. They figure they're better off going through the system and hoping to get good trucks."

"Can I get a copy of the contract?"

Baron got up from her desk and headed into the main office. Canterbury heard her ask one of the staff to print out a copy of the contract. Canterbury put his notebook away and looked around the office. The walls were gray and drab. There was a company calendar on the wall next to the desk, a whiteboard used to track tasks behind the chair, and a massive laminated calendar with deadlines scrawled on it on the opposite wall.

Tucked next to Baron's computer was a picture of her and a family in front of some suburban house in Ohio or somewhere. Something sickened Canterbury about the office and Baron. He couldn't put his finger on it until after he got back in his truck with a copy of the sole-source contract and the memorandum—signed by the Special Forces task force commander—authorizing it.

Baron was like every middle manager. She wasn't particularly talented but kept the trains going. She wasn't part of the war effort. She was just pushing papers. Canterbury got up every day ready to do battle to protect the base. Baron got up every day to collect a paycheck. This is what happened when war was outsourced. No sense of service or the feeling of being part of something bigger than a single man or woman.

Turd, Canterbury thought.

Back at the office, Canterbury was stopped by Captain Voss, a slight man with close-cropped black hair and olive features. Fresh out of college and officer candidate school, he was as by-the-book as it got. A perfect follower who wouldn't dare rock the boat.

"Where have you been?"

"Checking on a tip, sir," Canterbury said.

"Oh, a tip about what?"

"Fraud," Canterbury said. "A contractor is stealing, working for the Taliban, and maybe bribing Special Forces soldiers."

"Yeah," Voss said. "Well, call Task Force 2010 or SIGAR. We're here to protect the base."

"Yes, sir," Canterbury said. "But I figure since the contractor had access to the base, we had the jurisdiction to check him out."

Voss stared at Canterbury. It was the disapproving look of a parent. Voss treated all of his men like children, constantly checking behind them and micromanaging their movements.

"How are you doing on the background check review?" Voss said, ignoring Canterbury's explanation.

"It is ongoing," Canterbury said.

"Well, those files aren't going to review themselves," Voss said.

"Yes, sir," Canterbury said.

Back at his desk, Canterbury popped open his laptop and looked up Task Force 2010's tip line. He typed out an email about Wali's company. He hit send and turned to the pile of background checks. Canterbury pulled the first packet off the top and opened it. The company provided maintenance for the civilian aircraft ferrying supplies to Afghanistan. He was five names into his check when he stopped. Putting the file aside, he started to sort through the pile until he found it.

Wali's company roster.

Canterbury flipped open the file to the roster and started checking names.

He typed in Denise McKenna's name and waited.

A military police report about some alcohol-related issues popped up. Contractors were buying and selling liquor. The bottles would come on flights from Dubai and be sold for between $50 and $150 apiece. McKenna helped run the ring, according to the report. Canterbury printed off a February 2011 statement where she admitted to drinking vodka at least twice and to drinking with some of her colleagues. Even Canterbury thought the charges seemed weak. Anywhere else they wouldn't be against the law, but on Bagram—a massive base north of Kabul—drinking was banned. Under the regulations, the charges barred McKenna from working in Afghanistan. Canterbury could ban McKenna from Kandahar too, but that wouldn't help him get Wali.

Canterbury started the paperwork to ban McKenna, just in case. But first he wanted to talk with her.

ꕥꕥꕥ

The next day, Canterbury was an hour into his checks when his phone rang. It was Major Harvey Weston, who explained that he oversaw a task force of investigators looking into corruption allegations. His men had checked out Wali's company, and two points caught their attention. The first was that Wali was being used exclusively by the Special Forces. The second was that he was charging much more than his competitors. Weston asked Canterbury to verify Wali was still operating out of Kandahar Airfield.

"Yes, sir," Canterbury said. "I was at the TWOFOR office yesterday talking to them about this company."

"Good," Weston said. "We've got it from here."

"Sir?"

"We'll do an audit and stick a microscope up his ass and see what we can find," Weston said.

"Then what?" Canterbury asked. "We have a concurrent investigation into possible ties to the Taliban."

"If he's crooked," Weston said, "we'll freeze his bank account, ban him from working with the coalition, and try and recover some of the money. But we're a long way from there."

Canterbury smiled.

"Roger, sir. I'm here if you need anything more. In the meantime, I will keep investigating."

"Sounds good," Weston said. "Good work."

Canterbury hung up the phone. If he got his way, Wali was not only going to lose his freedom but his business as well. For the rest of the day, he worked through the pile of background checks.

But his mind was on how to turn McKenna.

CHAPTER 19

Wali was pacing when Charlie arrived at his compound. The young Afghan looked haggard.

"How did the meeting go?" Charlie asked.

Wali motioned for Charlie to sit down. A tray with tea and some sweets sat untouched on the table in the sitting room. Instead of sitting across from him, Wali sat next to Charlie.

"We have big problems," Wali said.

"Is your uncle OK?"

"Yes," Wali said. "He is fine. But he wants to go to America now."

Charlie exhaled, exasperated.

"I know he wants to go," Charlie said. "But one bomb maker isn't going to do it. I need more."

"I have more," Wali said. "Much more. But first, you have to promise you'll get him out."

"I can't promise that," Charlie said. "You know that."

Charlie took a sip of tea and let the silence hang in the room for a bit. Wali fiddled with his phone.

"I want out too," Wali said.

"Why do you want out?" Charlie said.

"Because no one is safe."

Charlie put down his cup.

"Enough with all the cryptic shit," Charlie said. "What the fuck is going on? Are you in danger?"

"We are all in danger," Wali said. "The Taliban have a nuclear bomb."

Charlie's eyes narrowed. He exhaled and smiled—not one of happiness but discomfort. The Taliban have *what?* He didn't believe it, but when had Wali ever lied to him?

Wali handed Charlie his phone. On the screen were pictures of a box and some wires. Charlie had no idea what he was looking at. He'd worked with explosives, but whatever this was looked like a cartoon science experiment. The wires were worn, the box containing the contraption was busted, and a thick coat of dirt and dust covered everything. It was impossible to confirm anything through the pictures.

"Let's say this is a bomb," Charlie said. "How did they get it?"

"They found it," Wali said. "My uncle said a farmer discovered it buried in a field. It was left behind by the Russians. The Quetta Shura want to sell it to al-Qaeda."

"What?"

Wali looked away. Charlie saw how the stress was piling up on him.

"They want to give it to the same fuckers that started all this. Can you imagine what they'll do with it?"

Charlie closed his eyes and took a deep breath. This was his worst nightmare if it was in fact a nuclear bomb he was looking at on the phone.

"Where is it?" he said.

"My uncle has it," Wali said. "But the Shura has a deal with the camels."

"And your uncle is sure it's a bomb."

Wali nodded.

"Yes."

"How?"

"He didn't tell me. But the Shura has a meeting set up in Dubai to make the deal. Why would the camels buy it if it wasn't a bomb?"

Charlie didn't argue with that.

"We have to get it first," Charlie said. "Tell your uncle not to move it. And don't let the Taliban give it to al-Qaeda."

Wali reached out and grabbed Charlie's arm.

"Is this enough to get us both out? If I help get this bomb, I won't be safe here. We both need to go."

Charlie stood up to leave. He'd just found his football. This was the victory. Stopping al-Qaeda from detonating a nuclear bomb was exactly what the war effort needed. This proved the sacrifice was necessary.

"Welcome to America," Charlie said. "I'm sure we can get you out once we get the bomb."

Wali's shoulders relaxed.

"I'm scared," he said just before Charlie reached the door. "If they do get the bomb, what will stop them from using it?"

Charlie paused at the door.

"Me."

CHAPTER 20

Canterbury sat next to Anabel. They were sharing a milk shake on the Boardwalk. She'd just closed the store and he had been waiting outside.

This was their fourth date, not counting several stops at the store, and something had changed. She was excited to see him. After a long day of dealing with cocky soldiers and crabby civilians, she welcomed the chance to hang with her boyfriend.

The label shocked her when she thought about it. She had come to Afghanistan looking for something. She didn't know what it was and still didn't. Maybe a closer look at her roots. A little adventure. A little money to start life in the United States. She really hadn't found all of that yet. But she found something with Neil. He wasn't like the others. He was gentle. But strong in his own way. She liked his ambition. He was serious but vulnerable at the same time. When she agreed to go out with him the first time, she did it for the story. He seemed harmless. But over the last couple of weeks, she'd come to depend on him for company.

"Hey," Canterbury said. "Kind of quiet over there."

Anabel blushed.

"Sorry," she said. "I told my mother about you."

Canterbury's face turned red. He took another sip of the milk-shake as he regained his composure.

"Yeah? What did you tell her?" he asked, trying to act cocky but failing to pull it off with a flushed face.

"That I'd met a nice American boy," Anabel said. "And that he's from Massachusetts, and I like him a lot."

"I'm not a nice boy," Canterbury said.

Anabel hit him on the shoulder.

"Yes, you are," she said. "You're not a cocky dick like the guys who come into the store. I wish they'd buy something instead of just gawking at me."

"I'm a gentleman," Canterbury said. "And if they keep gawking at you, I'll come and arrest them."

"Thank you, officer," Anabel said. "But I can handle myself."

"What did your mother say?"

Anabel shot Canterbury a confused look.

"About what?"

"Meeting a nice boy."

"To be careful," Anabel said.

Canterbury laughed.

"Be careful of what?" he asked. "You're in a war zone. I'm probably the least dangerous thing out here."

"Of falling in love," Anabel said.

Canterbury was silent. He was no longer embarrassed. A strange calm came over him. He looked into Anabel's eyes.

"Did you tell her it's already too late?"

Now Anabel's cheeks flushed red.

"No," she said. "But I told her that when you leave Kandahar, I'm going to leave too."

"So you're going to climb into my duffel bag and come home with me?"

"If that is what it takes," she said.

Canterbury was shocked. He had about a month and a half left on his four-month deployment. Wherever he was going next, she was coming.

Anabel slurped down the last of the milkshake.

"Do you want to go back to my room?" Anabel asked. "I just got a new movie from the exchange. We can watch it."

Canterbury didn't want to watch a movie. And by the look in Anabel's eye, she didn't either.

CHAPTER 21

Razaq sat on a rug on the floor near the back of an apartment in Kandahar City. He was sipping tea and waiting for Mullah Dadullah. They'd known one another during the Soviet invasion. Dadullah had lost a leg in that fight. He'd stayed out of harm's way since, hiding in Pakistan while Razaq and the others took the fight to the Americans.

Dadullah was coming to talk about the "device," as they called it, and give him an update on what he was to do with it. The topic made Razaq's heart hurt to think of what the camels would do. Their brazen attack on New York killed thousands and cost him his country. Now, his commanders wanted to give the camels more killing power and believed that it wouldn't come back to them.

It was insanity.

A plate of french fries from the restaurant on the bottom floor sat in front of him. Razaq pushed a few soggy fries around the plate. He wasn't hungry, but Zahir had insisted on getting something to eat. He noticed the boy was worried about him. But Razaq just didn't have an appetite.

Zahir was dozing in a chair near the door when a knock startled them both. Zahir opened the door and held it as three bodyguards and Dadullah walked into the apartment. The guards were all just kids like Zahir. And they all had scowls in an attempt to look menacing. Dadullah, like Razaq, looked old. A short man with stooped shoulders and a white beard stained with henna, he walked with a pair of canes to try and hide his limp. His prosthetic leg was hidden under his baggy pants.

Dadullah's canes clicked against the tile floor as he limped into the room. Razaq met him and the men embraced and kissed one another on the cheek.

"Hello, brother," Razaq said. "I trust your trip across the border was uneventful?"

"Allah blessed us," Dadullah said.

Dadullah kicked off his sandal and left his prosthesis with one of his guards. Razaq retreated to his corner as Dadullah took a seat on the floor, resting his back against the pillows that lined the room.

"How is your family?" Razaq asked.

"They are well," Dadullah said. "My son is commanding a unit in Zabul."

"I heard," Razaq said. "When I think of your son, I hear the words of a poem about how mujahedeen come to free villages from occupiers at the point of a bayonet. I hear he is living that poem."

"He is," Dadullah said. "He didn't want to go. He wanted to stay and protect me. I told him before he left that it didn't matter whether I am alive or dead, but to remember this: the resistance will become greater than your greatest expectations."

"*Inshallah*," Razaq said.

God willing.

Zahir brought in a tray with tea. He offered Dadullah a glass and then handed one to Razaq. Dadullah took a sip.

It was time to get down to business.

"Allah has delivered a clear path to victory," Dadullah said. "With the money and resources from the device, we will be able to fight until we control our nation again."

Razaq nodded along, not believing a word of it.

"The Shura want you to go to Dubai and meet with our buyers," Dadullah said.

"Dubai? Why me?" Razaq asked.

"Because you've seen the device," Dadullah said. "You can tell them what they need to know."

Razaq looked away. He didn't want to meet with anyone, nor did he want to fly to Dubai. If he was leaving, it was to go to America.

"But our sources in Kabul say you're on a watch list," Dadullah said. "We fear you'll be arrested before the meeting. So I'm going to send one of my bodyguards."

Razaq looked toward the door where the young guards waited trying to look hard in front of their bosses.

"One of those kids?" Razaq said. "They are going to represent our movement?"

Dadullah shrugged.

"You have someone better?"

Razaq had anticipated this mission. He figured someone would have to meet with the camels since they weren't going to risk crossing the border from Pakistan or Iran. He figured the meeting would be in Pakistan. But Dubai was a new wrinkle. Razaq let the question hang in the air between them. Then he spoke.

"What about my nephew?"

Dadullah looked at Razaq, waiting for the punch line. It didn't come.

"The nephew that works for the Americans?"

Razaq took a second to gather his thoughts. If this was going to work, his delivery had to be perfect.

"I've been meeting with him for years," Razaq said. "He loves his country first, but he is a businessman second."

Dadullah shook his head.

"He works for our enemy," Dadullah said. "He doesn't love his country enough not to help them."

"He gives the money to the poor and sends medicine to the villages," Razaq said. "He has given me money to get food and gear for my men. The money is going a long way to help our people. Plus, he travels to Dubai once a month. It wouldn't be suspicious."

"And he will do it?" Dadullah asked.

Razaq had Dadullah on the line now.

"He will," Razaq said.

"Why? He hasn't changed sides. He isn't one of us. Why would he help us fight?"

Razaq had anticipated the question.

"Because war means profit," he said. "What incentive does Wali have to bring peace to Afghanistan? He can continue to overcharge the Americans and use the money to help his people. And when the Americans go, he will charge Kabul. He doesn't care about politics."

Dadullah sat for a while sipping his tea. He looked out the window and rubbed his stump.

"When can you move the device to Quetta?"

"Do you remember my last visit to Pakistan?"

Dadullah nodded.

"We were stopped and searched by the Americans. What would have happened had I been traveling with the device?"

Razaq paused to let the facts of the story register with his boss.

"We just lost a shipment of explosives. The Americans are watching the border. I don't think it is wise to transport the device. If the camels want it so badly, they can come and pick it up."

Dadullah rubbed his beard and then shook his head.

"I see your wisdom," he said. "But the leaders don't want to lose the device."

"It is safe," Razaq said. "Safer than driving it around the countryside. What if the Americans have detectors at the border? I've provided pictures. That is all they get."

Dadullah seemed satisfied with the answer.

"I am glad it was you who got the device," Dadullah said. "You've always been the wisest of my commanders. Tell your nephew to go.

All he has to do is meet and show them the pictures of the device. Once everything is set, I will send you the contact and meeting time."

Razaq nodded. He helped Dadullah up from the floor. His guards kept Dadullah steady while he put his leg back on. Zahir opened the door and Dadullah and his guards filed out. Before Zahir shut the door, Dadullah looked back at Razaq and nodded. Recognition of his service and their shared sacrifice. No matter what they told themselves, both men knew they were just cogs in the same machine.

Theirs was not to question.

Razaq waited until Dadullah left before he left the apartment building. Zahir was in front and stopped halfway down the stairs. Two of Jan's police were waiting. Razaq held his breath and waited for them to speak.

"The general wants to see you," one of the officers said.

The other officer took Zahir's rifle.

Zahir looked at Razaq.

"OK," Razaq said. "Where is the general?"

Once outside, the first police officer opened the back door of a Ranger pickup truck's crew cab.

"Not far," the office said. "Tell your man to follow us."

The second officer climbed into the driver's seat. He put Zahir's rifle between him and the passenger seat. Razaq rode in silence as the officers fought through the accordion-like midday traffic.

Zahir followed in his truck.

Jan was waiting for Razaq at a police station on the eastern side of the city. The police were gone; only Jan's men were there. Zahir waited outside as Razaq was escorted into a back office used by the station's commander. The general was sitting behind a desk. He got up when he saw Razaq.

"Hello, old friend," Jan said as he embraced Razaq. "You look good."

Razaq sat in a chair opposite the desk.

"As do you," Razaq said, patting his belly. "Being a general has served you well."

Jan smiled, returned to his chair, and slid a brown envelope stuffed with bundled $100 bills across the table.

"For my trucks," Jan said.

Razaq slid the money into his pocket.

"Tell your men to check back in the village," Razaq said. "There is a cache there. Some rockets. An old recoilless rifle. The Americans will be pleased."

Jan made a note.

"You need to tell your nephew to be my partner," the general said. "He stole a lucrative contract from me."

Razaq laughed.

"You know I can't tell that boy anything," Razaq said. "He doesn't respect the old ways. Too much America."

Jan nodded in agreement.

"This new generation has no respect," he said. "We are the elders. We are wise. Your nephew insults the memory of his father."

Razaq hated to hear Jan talk about his brother, but he had bigger issues. It was easier to agree for now. Jan always liked to hear himself talk anyway.

"Take your nephew," Jan said. "He didn't follow his uncle. Instead, he lived like an orphan until the Americans came. Then he let them adopt him."

"My nephew is a successful businessman," Razaq said. "Nothing more. He is not like us. Afghanistan has been under a black umbrella since the Soviets came. He dares to peek out from underneath. You know the saying about Jesus visiting hell with the archangel Gabriel?"

Jan didn't answer. Razaq took his silence as an invitation to continue.

"Jesus was taken to the seven hells and seven paradises. At the mouth of the first hell, he saw fire and people shouting and lots of guards. When people tried to escape, they were thrown back. Each hell got worse and worse until they reached the mouth of the last one. There were no guards. 'Those six hells have guards. Why are there are no guards here?' Jesus asked. Gabriel said, 'This is the hell for the Pashtuns. When one tries to climb out, the others grab hold of his feet and drag him back.'"

Razaq paused to make sure the lesson wasn't lost on the general.

"Stop grabbing my nephew's feet," he said, putting a cap on the discussion.

Jan folded his arms and glared at Razaq.

"I know you and Wali meet often," he said. "Why?"

"He is my nephew," Razaq said. "We might not be on the same side, but in the eyes of Allah we are one."

Jan's phone rang. The general looked at it and then looked back at Razaq.

"I am sorry but I have to take this," he said. "You can go for now. But tell your nephew to learn some respect."

CHAPTER 22

Charlie drove back to Kandahar Airfield on autopilot. His mind was trying to make sense of what he'd heard. This was the most important mission of the war. Taking a nuclear bomb off the battlefield before it fell into the hands of terrorists was why he'd joined the Army.

Instead of going back to Camp Brown, Charlie headed for Felix's office. It was located in a compound near the NATO headquarters building. The one-story building had several offices and a command center where the agency managed its drones and militia forces. It was surrounded by a wall with a gate manned by an American contractor dressed head to toe in 5.11 garb.

Charlie stopped at the gate and showed his ID.

"I'm here to see Felix Van Owen."

The gate guard was tan, had sunglasses propped on his head, and didn't look like he'd eaten a carb in a decade. He made Charlie—with his thick linebacker physique—feel fat. Charlie figured he was a former SEAL.

The guard picked up a phone and, after a short conversation, motioned Charlie inside the gate.

"You need directions?" the guard asked.

"I know the way," Charlie said, walking into the building. He worked his way down the beige hallway and stopped at the last office.

Felix looked worse than Wali.

He was wearing a ratty Black Crowes concert shirt from the 1990s, baggy cargo pants, and flip-flops. Felix motioned for Charlie to sit on a fold-out chair in front of his desk.

The office was cramped, with a worn desk and a threadbare chair that barely rolled on the concrete floor. The walls were bare except for a faded Afghanistan tourism poster. A dusty red Oriental rug was the only item of color in the room.

"What's up, Charlie?" Felix said, reaching into the refrigerator next to his safe and getting out a fresh Diet Coke. His desk was covered with at least a six-pack of finished soda cans.

"You look like shit," Charlie said.

"Back on vampire hours," Felix said. "You know the transition is a bitch. Three strikes last night. Waiting for BDA, but pretty sure we got rid of some shitheads."

Battle damage assessment. Basically, did the missile hit the target or not?

Charlie smiled.

"Nice work," he said.

"Yeah," Felix said. "But you know as well as I do we can't shoot our way out of this mess."

"No," Charlie said. "But it doesn't hurt to thin the herd."

"As much as I'd love to bullshit, I'm tired," Felix said. "And I'm late for a meeting. What's good?"

Charlie leaned back in his chair and closed the door to Felix's office.

"It's big."

"Wali's uncle?"

Charlie nodded.

"What do you know about Soviet suitcase nukes?"

Felix took a sip of his soda.

"Dick. Why?"

"Because Wali's uncle has one."

Felix put down the can and leaned forward. He looked fully awake.

"The Taliban have a suitcase nuke? You're sure?"

"No," Charlie said. "But that is what Razaq told Wali. The Taliban are trying to sell it to AQ."

Charlie showed Felix the pictures Razaq had finally sent Wali of the device.

"This could be anything," Felix said, zooming in on one of the photos. "Then again, I have no idea what a Soviet suitcase nuke looks like. Can I get these photos?"

Wali nodded.

"Where is it now?" Felix said.

"Razaq has it," Charlie said. "They dug it out of a field."

Felix handed Charlie his phone and started to type on his computer.

"A field?"

"Yeah," Charlie said. "Some farmers found it."

Felix hit send and looked up from his computer. The photos were already on their way to Langley for analysis.

"What about Wali and Razaq?"

"They want out," Charlie said. "Wali was really spooked. I told them this would be enough."

Felix took a sip of his soda.

"Doable," Felix said. "I think. Bringing us a nuke should be enough for a visa, right? Got to run it up. But let's not promise too much until we see what this is."

Charlie stood up to leave.

"How long?"

"I put a priority designator on it, so not long. You going back to Brown?"

"Yeah," Charlie said. "I've got to report it up my chain too."

"Can you wait one?" Felix said. "Let me get the analysis back first. We can brief it together."

Charlie shrugged. It was Felix's operation.

"Roger," Charlie said. "You've got twenty-four hours."

Felix smiled and gave Charlie a little "cheers" with his soda can.

ꝹꝹꝹ

Just after lunch the next day, Charlie and Felix were in Lieutenant Colonel Kyle's office. Spread across his desk were photos of the device. Kyle was reading through an analysis report.

"They aren't buying it," Felix said. "My guys think the bomb is a hoax."

Kyle looked up from the report.

"It says here it all goes back to a GRU defector named Stanislav Lunev," Kyle said.

Felix flipped through his briefing slides until he landed on a picture of Lunev.

"Right, sir," Felix said. "Lunev claimed Russian-made suitcase devices exist. They were called RA-115s and weighed between fifty to sixty pounds. The bombs were wired to an electric source and a battery backup. When the battery runs low, the weapon has a transmitter that sends a coded message to the Russian embassy or consulate."

Charlie looked at Felix and then at Kyle. *So this thing is all bullshit* was written across Kyle's face.

Felix continued to brief Kyle.

"So Lunev wrote a book and suggested that suitcase nukes were hidden by the KGB in other countries. We never verified if Afghanistan was on the list. Lunev said that he personally looked for hiding places in the Shenandoah Valley area and claimed the bombs were smuggled across the Mexican border. Of course, the FBI went nuts and searched all over the country. At the end of the day, Lunev probably exaggerated things. It's unlikely, based on Langley's analysis, the Taliban have a nuclear bomb."

Kyle put down the report and looked at Charlie and then Felix.

"So you guys are out?" Kyle asked. "Great. Charlie, get Frank and let's start putting together an op to get this thing."

Charlie paused for a second and looked at Felix.

"We're not out," Felix said. "Our analysis says this isn't a bomb, but that doesn't mean it isn't valuable. If the Taliban are trying to sell it, we have a chance to catch an AQ financier. That has value."

Kyle folded his hands.

"So since this is an agency operation, what's the next move?"

"We're calling it Corona," Felix said. "We're naming everything after beer right now. Charlie and I are headed to Kabul. Station chief wants us to come up and brief next steps."

Felix looked at Charlie.

"Excuse us, sir," Felix said. "We've got a flight to Kabul to catch. But I wanted to make sure we kept you read in."

℘℘℘

Dewayne Church looked like a college professor. He was dressed in a white oxford shirt and stained khakis. He wore hiking books, and readers hung around his neck. His skin was tan from years in the Central Asia sun. He wore his curly hair long and shaggy, and a thick gray goatee covered his chin.

He was sitting at a small table when Felix and Charlie entered the small conference room on the military side of the airport. Because of the sensitivity of the mission, Church met Felix and Charlie at the airport instead of the embassy. This way, the pair could get on a plane and head back to Kandahar when the meeting was done.

Felix put the mission briefing slides on the table.

"So I doubt you need for us to go over this whole thing in detail again," Felix said. "The thumbnail version is pretty straightforward. We're going to send a highly vetted agent to Dubai to meet with an AQ financier. We'll have a team in place for surveillance, and I'm going to be on the ground. Once we ID the financier, we will work with our agent to set up a buy in Afghanistan. When the AQ financier crosses the border, we'll either kill or capture him, depending on conditions on the ground. Charlie's guys will simultaneously secure Corona and deliver it to our team for transport to a facility in Doha for analysis."

Charlie started to brief his part when Church cut him off.

"Here are my concerns," he said. "One, who is this agent? Two, are we sure Corona is what they claim? I got a cable today asking if we could get a sample. I know you sent back pictures, but Langley hasn't completely signed off on it yet. They haven't even briefed the president because they're afraid of leaks, especially if this thing turns out to be bullshit."

Charlie and Felix exchanged glances.

"This operation is set to kick off in forty-eight hours," Felix said. "There is no chance we can get a sample. Pictures will have to suffice. As for being bullshit, the Taliban and al-Qaeda think they have a bomb. That's enough for me."

Church rubbed his nose and closed his eyes as if that would melt away the stress.

"That's what I told them," Church said. "I don't think that's going to be a deal breaker. But command and control is."

"Sir?" Charlie said.

Church slid on his readers and flipped through the mission briefing.

"I can't tell if this is a CIA operation or a military operation."

"It's a joint operation," Felix said. "We have our part and the green suiters have theirs."

Church closed the file.

"Seems like a lot of chiefs," he said. "Langley is confused too. We're waiting on a response from the military. Until we get it, the operation is on hold."

Felix leaned back in his chair and smiled. This was a dick-measuring contest. Before Felix spoke, Charlie cut in.

"Why not make it an agency operation?" Charlie asked. "Look, I don't care who's in command. We have a chance to remove a weapon of mass destruction from the battlefield. You guys take credit for it. We take credit for it. Who gives a fuck? I just want to get this bomb."

Felix looked at Charlie, who shrugged.

"I agree, sir," Felix said.

"Are you able to make that call?" Church asked.

Charlie smiled.

"No, sir," he said. "But I also don't want to miss our window because the head shed can't pull the trigger. I talked to my colonel, who ran it through his chain of command. I brought a memo agreeing to OGA control, with one caveat: Wali remains a Special Forces asset."

"I think we can live with that," Church said. "If your commander can."

"Can I use your phone, sir?" Charlie asked.

"Of course," Church said.

ꕥꕥꕥ

A few hours later, Charlie and Felix boarded a C-130 for Kandahar with a briefcase full of CIA money. As other soldiers walked up the ramp and found seats, Felix slid the money under his seat and found his seat belt.

"How did you get Kyle to agree to agency control?" Felix asked.

"It didn't take too much arm twisting," Charlie said. "Kyle hated the op. We had to go around him to do the meet the first time. I just told him if it goes south, our hands are clean, and if it works, it was our source."

Felix smiled at the manipulation.

"Smart," he said. "You meeting with Wali today?"

"Roger," Charlie said. "As soon as we get on the ground, let's head over to his compound."

The sound of the aircraft's engines made further conversation impossible. Felix fell asleep before the plane even took off. Charlie couldn't sleep with fifty thousand dollars in cash at his feet and the thought of al-Qaeda with a nuclear bomb in his head.

Charlie's first deployment was simple: get the terrorists who attacked his nation. But the mission kept changing each time he returned. The Taliban became the new target after al-Qaeda fled. Then propping up the government in Kabul. Each year the policy makers moved the target or changed it. Charlie often returned to Fort Bragg unable to tell his wife and kids what he'd accomplished. He knew the talking points, but in his heart, he didn't know. He told them why he went into harm's way. Was it so Afghan girls could go to school? Maybe. That was as good a reason as any. Sometimes he heard guys say it was to make sure "they" didn't come to the United States. But they already did, and killing the Taliban in Afghanistan probably did little to protect Middle America.

But the bomb changed everything.

It was a goal he could accomplish and with tangible benefits. The thought of being on a mission of that magnitude energized him. Only shooting bin Laden would reach the same height.

A truck was waiting for them on the tarmac when they landed. Charlie drove it to Wali's compound. Wali met them at the gate, and the trio retreated to his office.

"You remember Felix," Charlie said.

Felix and Wali shook hands. Felix sat in the chair across the desk from Wali. Charlie took the chair in the corner behind the desk.

"I've got good news," Charlie said as Wali slipped into his office chair. "The operation is a go. But we need to do some things first."

Felix took a small GPS tracker out of a backpack.

"We need your uncle to hide this on the device," Felix said. "This way we can never lose it. Also, we need to know about the buyer. Who is he? Where is the meet? Can you do that?"

Wali nodded.

"I think so," he said. "When are you going to get it?"

Felix looked at Charlie.

"We're not," Charlie said. "We're going to wait to see who the buyer is and track them back to the al-Qaeda leadership."

Wali was confused.

"Why? This is a nuclear bomb."

Charlie started to talk, but Felix cut him off.

"Yes," Felix said. "But our analysts think it isn't armed yet. It needs a detonator. So while dangerous, without the missing piece it is harmless. The GPS will allow us to keep track of it. All your uncle has to do is complete the transaction."

"And then what?" Wali asked.

Felix smiled.

"Then we get your uncle to one of our safe houses and fly him to America."

Wali seemed relieved.

"And me?"

Felix shrugged.

"Up to you."

Charlie patted Wali on the shoulder.

"If you have any other questions, you know how to contact me. It's real important we get that GPS onto the bomb. Call me when it's done, and tell your uncle we need details on the buy as soon as possible."

Felix excused himself to use the bathroom. Wali waited until he was out of earshot.

"Is this his mission or yours?" Wali asked.

"It's both," Charlie said. "Technically, it is OGA run, but you're my source. So we both have a vote."

Wali checked the door and leaned in as if to make sure Felix couldn't hear anything if he came back in while they were talking.

"Do you trust him?" Wali asked.

"Yeah," Charlie said. "He's a good dude."

Wali leaned back.

"OK."

Felix came back into the office and closed the door. He was carrying a high-end roller suitcase with a lock. Felix opened the lock and laid the open suitcase on the desk.

"This will be your bag," Felix said. "We're giving you some cash now just in case your contact picks you up right from the airport. This is for expenses. You're a high roller. Don't be afraid to throw it around."

Charlie took the money from the kit bag and slid the bundles of cash under the suitcase's false bottom.

"And you spoke to your uncle?" Charlie said.

Wali helped arrange the stacks of bills for Felix.

"He called me yesterday," Wali said. "I'm supposed to check in at Roda Al Bustan near the airport and wait to be contacted."

Felix packed the last bundle.

"I'll be on the ground," Felix said. "If you need anything, here's a number to call."

Wali looked at Charlie, who shook his head in approval.

"Look," Charlie said, "you're getting into some heavy shit here. These guys are al-Qaeda. These guys are true believers. They are terrorists that want to bring harm to my country. They aren't afraid to fly planes into buildings and plant bombs on trains full of innocents."

Wali shook his head in agreement.

"I understand," he said. "These are the same men that destroyed my country."

Wali put the number into his phone.

"When do I call this number?"

"Don't call it unless you're in danger," Felix said. "Ask for Tamer. The operator will put you through to me. We will be less than a minute away."

Wali sat down.

"What if he sees you?"

"Who?" Felix asked.

"Al-Qaeda," Wali said. "What if you spook him?"

Felix looked up from the bag.

"We won't," he said. "You won't even know we're around. Now it's very important that you take this phone with you."

The smart phone looked normal as Wali studied it. Felix was fiddling on his laptop. A few key strokes and a song was playing over his computer's speakers. Wali looked at Felix.

"Sound familiar?" Felix said. "You were listening to it..."

Felix paused to check the file.

"...around ten a.m. this morning, right?"

Wali nodded.

"You see that phone," Felix said. "Get it within range of other electronic devices and we can break in. I can turn on laptops and phone cameras, steal files, and leave software to capture keystrokes."

Wali dropped the phone on the table and moved away from it.

"Don't worry," Charlie said. "It won't bite."

Felix laughed.

"Not in a literal sense," Felix added. "At the end of the day, your goal is to make a deal. A deal that brings the buyer into Afghanistan. We'll take care of the rest."

"OK," Wali said. "I understand."

There was a knock at the door, and Denise popped her head inside.

"Do you have a minute?"

Everyone froze. Denise saw the money and then looked at the men. Wali looked at Charlie and Felix. Charlie finally spoke up.

"We're almost done," he said. "Give us a minute."

Denise shut the door. Charlie looked at Wali.

"Next time lock it," he said.

Felix replaced the false bottom and grabbed his gear.

"Is she going to be a problem?" Felix said.

Wali shook his head no.

"She works for me. She knows to keep her mouth shut."

Charlie shot a glance at Felix telling him everything was all right.

"OK," Felix said. "I'll see you on the ground."

Wali shook Felix's hand.

"But I won't see you," Wali said.

Felix chuckled.

"Now you're getting it," he said.

Wali reached out to shake Charlie's hand, but the Green Beret pulled him in for a bro hug.

"Take care of yourself, brother," Charlie said. "I know you can do this. You're saving lives. Thank you."

Wali didn't know what to say. He felt tears welling up in his eyes.

"It is my duty," he said. "I have no choice. Allah wills it."

❧❧❧

Wali walked Charlie and Felix to their truck and then went back inside. He had started packing for his trip to Dubai when McKenna came back. She knocked softly and then poked her head into his bedroom.

"All done?" she asked.

Wali stuffed a shirt into the suitcase.

"Yes," he said. "What do you need? I have to finish packing."

"Nothing," McKenna said. "I just had a question, but I took care of it."

McKenna started to leave but stopped. She looked down, avoiding eye contact.

"What was all that money for?" she asked.

Wali turned to look at her.

"Nothing," he said.

McKenna tried to meet his gaze but looked away again.

"That was a lot of cash," she said.

Wali felt his heart pound. He didn't know what to tell her. If only she hadn't burst into the office. He felt her eyes on him, demanding an answer. He blurted out the first thing to pop in his head.

"I was paying them off," Wali said, regretting it as soon as it crossed his lips. "You know how all this works."

"Paying them off?" she said. "Are you serious?"

"No, I'm not serious," Wali said, walking over to get some clothes out of a drawer. "Look, it was just business. Nothing you need to worry about. You better go."

McKenna looked at him for a second. She hesitated. When Wali turned back toward his bag, she started to back out of the room.

"I guess I'll go," she said.

Wali just waved as McKenna closed the door. His mind was already on Dubai.

CHAPTER 23

The weather outside the black Lexus SUV was scorching. Wali asked the driver to turn up the air-conditioning as the truck raced down the highway. To his left, he watched the buildings of the Dubai skyline. The city looked like it was born out of the sand. A fully formed modern civilization. Wali felt like he was looking into the future.

Once he started to make money as a contractor, Wali began coming to Dubai to relax and do business. He liked the resorts and shopping, but he didn't really like Gulf Arabs. There was something about their hypocrisy that got on his nerves. One minute they were denouncing the West and the next minute they were gorging themselves on Shake Shack burgers and Outback steaks.

After landing, Wali had exchanged his cargo pants and T-shirt for a perfectly pressed shalwar kameez—the long shirt and baggy pants worn in Central Asia—and a black Quiksilver military-style cap.

He carried both phones but used his cheap Afghan phone to make calls, leaving the smartphone on the seat next to him. Wali received a steady stream of calls from Denise and Khalid. The phone rang over and over again. Between calls, Wali kept a watchful eye for Felix, but he didn't pick him up on his tail.

After Wali hung up on hopefully his last call of the day, the driver looked back at him in the rearview mirror.

"Why do you keep using that cheap phone when you have a nice phone on the seat?"

Wali looked at both phones and shrugged.

"I can throw it when I get angry," he said, waving the cheap phone back and forth.

ᏰᏰᏰ

The restaurant was in a shopping center. Wali spotted a prayer area set off in a corner just inside the lobby. Wali didn't pray a lot. He was a Muslim, but not a good one, yet something drew him to the area.

He was nervous.

Playing James Bond sounded better than doing it. In a few minutes he would be face-to-face with a terrorist. And the terrorist would consider him a member of the Taliban. But Wali hated the Taliban.

No one knew who the Taliban were when they stormed the streets of Kandahar in 1994. A new warlord was in charge from street to street. He figured they were just the next warlords up. But the Taliban brought order when they first arrived.

When the first Taliban fighters showed up in his neighborhood, Razaq was eager to help.

"Give me the radio," his uncle had said. "The Taliban needs the radio."

Razaq hung around the fighters and soon joined them. He told stories about Taliban fighters marching from Maiwand in southern Afghanistan to capture Kandahar City. He talked about seizing an ammunition dump owned by the warlords. Soon, Wali watched his uncle climb into a truck and head for Kabul. When he returned, Razaq was a commander in charge of dozens of fighters.

It wasn't until Wali was a teenager that reality set in for him. It was winter 2000. One afternoon, after school, Wali and his friends were listening to his favorite Indian music tape when two Taliban walked past. They noticed the music and started to walk toward Wali and his friends.

"What do you have?" one of the Taliban asked. "What are you listening to?"

Wali ejected the cassette. He was wearing a black jacket. He palmed the cassette and put his hand next to his jacket to conceal it. The Taliban fighters checked the cassette player, but it was empty. One of the soldiers noticed Wali's hand.

"Give me what you have in your hand," he said. "What do you have?"

"Nothing," Wali said.

The Taliban slapped Wali, who threw the tape on the ground as the fighter grabbed him and began pulling him toward the district office. Once there, the guard shoved Wali and his friends into a Conex container in the building's courtyard. A few minutes later, more than a dozen kids—all boys—were pushed into the Conex. Wali and the other prisoners waited for more than five hours in the dark. Occasionally, the guards would give them water.

Finally, the guards returned to the Conex and recorded the prisoners' names and the names of their fathers. When they were done, the guards started to take the boys out one by one. Wali fought his way to the back of the container. He heard some of the boys crying.

Wali's turn finally came, and the guards led him into an office. There were ten to fifteen Taliban guards standing around the walls. Sitting at the head of the room was a mullah holding a stick. His gray beard was died bright red with henna.

The guards forced Wali onto his stomach in the center of the room and pinned his arms and legs to the ground. The Red Beard Mullah—as Wali remembered him—raised the stick and brought it down hard on Wali's hip. The pain shot through his body. Before he recovered, the mullah hit him again. The pain was a jolt to his system, but Wali stifled his cries. He wasn't going to give them the satisfaction.

"Oh, he is a hero," one of the guards said. "He is a champion. Beat him more."

The mullah continued to hit him. Three times. Four times. Five times. After the seventh stroke, Wali let out a cry and asked the mullah for forgiveness.

"Mullah, I swear I will not do it again," Wali said.

The mullah hit Wali three more times. The guards let Wali up, and he sat in the middle of the room recovering. His body hurt and he couldn't look up at the mullah, who was lecturing him about the Koran and that playing music was *haram*, which means forbidden in Arabic.

Wali wasn't listening. He couldn't get over the fact the mullah had beaten him without at least hearing his side of the story. Why beat him after the first offense? He understood a beating after he'd been warned, but the Taliban beat him first and then told him not to do it.

The memory put Wali in a bad mood as he walked to the restaurant.

What kind of people are they? he thought.

A replica cannon sat near the front door of Laal Qila (Red Castle in Urdu). Inside the dining room, the waiters were dressed in traditional costumes: parachute pants, turbans, and pointy shoes. It had the same feel as Disney's *Aladdin*. He scanned the room looking for Samir, the name of his al-Qaeda contact. Wali had no idea if that was his real name or not.

Wali hesitated in the lobby until he spotted an Arab man sitting near the back looking at his phone. He was the only single man in the room, so Wali took a chance. Samir had given him a code phrase.

"A friend said the chicken curry here is wonderful," Wali said in halting Arabic.

He waited for the response.

"I come for the hummus," Samir said with a smile.

He nodded toward the chair and Wali sat down. A waiter came over to the table. Samir was drinking orange juice, so Wali ordered the same.

"My Arabic is bad," Wali said. "Pashto or Dari?"

Samir shook his head no.

"English?" Wali said.

"Yeah, that works," Samir said.

Samir set his phone down on the table and folded his hands. He didn't look like a terrorist to Wali. He was slight with wavy black hair, a goatee, and a nice Italian suit.

"Should we eat first?" Samir asked. "I'm starving."

Wali wasn't hungry. They were about to talk about selling a fucking nuclear bomb! But he just nodded and followed Samir toward the buffet.

Under the nearly two dozen silver domes was a massive spread of Indo-Pakistani cuisine ranging from roasted lamb to chicken curry. The buffet also had Chinese dishes and a salad table with hummus and sliced vegetables. Wali filled his plate and returned to the table. He placed the phone Felix had given him on the table next to Samir's. When Samir returned, he picked up Wali's.

"This is the new Google phone," Samir said. "How do you like it? I'm an Apple guy, but I like some of the features."

"I just got it," Wali said, his voice sounding strained. "But I like it so far."

"Mind if I turn it on and look at the interface?"

"Sure," Wali said, the word coming out in a croak.

Wali held his breath as Samir powered up the screen. Was there any chance he'd detect Felix's spy tools? Samir scrolled through the apps. He seemed lost in the phone for a few minutes. Wali glanced around the room looking for the CIA man or his team. He wanted reassurance that the backup would swoop in and save him if Samir discovered the phone was a bug. Nearby was a table of women enjoying lunch. Across the room was a solitary businessman eating soup. No one was watching him. No one was there to save him.

"Mind if I try the camera?" Samir asked, holding the camera horizontally as he framed a photo of Wali.

Wali gave him a half smile as Samir took the photo.

"Send that to me," Samir said. "I want to see the picture quality."

Wali took the phone back and sent the photo. Samir's phone vibrated. Samir picked it up and checked the photo.

"That's nice," he said.

Samir typed on his phone for a bit and then set it back down. Wali looked at Samir's plate. It was piled high with food, but no hummus. He knew it was a code word, but he'd gotten an extra helping of curry.

"How is the hummus?" Wali said.

Samir looked over his plate.

"Right," he said. "To be honest, I don't care for it."

Wali smiled.

"Are you from Dubai?" Wali asked in between bites of curry and meatballs.

"Egypt, but I live here," Samir said. "I went to school in America and London. You?"

"Kandahar," Wali said.

"Where did you learn English?"

"The Americans," Wali said. "I own a trucking business. I bring supplies around for the Americans, so I had to learn the language."

Wali and Charlie had role-played this part of the conversation before he left. It was impossible to hide Wali's business, so they figured it was best to bring it up as soon as possible. Don't make it a secret. Wali knew Samir was taken off guard.

"You work with the Americans?" Samir said.

"Yeah," Wali said, sipping his orange juice. "My relationship means I have access to information, and the money they pay me helps our cause."

Samir smirked.

"That's a good business plan," he said. "No offense, but when I think of your people, I see guys in the mountains with big beards."

Wali ran his hand across his shaved cheeks. That was one of the reasons he shaved every other day. He wasn't some goat-fucking fundamentalist.

"Yeah, well, you're not some arrogant Arab who thinks because he lives near Mecca he is somehow more important," Wali said with a weak chuckle. "I watched as your kind raced around in your black luxury cars and SUVs with tinted windows and motorcycle escorts. The car's license plates had no numbers, just 'No Stop' written in Arabic."

Samir didn't seem insulted.

"Those aren't my people," he said. "My weapon is money."

Wali nodded. He agreed with that. He had gone from orphan to multimillionaire. Mullahs and warlords that previously wouldn't even spit at him now called upon him. He also had powerful enemies. But that only meant he had power.

But Samir was still a riddle to Wali. He spoke English like the Special Forces guys and didn't have the fire of the other Arabs he'd met in the past.

"What about you?" Wali asked. "Where did you learn English?"

"Philadelphia," Samir said. "I went to Wharton."

Wali sat with a blank face.

"The business school at the University of Pennsylvania," Samir said finally. "It's an Ivy League school. I studied finance."

Samir's phone beeped. He had another text message. Samir picked up his phone and checked it.

"You check out," Samir said.

"What?"

"I sent your picture to the brothers and they confirmed your identity," Samir said. "Now we can get down to business."

"Here?" Wali said.

Samir shrugged.

"I was just sent to meet you," he said. "I was supposed to get your picture. They are going to tell me the next step. I guess we just eat."

Wali still didn't have an appetite, but his mission was to keep Samir close. He choked down his plate of food and made small talk about movies and music and anything else to keep an awkward pause at bay. After the meal, neither man knew what to do. They couldn't sit at the same table all day drinking tea.

Wali was stumped. Samir seemed kind of cool, and Wali's job was to get the deal done. He'd already planned to visit Dubai Mall, a favorite stop when he visited. Why not take Samir with him?

"Want to hang out?" Wali asked. "I was going over to the mall."

"Shopping?"

"Yeah, I guess," Wali said. "It's hot. I just want to be in the air-conditioning. Plus, they don't have the same selection in Kabul or Kandahar."

"That's true," Samir said. "I'll drive. I just got my Ferrari out of the shop yesterday."

The Dubai air was muggy, and it felt like they were under a hair dryer as they walked toward Samir's car. It was a yellow Ferrari F430 with a yellow-and-black interior. It looked like a very fast bumblebee. Samir fished out some keys from his suit pocket, climbed into the sports car, and started the engine.

Out on the road, they joined other high-end cars—BMWs, Maseratis, and McLarens—driven by emirates in robes and keffiyehs white as snow. Wali was used to beat-up sedans and trucks. He always marveled at the car show on the roads around Dubai. The Ferrari's engine gave off a high-pitched shriek as Samir worked the gears, pushing the bumblebee into gaps in the traffic.

Guest workers—men from the Philippines, Bangladesh, and Indonesia—walked along the sidewalk past a Hardee's and KFC restaurant as Samir sped by. At the mall, they got Cold Stone Creamery, and both men purchased shoes at the Vans store. Wali got a winter jacket at H&M. Samir bought new running shoes at the Nike store.

They threw their bags in the car and headed outside the city for a drive. Once they cleared the city, Samir pushed the Ferrari. Soon, the brown sand was just a smear. They drove out to Fujairah on the east coast and sat on the beach before catching evening prayers at the Sheikh Zayed Mosque.

The whole trip was surreal to Wali. He forgot who Samir was. It felt like vacation with a new friend. He liked Samir, which wasn't something he expected when he left Kandahar.

When they arrived at the Sheikh Zayed Mosque, Wali marveled at its massive white minarets. Everything in the United Arab Emirates was over the top. It felt like the Arabs didn't do anything simply. It was all decorated to the hilt. Seeing all the wealth and comfort made Wali miss home. He wanted a simple time. But he also wanted this for Afghanistan. He felt ashamed as he kicked off his shoes and prepared to pray. The men around him didn't have to say it. They knew he wasn't an Arab. They all might pray to the same god, but he was looked down upon as an Afghan.

While the men around him prayed for salvation and forgiveness for one transgression or another, Wali prayed for strength and humility.

After prayers, Wali was finally hungry, his fear losing out to his body's need for energy.

"Now that that's done, let's eat," he said. "I know a great Afghan place."

***

Kabana was busy when they arrived, with waiters catering to several outdoor tables. Emirs and expats sat smoking hookah pipes. A waiter led Samir and Wali to a table outside in the middle of a patio overlooking the street. The chairs were love seats with brown cushions. A large square table that came up to their knees filled the space between the couches.

Wali explained that an Afghan woman owned the place. She'd used a million dollars from her ex-boyfriend to open it after the couple broke up. Wali said the owner was opening another location in Dubai soon.

"I guess she got a new boyfriend," he joked.

A waiter came over, and Wali started to order before Samir even looked at the menu. For two minutes, Wali ordered appetizers, salads, and entrées.

"What is America like?" Wali asked afterward. "I've never been."

Samir took a sip of his juice.

"Yeah, America is fun," he said. "I liked Philadelphia. It's fun city. Lots to do. You can get anything in America."

Soon the table was full of plates. Baba ghanoush, Afghan salad, lamb degi, kabuli palaw. The meal reminded Wali of home. He kept the conversation going between bites.

"You've got to explain something to me," he said. "What is a guy educated in the US doing here?"

"I got a good finance job," Samir said. "Plus, I got family here."

Wali didn't believe him. Samir lacked the radical passion he'd seen so many times. Wali remembered the rage in the eyes of the al-Qaeda fighters caught by the Special Forces. Samir wasn't a true believer—or he was doing a good job suppressing it.

"But you just said you liked living in the United States," Wali said.

"I did. But that doesn't mean I like their policies. I don't like them bombing my people."

Wali took offense to that. He'd never heard of American fighters bombing Egypt. But he watched the Taliban bomb his people daily.

"Who did the American bombs hit in Cairo?"

Samir was silent for a minute.

"Muslim people, I guess," he said. "I'm just doing this for my brother. This is his thing."

Wali had come to Dubai with hate in his heart. Samir was supposed to be some camel hell-bent on waging war against his friends.

Instead, Samir was just a dumb kid like himself. They were just trying to find their way. It was all kind of silly, really. Samir loved the United States and yet he was trying to help destroy it.

"But you're still here with me. Why?"

Samir shrugged.

"My brother got me the gig," he said. "I haven't really joined them. I just help manage their money. Make sure guys get paid. My brother, Hamza, is an imam. I think he was with bin Laden for a while in Afghanistan. Or at least that is what he told me. Sometimes I hear him talk about Tora Bora, but I don't really ask. I don't want the details."

Wali didn't know what to say. He was stunned. *Samir's brother knew bin Laden!*

"That's amazing," Wali said. "I would love to meet the sheik. To know the man who scared the Americans every day."

ꕥꕥꕥ

Samir dropped Wali off at the Crowne Plaza Dubai on the Sheikh Zayed Road, across from the Dubai World Trade Centre and only a short drive from the mall. Before he got out, Wali looked over at Samir.

"What are you guys going to do with it?"

Samir shrugged.

"That is way above me. I'm in finance. But I suspect we'll let other groups know what we have. My brother told me it will help with recruiting. Then maybe use it in America."

Wali was stunned. Samir checked his watch.

"I'll be in touch soon with details on the deal," he said as he put the Ferrari in gear. "It was great to meet you."

Wali climbed out in silence and watched the sports car speed off. Samir's voice echoed in Wali's head.

Maybe use it in America.

CHAPTER 24

Denise stopped at the gate and showed the guards her badge. She didn't notice at first that the Romanians had been replaced by Americans. Air Force. That was strange. They were never on the gate. An Air Force sergeant looked at her ID card without offering a greeting and directed her toward a covered carport.

"Head over there, please," he said.

"What for?" Denise asked. "What is going on?"

The Air Force sergeant wouldn't look at her.

"New security procedures," he said.

Denise put the truck in gear and drove over to the carport. Another Air Force sergeant was resting in the shade on one of the concrete barriers.

"Turn off the engine, please," he said, opening his credential wallet so she could see his badge. "I'm going to need you to get out of the vehicle."

Denise read the name: Neil Canterbury. She was confused. "What for?"

"Are you aware of your ban from all military installations in Afghanistan?" Canterbury asked.

Denise looked away. Canterbury smirked.

"Let's go."

He ushered Denise toward his 4x4 parked nearby.

"What about my truck?"

Canterbury took hold of Denise's arm.

"You've got other things to worry about now."

A jolt of fear shot through Denise. She didn't protest as she walked to Canterbury's truck. The minute the American put on the handcuffs, she was paralyzed. Her brain shut down. She rode in silence as Canterbury drove to his office.

Of course, Denise knew about the charges that had led to the ban, but she hadn't thought about them for years. How many times had she gone through the gate?

Countless.

Why was she being stopped now?

She glanced at Canterbury. He looked like such a boy. He had a weird smirk on his face as he drove. He was enjoying this.

❧❧❧

Wali was in Washington, DC—or at least the Washington of his imagination—visiting the Capitol. The white dome looked like freedom to him. He was overtaken by its beauty as he walked closer to it when he heard a thunderous boom. The dome shook for a second and then disappeared in a pillar of fire. A mushroom cloud started to form in the sky. Wali fell to his knees. He didn't move. The shock wave from the detonation was coming at him like a wave, leaving destruction in its wake.

Wali tried to run. He knew who'd done this horrible thing and wanted to tell someone. Charlie? Felix? But his legs were frozen in place. He tried to scream for help, but all he heard was his phone ringing.

Wali's hotel room was dark, the blackout curtains pulled tight. He didn't want any of Felix's men watching him. His phone rang again. He'd missed a half dozen calls from Kahlid.

It was him again.

"Hello?" Wali said.

"Where have you been? I've been calling for an hour!"

Kahlid's voice was strained. He never talked to Wali like this.

"What's wrong?"

"They arrested Denise?"

"Who? For what?"

Wali was confused.

"The guards. They arrested her at the gate. Anabel said she never came by the store, so I started looking for her. The Romanian guards told me the Americans arrested her."

Wali didn't have time to untangle this. He was under enough pressure working with Felix. There was no room on his plate.

"Call Charlie," he said. "He'll take care of this for us."

⁂

Less than an hour later, Charlie pulled in next to Canterbury's truck. He touched its hood as he walked past.

The engine was still warm.

Good, Charlie thought. *She hasn't been here long.* He'd left as soon as Khalid called. There was no way he was going to let anything get in the way of the mission.

One of Canterbury's unit mates showed Charlie to a conference room. He sat on the table and waited. Soon, he heard Canterbury's voice tell someone not to let Denise leave. The door opened and Canterbury came into the room.

"What do you want?" Canterbury said.

"Look, I didn't come here to fight," Charlie said. "I just came to pick up Denise."

"Who asked you to come and pick her up?"

"I got a call from her boss. This is all a misunderstanding."

Canterbury put his hands on his hips.

"The fuck it is," he said. "This is an ongoing investigation. Denise will be released once I'm done with my questions."

"And what are your questions?"

"This is all part of an ongoing investigation," Canterbury said. "I will warn you that you could be part of the investigation."

Charlie couldn't believe what he was hearing.

"What are you talking about? I read your report on Wali, and by no means am I telling you not to report stuff that you're getting. But I'm sure the accusations against Wali aren't true."

Canterbury folded his arms across his chest.

"*Accusations?*" Canterbury said. "Wali is *corrupt*."

This sounded personal.

"What happened, dude?" Charlie asked. "Did you try Special Forces but couldn't hack it? That why you're in the Air Force?"

Canterbury let a smile spread across his lips.

"That's what you guys always think," he said. "I have too much integrity to be in Special Forces."

Charlie already regretted the cheap shot about the Air Force. He just needed to get out of this office with his operation intact.

"You know that this is my guy," Charlie said. "He's providing vital logistical support to the task force. Denise is part of that effort."

Canterbury wasn't having it.

"Your *guy* is Taliban," he said.

There was no way this little prick was going to derail his operation. A city in the United States could get nuked all because this guy wouldn't give up his personal vendetta against Wali.

Charlie slammed his fist against the table.

"I'm warning you just this once," he said. "Back off. Do not get in the way of our operations."

"You need to get out of my office," Canterbury said, his voice cracking. He felt rage rising in his chest. "Keep pushing me."

Charlie wanted to keep pushing.

"I'm going to leave, but I need to know what the fuck your problem is with Wali and why you're disrupting my fucking operations."

"Wali is a threat to the security of this base," Canterbury said.

Charlie laughed.

"You've been talking to Jan, right?" he said. "You should have told me. We've been over his Taliban accusations over and over. I dealt with all this on a previous rotation. It's bullshit. It's not like every week there is a whole new guy that comes in. It's the same dude every time. Should I just go over and tell Jan to stop?"

Canterbury tried to hide his surprise. Jan was the source, but how did Charlie know?

"I am not going to confirm anything about my possible sources," Canterbury said. "But we know he's meeting with the Taliban. He's paying them to protect his trucks. And he is overcharging your unit to move supplies and sending the proceeds to the enemy."

Charlie just shook his head.

"You have no idea what's really going on," he said. "And if you're not careful, you could mess up some important things. Operations that could cost the lives of millions of Americans."

Canterbury was tired of dealing with these special operations guys.

"Stop talking to me like I'm not protecting people," Canterbury said "It sounds to me that you have something to hide. Maybe I need to bring you in too. You want to tell me anything, Chief? How much is Wali paying you to fight his battles?"

Charlie lost his composure and lunged across the table, sending chairs flying.

"Who the fuck do you think you're talking to?"

Canterbury scrambled away. The sound of crashing furniture brought Canterbury's unit mates to the door. Charlie shoved past them, glaring at Canterbury the whole time. Canterbury followed Charlie out of the office and stood in the doorway. He smiled as he watched Charlie climb into his truck.

"Get in my way and I'll beat your ass," Charlie said. "You're fucking around with something much bigger than all of us. I'm not going to warn you again."

CHAPTER 25

The next morning, Samir called Wali from the lobby of the hotel.

"I'm coming up," he said. "How fast can you get ready?"

There was an urgency in Samir's voice. The words came out like machine-gun bursts. He was nervous.

Wali met Samir at the door of his suite and let him inside. Samir walked to the center of the room and turned to face Wali.

"He wants to meet today," Samir said.

Wali waited a beat.

Neither of them had anticipated this meeting happening so quickly. But it was happening, and it was exactly what Wali had hoped for after spending the day with Samir.

"Your brother?" he asked. "He wants to meet me? Today?"

"He wants to meet you *now*," Samir said. "Let's go. He's waiting."

"I need to change. Give me five minutes."

Wali went into the bedroom and pulled on jeans and a T-shirt. Samir was waiting at the door. Wali reached for his phone, but Samir grabbed his arm.

"Let's leave it behind," he said.

Wali looked at the phone Felix had given him and then back at Samir.

"Of course."

They rode the elevator in silence.

The playboy from the day before was gone. Wali noticed Samir's head was on a swivel. He eyed everyone that came within twenty feet of them. A black SUV was waiting at the door. Two large Arab men in suits, obviously armed, were standing outside the vehicle. They didn't say anything as one of the men opened the rear passenger-side door. Samir slid over behind the driver and Wali climbed in after him. As soon as the door shut, the SUV started to move.

The bodyguards followed in a sedan.

Wali watched the streets of Dubai through the tinted glass. It was Friday, and families were in the market enjoying the cool morning. Tables at the outdoor cafes were filled with men smoking hookahs.

They drove in circles for half an hour. The driver pulled over several times to make sure they weren't being followed. Finally, they drove to a secluded town far from the hustle of downtown Dubai. There were many apartment buildings, and the roads were more sand than pavement. The small convoy pulled into an underground garage and parked in a dark corner. The truck's tinted glass made Wali feel like he was at the bottom of the ocean. He could barely see his hand in front of his face.

When Samir opened his door, and the inside of the truck exploded with light from the dome in the middle of the cabin, blinding Wali for a second. As he regained his night vision, a man in a white robe and kufi opened the rear passenger door and pushed into the seat next to him. A set of brown prayer beads was threaded through the man's right hand. He had a long scar across his cheek and huge bags under his eyes, undoubtedly because he lived on the run. He seemed to be in decent shape, though, considering all he had done and been through.

It was Hamza, Samir's brother.

"*As-salamu alaikum wa rahmat'Allah wa barakatu*," Hamza said, the extended religious greeting in Arabic.

"*Wa alaikum...*" Wali started to say in his bad Arabic, but Hamza cut him off.

"We can speak in English. I've heard many wonderful things about you, my son," Hamza said. "It is truly an honor to finally meet you."

Wali was stunned by the man's words. He was honored?

"Sheikh, the honor is absolutely all mine," Wali said in his best Arabic. "I pray for you and your family every day. I am at your service, sir."

Hamza smiled and shook his head.

"We are all in the service of Allah, dear brother," he said. "The honor lies in the path of Allah."

"By the grace of God," Wali said.

"Samir tells me that you are a very successful businessman in Afghanistan and that you work with the Americans," Hamza said. "But what really impressed me is the fact that you never forgot who you are or what matters most. May Allah reward you for your deeds, dear brother."

"This world is just a test for the afterlife, God willing," Wali said, digging deep into his fundamentalist repertoire.

This wasn't him. He didn't believe any of it. But he also knew the only way he was getting out of that truck was if he made them believe.

"By the grace of God. You are wise beyond your years, Wali," Hamza said as he put his hand on Wali's shoulder.

Hamza turned to Samir.

"Have them bring us some tea."

Samir got out of the SUV. Hamza turned his attention back to Wali.

"You have taken a great risk coming here and meeting with us," the sheikh said. "This has not gone unnoticed by me or our friends in Quetta. But more importantly, by Allah."

Wali looked away. He couldn't hold the man's gaze any longer.

"Thank you, Sheikh. But I hope to do more."

Hamza snapped his prayer beads.

"You will, God willing, my boy," Hamza said, patting Wali's leg. "That's why you are here. I don't travel to meet just anyone, you know."

Samir returned with a thermos and a tray of glasses and rejoined the others in the SUV. He filled each glass with scalding-hot tea. Hamza took the first glass. Wali took the second. Samir loudly sipped from the last one.

All three drank tea for a while. No one spoke. Hamza finally nodded to Samir, who got out of the truck.

"It's time to go, Wali," Samir said.

"You are the reason we are going to win this war, my son," Hamza whispered to Wali before he got out.

Samir came around to Wali's side of the truck and shook his hand.

"I have some more business to discuss with my brother before he travels again," Samir said in English. "The driver will take you back to the hotel. I'll call you later."

The driver climbed behind the wheel of the truck. Wali tried to see where Samir and Hamza went, but it was impossible in the dark garage.

An hour or so later, the skyscrapers of Dubai filled the windshield.

Wali exhaled. It felt like he'd been holding his breath since he first got into the SUV.

CHAPTER 26

Canterbury went back to the interview room.

Denise was sitting at a table. When he entered the room, her shoulders slumped. Canterbury sat down and put a piece of paper in front of her.

"According to this report, you were banned from Afghanistan after an alcohol violation in Bagram," Canterbury said. "You can deny it again, but it's all right there."

Denise pushed the paper away.

"I should have fought it," she said. "I had a couple of drinks. I wasn't doing the other stuff."

Canterbury picked up the paper.

"You didn't smuggle alcohol or drugs onto the base?" Canterbury said. "You weren't one of the girls suspected of trading sexual favors for cash or drugs?"

Denise looked Canterbury straight in the eye.

"I'm no whore," she said. "I fuck who I want."

Canterbury gave the last comment a little half smirk.

"I don't care who you fuck," he said. "I don't even care about you."

Denise exhaled and sat back in the chair, her arms crossed in front of her. She caught her second wind.

"So why am I here?"

Canterbury returned the paper to the table.

"Because your boss is a threat to this base. Do you know who just came to the office?"

Denise shook her head no.

"Of course you do," Canterbury said. "Your boss's SF friend."

Canterbury paused and flipped some pages in his notebook. He knew Charlie's name, but he was playing it for dramatic effect.

"Chief Warrant Officer Charlie Book," Canterbury said. "So how much is Wali paying him to be an enforcer?"

Denise didn't know what to say. She just stared at Canterbury.

"Come on," Canterbury said. "You know things. You've seen things. There's no reason why you should be sitting here for having a drink after work while he steals and bribes his way to the good life."

Denise looked at the charge sheet lying on the desk again and then back at Canterbury. He had her.

"OK," she said. "But once we finish our talk, I'm free to go. No bullshit. I just want to get the fuck out of here."

"Depends on what you tell me," Canterbury said.

"I just want to go home, OK?" she said.

Canterbury just stared at her.

"Look, Wali is a good guy for the most part."

Canterbury smiled at that.

"I don't care about the most part," he said. "It is the other part I'm interested in talking about."

Denise looked away. Canterbury saw she was nervous. She knew something, but she needed to screw up her courage first.

"Have you ever seen him pay Charlie or another Special Forces soldier?"

Denise looked down at her clinched hands. She squeezed them together like she was praying with all her might. Canterbury let the silence sit. When it got unbearable and Denise's hands were white from the pressure, she looked at him.

"Once," she said through a clenched jaw. "He was in with Charlie and another guy. I don't know who he was. They had a bunch of money on the table. Lots of cash. They got weird when I came into the room. When I asked Wali about it later, he dodged my questions."

Canterbury was scribbling down the details.

"When did this happen?"

For the next hour, Denise and Canterbury went over the meeting with Charlie and Felix. Canterbury got every detail. He wanted to know the layout of the room, where Charlie sat, and where Wali sat. Denise kept talking and adding details. After a while, Denise wouldn't stop talking.

"Once we stopped at the gate and Wali let the guards hold his bankroll," Denise said. "He bragged afterward that he was untouchable. He told me nothing could happen to him as long as the Special Forces were around."

Canterbury didn't believe what he was hearing. His case was coming together in front of his eyes. Denise's statement paired with Jan's intelligence sealed the deal.

"Where is Wali now?" Canterbury said.

"Dubai, I think," Denise said. "He left in a hurry. Didn't say why, but I expect he will be back in a few days. He doesn't like to leave the business for long."

Canterbury closed his notebook and smiled at Denise for the first time.

"You have to let me know when he gets back," Canterbury said. "And tell no one what we talked about. It won't be long now. I just need to type up your statement and once you sign it you can go. Do you need anything?"

"Just some water," she said. "What am I supposed to tell them if they ask me what happened?"

Canterbury was at the door of the room.

"Just tell them the truth," he said. "You got busted for drinking and you've got to go home now. They don't have to hear about the rest."

Denise smiled when she heard the word "home."

Canterbury made a copy of Denise's signed statement and drove out to see Jan that evening. They met in the general's office over tea and sweets.

"What is this?" Jan said as Canterbury handed him Denise's statement.

"It is the smoking gun we've been looking for," Canterbury said. "One of Wali's employees confirmed everything."

Jan scanned the paper and gave it to Basir, who held it in his lap.

"What do you mean everything?" Jan said.

Canterbury was too excited to realize neither Jan nor Basir could read the statement.

"He is bribing Special Forces soldiers," Canterbury said. "Or at least two took his money."

Jan nodded in agreement like a true believer hearing a sermon.

"And what of the Taliban?" Jan asked.

"She didn't know anything about them," Canterbury said. "But this evidence alone means I can arrest him and we can have his business barred."

Jan stood up from his chair and walked over to his desk. He opened a drawer and took out a bottle of whiskey. Basir got two glasses. Jan poured two fingers into each one and waved Canterbury over.

"First we drink," Jan said. "Then I have some information."

Canterbury approached the desk warily. Drinking was forbidden under General Order Number 1, but how could he decline? This was rapport building. Not taking the drink would risk insult. Canterbury took the whiskey and smiled.

"Manana," Canterbury said. "Thank you" in Pashto.

Both men took a sip. Canterbury felt the whisky burn all the way down. He hadn't eaten, and his stomach was doing cheetah flips. Canterbury tried not to cough, but his body forced him. Jan didn't seem to notice, but Canterbury caught Basir's smirk.

Jan waved Canterbury back to his seat. Back behind his desk, Jan flipped open a file.

"My sources confirmed Wali is meeting with the Taliban," Jan said. "We've known it, of course, but we didn't know who. Well, his Taliban contact is his uncle. The man's name is Razaq. He is a known Taliban commander. He and Wali meet in Kandahar often. It is there Wali pays for protection and gives his uncle information about the coalition."

Canterbury choked on his whisky again. This time out of shock. He put his glass down on the desk.

"How do you know this?" he said, leaning forward to see the paper in the file.

Jan picked up Canterbury's glass, shielding the file, and handed it back to him to finish.

"Because we caught Razaq and he admitted it," Jan said.

"Where is Razaq now?" Canterbury said.

"Back with his men," Jan said.

Canterbury put his glass down.

"You let him go?"

"He has no value in a jail," Jan said. "Plus, he owes me. He works for me now."

Canterbury tried to hide his anger. They had a Taliban commander in custody and the Afghans let him go. It could have been one less shithead on the battlefield.

"But he is a Taliban commander," Canterbury said. "He is actively plotting against us, and you let him go."

Jan took a sip of whiskey.

"He is Taliban," Jan said. "But he is also a wise man. When the Taliban fall, he will come back to Kandahar looking for help. I am that help. His allegiance is to himself. So, if he gives us information that leads to the arrest of real threats like Wali, he is Taliban in name only."

Canterbury wasn't tracking. The whiskey on an empty stomach was starting to have an effect. He needed to eat. He needed to sleep. He needed to get his report ready. The Razaq question could wait for another day. If what Jan was saying was right, they could get him another time.

"I understand, sir," Canterbury said. "Thank you for the drink. I need to get back and start the process so we can get Wali. Once we take Wali off the battlefield, we can work on Razaq."

Canterbury got up. Jan had Denise's statement in his hands.

"I need to get that statement back, sir," Canterbury said.

Jan looked at Basir.

"It is your only copy?" Basir said.

"No, but it is classified," Canterbury said.

"We need a copy for our files," Basir said. "Don't worry, we will protect the document."

Canterbury started to protest, but Basir escorted Canterbury toward the door.

Meeting over.

CHAPTER 27

Wali watched the Arabs ski down a slope.

The buildings inside the ski slope area were meant to look like an Alpine ski village. The window glass was frosted over and difficult to see through. He watched as a few children snowplowed their way down the slope.

Wali laughed.

Gulf Arabs skiing inside a mall. *This is what camels look like in the snow*, Wali thought as he sipped his orange juice. Samir appeared at the front of the restaurant and walked over to his table.

"Do you ski?" he asked, sitting down.

"No," Wali said.

"But you have snow in Afghanistan."

Wali smiled.

"Yes," he said. "But we have more important things to do."

A waiter came by and took Samir's order. He got a juice like Wali.

"I just learned," Samir said as the waiter left. "It is good fun. Maybe next time you're here, we can try it together."

Wali smiled and took a sip of his juice.

"Maybe."

"You must find this all amusing," Samir said. "Skiing in a mall. No war. Just frivolities." He chuckled.

"But this is my hope for Afghanistan," Wali said. "We don't want war. We want peace. We want joy and hope for our families. We want to ski."

The waiter brought Samir a glass of juice. Samir raised his glass.

"To skiing when the Americans are gone," he said.

"Indeed," Wali said.

Samir took a sip of his juice and then reached into his briefcase. He had a stack of papers.

"This is for the money transfer," Samir said. "We'll deposit five hundred thousand dollars into your account. This is a good faith payment. My people will send a representative to Pakistan next week to finalize the rest of the money. When it is time, our people will then travel to pick up the bomb. I hope you will find that acceptable."

Wali flipped through the paperwork. His heart was beating through his shirt. He didn't believe Allah was going to allow this. These men were ready to pay millions for a bomb to commit mass murder.

Samir handed him a pen. Wali's hand shook as he signed the paperwork to authorize the transfer.

"I'll need some time to make arrangements," Wali said.

Samir put the paperwork back into his briefcase.

"My brother will be coming," Samir said. "He will be traveling with one of our experts. They will stay no more than one night."

"That is doable. How do I contact them?"

Samir put an envelope on the table.

"We will contact you," Samir said. "Directions are right here."

He slid the envelope over to Wali, who put it into his pocket.

"Anything else?"

Samir called the waiter over.

"Only lunch," he said. "When do you fly out?"

Wali didn't want to stay for lunch. He just wanted to get back to his life. He wanted to talk with Felix and wash his hands of this bomb.

But he didn't leave.

"Tonight," Wali said.

"Great," Samir said. "We aren't in a rush."

After a filling lunch of German bratwurst and fried potatoes, Wali finally returned to his hotel. He was exhausted. All he wanted to do was catch a nap and then head over to the airport.

Wali slid the key into the lock and walked into the room. Felix was sitting on the bed watching CNN. His sandals were on the floor.

"How was lunch?" Felix said. "My guys said you had a feast."

Wali wasn't sure he liked Felix, if that was even his name. He was too familiar. Too friendly. But he hadn't earned it. Wali wanted to talk with Charlie. That was the deal.

"It was good," Wali said. "But it was hard to eat with Samir."

"I'm not a big fan of German," Felix said, slipping on his sandals. "Too heavy for lunch. All I want to do is take a nap afterwards. I tend to avoid meat midday. Salads and that sort of thing, you know?"

Felix took a seat in a chair near the balcony that overlooked the Persian Gulf.

"Where is the envelope?"

Wali fished it out of his pocket as thoughts swirled around his head. He was shaken. Felix knew his every move and yet he never saw the CIA man or his team. Was the man eating soup at the restaurant the first day watching him?

Felix held out a plastic bag, careful not to touch it. Wali dropped the envelope in the plastic bag.

"You did good, my friend," Felix said. "Took balls to go into that parking garage. You did good."

"Good enough to get to America?"

Felix sealed the bag. He took out his phone and sent a text.

"Yeah, man, good enough in my eyes," Felix said. "But I don't make that decision. But you have my vote."

There was a knock at the door. It made Wali jump. Felix stood up, checked the peephole, and then just cracked the door and slipped the bag through.

"Thanks, brother," he said to an unknown ally.

Felix returned to his seat across from Wali, who sat on the bed.

"I need that envelope," Wali said. "Those are the directions for the exchange."

"Yeah, I know," Felix said. "We just want to get DNA off of it. We'll return it before you leave. Now, let's talk about the money. We know they just wired you half a mil," Felix said.

Wali had no idea they were watching his accounts.

"Just leave the money there," Felix said. "We'll collect it up once this thing is done. It is important that you don't let your uncle's guys get it. You think you can do that?"

Wali had no idea.

"Sure," he said, hoping to get Felix out of his room so he could sleep.

"Great," Felix said. "You did good work here. Now your uncle has to come through."

Felix got up and headed for the door. He patted Wali's shoulder as he passed.

"Have a good flight," Felix said. "I'll see you back at KAF."

Wali was asleep seconds after his head hit the pillow. Two days of stressful meetings caused his body to shut down. When he woke up a few hours later, he found the envelope on the floor near his door. Someone must have slid it underneath while he slept.

First class was empty, and he enjoyed a movie and a curry dinner. Wali was first off the flight and shouldered his bag in the terminal when Basir and one of Jan's men sidled up to him.

"The general wants to see you," Basir said.

Wali was too exhausted to argue. Outside, he climbed into the truck and sat silently as they drove to Jan's compound. Basir marched Wali into Jan's office. The general was in uniform sitting behind his desk.

Basir stood behind Wali.

"How was your flight?" Jan said.

Wali wasn't in the mood for this bullshit. He just smiled.

"You've been very busy," Jan said, ignoring Wali's silence. "You're running one or two convoys for the Special Forces a day. That is on top of your other businesses. I figure you're making fifteen to twenty million a month. Does that sound right?"

"Check your math," Wali said. "You tell me."

Jan slid out of his chair and walked around to the front of the desk.

"You're doing very well," Jan said. "But you have enemies now."

Basir took out a folded piece of paper and slid it across the desk to Jan. He picked it up and started to read. It was Denise's statement. Wali listened as someone accused him of bribing Charlie and Felix. Every word made him angry. He was so mad he didn't even hear Jan.

"Wali," Jan said, snapping him out of his rage. "The Americans are after you. They want to put you out of business. Your own people have no loyalty."

"So you say," Wali said. "What does any of this have to do with you?"

"We're Afghans," Jan said, trying to relax him. "They are Americans. If this was 2001, I'd agree with the Americans. But it is not. I don't trust the Americans anymore."

Wali folded up the statement and put it in his pocket. Basir started to ask for it back. Jan silenced him with a wave of his hand.

"The Americans are coming for you," Jan said. "They think you stole from them. You bribed them. You tricked them. I told them no, but they insist you're Taliban. You're not safe."

"And you're going to protect me?" Wali said. "What is that going to cost me?"

He started to get up.

"We can be partners," Jan said. "You have the trucks. I have the security. I have the ear of the Americans. This will all go away once you are with me. We can make a fortune together."

Wali folded his arms across his chest. He had to respect the general's persistence. This was a new pitch. Join forces so I can get half of your wealth.

"Don't you protect me anyway?" Wali said, pausing to let Jan ponder the question. "You wear the uniform of Afghanistan. Isn't that your job?"

Jan didn't say anything. Wali was sure he didn't have an answer. The thought of serving his country instead of his wallet never crossed his mind.

"It is your duty to protect me and all Afghans," Wali said.

Jan walked out from behind his desk.

"Of course," Jan said. "But this isn't about my service. This is business."

"It always is," Wali said. "And like always, I don't want to be your partner. I don't owe you anything."

Jan smiled. Wali grit his teeth. The smile told him everything he needed to know. He was fucked. This wasn't an offer. It was a shakedown. Either you were with Jan or against him.

Wali was firmly against him.

"Fuck you," Wali said. "This meeting is over."

Wali turned to leave. Jan slammed his hand on the desk.

"You are just a naïve kid," he said. "Listen to how you talk to me. You think you're an American. You believe your friends will take you home with them. But they have grown tired of Afghanistan. Their politicians talk about leaving. When they leave, you will be here. It will just be us. Remember that. The Americans don't live here. Only Afghans. You will have no friends."

CHAPTER 28

Wali's compound was quiet. Most of the workers were in their rooms. The last convoy had left hours before.

Wali stopped at the door of his office.

"Get Denise," Wali told the guard at the gate.

He walked straight back to his bedroom and tossed his bag onto the bed. He heard the front door open.

"Take a seat," he said.

"Wali," Denise said.

She started to come back to the bedroom until Wali poked his head around the doorjamb.

"Take a seat in the office," he said, pulling a clean T-shirt over his head.

Denise was standing near the door when he walked into the office. Wali walked straight to his desk and sat down. He pulled the folded statement out of his pocket and made a copy.

"Ms. McKenna, please take a seat," he said.

He heard her sobbing.

"You're fired," he said. "I saw the statement. I read the allegations. It is hard to believe you'd make up these things."

Denise wouldn't look at him.

"Why did you do it?"

Denise started to cry harder.

"I don't know," she said. "I was scared. I didn't know where you were. You won't tell me anything. I didn't know what to do. They arrested me."

Wali started to read from the statement. He read about how he bribed Charlie. He read about showing the guards his bankroll.

"Stop," she said. "Please. I know what I said."

Wali looked up from the paper.

"And what about this charge in Bagram? You never told me you were banned."

Denise finally looked up at Wali.

"They made me sign a confession," she said. "The others accused me of smuggling alcohol. I didn't do it."

"So now you know how it feels."

Denise grabbed for Wali's hands. He jerked them away.

"I'll make it better," she said. "I'll recant. We can make this better. Ask your friends to help with the Bagram charge."

Wali looked at the wall.

"I'm going to get you on the next flight to Dubai," Wali said. "Get your stuff packed."

"Wait," Denise said. "I can help you. The Air Force guy, Canterbury, wants the Special Forces guys. He doesn't want you. Let's go see him together. Tell him the Special Forces guys wanted money. You had no choice."

Wali stood up and grabbed Denise by her arm. He wrenched her out of the chair.

"Get packed," Wali said.

CHAPTER 29

Ebony walked over to Charlie's desk. She'd just returned from the DFAC.

"Yo, Chief, check this out."

Charlie took the paper from her and scanned it. It was an investigator's report. He stopped when he saw Wali's name. His eyes shot down to the end. The report was authored by Canterbury.

"Ain't that your guy?" Ebony said. "Sounds like he turned into a bad apple."

"The fuck he is," Charlie said, getting up from his desk. "Where did you get this?"

"I've got a friend," she said. "Keeps tabs on things for us, you know?"

Charlie didn't want to know. He stopped reading when he got to the first source. Ebony was still standing by his desk.

"Sorry," Charlie said. "Thanks for this. He is our guy, but this is bullshit."

Ebony started to walk back to her desk.

"I've seen reports like this in the past," she said. "Same kind of stuff."

Charlie put the report on his desk.

"Hey, can you look them up for me? I want to check something."

Ebony started to compile the reports. Charlie punched in the informant's code in a database. It was Jan. Charlie kept reading but stopped when he got to the second informant. A quick check of the database revealed what he thought.

Denise.

"Hey Chief," Ebony said. "I've got those reports you want."

Charlie didn't look up.

"Just tell me the source."

He read her the number. She nodded.

"Yeah," she said. "Same guy, just different AFOSI guy."

Charlie shook his head.

"Fucking clowns," he said. "Jan has been feeding them the same lie. He finds the new guy and pushes this line of garbage."

Ebony laughed.

"They're like mushrooms," she said. "Keep 'em in the dark and feed 'em shit."

"You couldn't be more right," Charlie said.

He lifted his phone and called Felix.

"We've got a little problem," Charlie said. "You have a few minutes to take a ride?"

Charlie hung up the phone and grabbed his ball cap.

"I'll be back," he said.

Ebony clapped her hands and let out a hoot.

"Go get 'em, Chief," Ebony said.

Felix met Charlie outside the gate and they drove over to Canterbury's office. He sipped a Diet Coke as they drove. This was a real one from America, not the international "lite" version.

"I can't drink that Coke lite anymore," Felix said, getting the last drop out of the can. "I miss that chemical burn you get from the real thing."

Charlie just nodded along. He wasn't listening. He was mad but wanted to keep his composure. Last time he met Canterbury, it almost ended in a fight. A beatdown, more likely.

"Before we go in, let me get this straight," Felix said. "This Air Force guy wants to arrest Wali for bribery and working with the Taliban. Our Wali. The guy we told to meet with the Taliban."

"Right," Charlie said. "But he doesn't know that."

"Of course he doesn't," Felix said. "Why would we tell him?"

"We wouldn't," Charlie said.

"So, why am I here?" Felix said. "I don't care about some Air Force cop. Just shred it."

Charlie shook his head.

"We can't."

Felix was confused.

"I thought you handled this," he said. "Didn't you talk to him already."

"Yeah," Charlie said. "But it didn't stick. That's why you're coming."

Felix shook his head.

"Ah," he said. "You're going with the secret squirrel routine. Shit, man. Why didn't you tell me? I would have changed."

Charlie looked over at Felix. He was wearing North Face khakis, a Captain America T-shirt, and flip-flops. He couldn't have been less intimidating.

"You look like you're late for class," Charlie said. "Is that any way to fight a war?"

Felix looked over at Charlie in his uniform, the puke-green digital print.

"You look like my grandmother's sofa," Felix said. "Let me at least borrow your shades."

Charlie slid the transmission into park and climbed out of the truck.

"And violate one of the SOF rules?" Charlie said.

"Right. Always know where you are, always look cool, and if you don't know where you are, look cool," Felix said.

Charlie slid his sunglasses down from the top of his head.

"Can't look cool without shades."

Charlie walked into the office first. Felix followed. He tossed his empty soda can into an empty trash can. The can made a loud bang as it hit the bottom. Everyone in the office looked up. Charlie looked back at Felix.

"Sorry, Dad," Felix said.

Turning his attention to the office, Felix smiled and stretched out his arms.

"We're looking for Special Agent Canterbury."

Canterbury popped his head up over his cubicle wall.

"Here, sir," he said.

His military bearing melted away when he saw Charlie.

"You need to leave, Chief Warrant Officer Book," Canterbury said. "We have nothing to talk about."

Charlie mouthed "fuck you" to Canterbury. Felix ignored both of them. He walked over to Canterbury's desk and stuck out his hand.

"Hey, man," Felix said. "Just here for a quick chat. It doesn't have to be like that. Let's find a place to talk."

Canterbury wasn't sure what to do. He shook Felix's hand.

"What do you want to talk about...sir?"

Felix scanned Canterbury's desk. A few papers. A Green Beans coffee cup. Pens. Computer. A picture of his parents at some state fair. A Filipino girl at the KAF Boardwalk. Felix stopped. The picture of the girl didn't fit in Canterbury's white-bread narrative.

Captain Voss interrupted their meeting.

"Can I help you guys?" Voss said.

"Maybe," Felix said. "We need to talk with you guys about some reports."

Voss wasn't sure what to do. This was irregular.

"I didn't catch your name," Voss said.

"That's because I didn't give it," Felix said. "My initials are OGA."

The color in Voss's face drained. He ushered Felix, Charlie, and Canterbury into his office. Canterbury sat in a chair to the captain's right. Charlie sat opposite the captain. Felix closed the door and then turned to face the captain and Canterbury.

"It is important that what is said in this room stays in this room," he said. "Am I safe to assume we all have top secret clearance?"

Felix waited for nods all around.

"OK," he said. "Any mention of this to anyone outside of this room will get you thrown in jail."

Felix leaned in toward Canterbury.

"My office wanted me to bring over some NDAs," he said. "The big ones that basically send you to Gitmo if you breathe a word of this to anyone, but I said no way. We're one team, one fight. Right?"

Canterbury was nodding along. But Voss saw through the bullshit.

"OK, get on with it," he said. "We understand."

Felix turned his attention to the captain.

"Sorry, sir," Felix said. "OK, I understand your office generated a report about Ahmed Wali. The report makes accusations about collaboration with the Taliban."

The captain looked at Canterbury.

"Yes, sir," Canterbury said. "I am in the process of putting together a packet on him. He is meeting with the Taliban. His uncle is a commander. The money we pay him to move supplies is funding the insurgency."

"Bullshit," Charlie said, unable to contain himself. "I told your dumb ass..."

Charlie stopped when Felix put his hand on his shoulder. Charlie looked away, took out his can of Copenhagen, and packed a thick wad into his cheek.

"What my colleague is trying to say is Wali isn't what you think he is," Felix said. "He is an important intelligence asset and isn't to be touched."

"But sir..." Canterbury started to protest.

Voss looked over at Canterbury and then at Felix.

"Do you have anything in writing?" Voss said. "When did your operation start? My investigator has been looking into Wali's activities for a while, and we've uncovered some troubling things. His sources are confident he is a Taliban sympathizer."

"I can't reveal details about our operation, but..."

Before Felix finished, Charlie jumped into the conversation.

"His sources?" he said. "You mean a warlord who has shoveled you guys shit for years. He is Wali's main competitor. You think he has an agenda? Who would benefit from Wali losing his contracts? You know Jan buys those rockets from the Taliban so that he can turn them in to you and look good."

Voss folded his hands like a teacher waiting out a child's outburst.

"We have more than one source," the captain said.

Charlie tried to stifle a laugh, but failed.

"You mean Denise?" Charlie said. "The ex-employee? The one that lied about being a whore and smuggling booze to fat contractors in Bagram? That source? This is a fucking clown show. Just get out of the way and let the adults win this war."

Felix watched as Voss's face went from being flushed to beet red as he tried to figure out what to say to Charlie. Canterbury looked at his commander like a child waiting for his father to defend him. Felix opened the door and looked at Charlie.

"Why don't you take a break," Felix said.

Charlie didn't want to leave, but the damage was done. He stood up and walked out of the office. Charlie felt the eyes of the office on his back as he left.

Fuck them.

They didn't understand what was going on.

A few minutes later, Felix came out of the office with a big grin and a cold Coke lite. Charlie was standing next to the truck, his arms folded across his chest.

"Let the adults win the war," Felix said. "Is that how they teach rapport building at the qualification course now?"

Charlie spit a stream of tobacco juice into the dust.

"Was I wrong?"

Felix shook his head as he climbed into the truck.

"They have a job to do," he said. "It might not be the job you want, but it is part of the war effort."

Charlie didn't want to get into it with Felix, mostly because the CIA man was right. But Charlie was a meat eater. He defined his war by successful operations, finding, fixing, and finishing the Taliban. His war was about making an impact with a bullet. Canterbury's war was background checks and speeding tickets. If you're going to come all this way to Afghanistan, you might as well fight. Everyone else was a fucking war tourist.

Felix took a pull from his soda.

"Where did you get that?" Charlie said.

"They were kind hosts," Felix said. "Once you left, of course."

Charlie guided the truck into the traffic.

"So, where does this leave us?" Charlie said.

"We're good," Felix said. "I convinced the captain that we vetted Wali and he is on the up-and-up. But by no means should his office stop investigating."

Charlie pulled the truck over and threw it into park.

"You what?" he said. "What the fuck are you talking about?"

Felix turned to face Charlie.

"Canterbury agreed to find a new source," Felix said. "He also promised to run the case by my office. At first, I said you guys because Wali is your guy, but they fucking hate you. So, if they find anything, and they won't, then they'll call me."

Charlie put the truck back in gear and joined the line of traffic again.

"I guess that makes sense," he said.

Charlie's phone rang. He fished it out of his shoulder pocket and showed Felix the screen. It was Wali.

"What's up, pimp?" Charlie said. He listened for a moment. "We're on the way."

Charlie hung up the phone and turned to Felix.

"The exchange is set," he said. "We're on."

Wali was pacing in his office when Charlie and Felix arrived. Charlie sensed it immediately.

"Hey, man," Charlie said. "You cool?"

Wali looked at Charlie and then Felix.

"Yes," Wali said. "I'm OK."

Felix fished out his phone and headed for the door of the office.

"I've got to take this," he said. "Back in a minute."

Charlie watched the door shut. Wali was seated in a chair. He had a cup of tea in his hand.

"I fired her," Wali said. "She lied to me. She didn't tell me about Bagram. Then she lied to the investigators. They think I bribed you. They think you're a bad guy. We need to go tell them everything."

"Wali, I am a bad guy," Charlie said. "I'm a bad motherfucker."

Wali didn't know what to say. Was his friend making a joke? This was a serious time. Charlie smiled at him.

"We talked to Canterbury today," Charlie said. "You don't have to worry about me. This will all be over soon."

Wali relaxed.

"I was worried," he said. "I was afraid you were in trouble."

Felix cleared his throat.

"Gentlemen, I know we're all mad at the Air Force, but we have a bomb to get, don't we?"

"I have a lot to share," Wali said.

Wali spread a map out on the desk. It covered Kandahar Province from the Pakistan border to the border of Helmand Province. Wali folded the map so it only showed an area west of Kandahar City.

"The device is in a compound here," Wali said, pointing to an area in the center of the Panjwai Valley. "My uncle's bodyguard is watching it."

Wali took out a handwritten note and spread it out on the desk next to the military map. Printed in Arabic was a date, GPS coordinates, times, and dates. The make and model of the car was also provided so the Taliban could grease the border guards.

"Samir's brother's is coming from Quetta. He will travel by taxi from Spin Boldak to Panjwai. Once the money is exchanged, one of my trucks will take the device across the Red Desert to a link-up point near the border. AQ will take it from there."

Felix and Charlie studied the map for a few more minutes.

"And what about Samir's brother?"

"They didn't share how he'd get back to Dubai," Wali said. "And I didn't ask."

"Smart," Charlie said.

Wali nodded in agreement. "We have four days."

There was a knock on the door. Charlie covered the map and the message with a blanket from a nearby couch. One of Wali's workers came in with trays of food.

"I haven't eaten," Wali said. "Will you join me?"

Charlie wanted to leave. They had so much planning to do. But they couldn't leave without insulting Wali.

"Sure," Charlie said. "Can I wash my hands first?"

He got up and walked down the long hall to the bathroom. Charlie took a piss and then washed his hands. When he opened the door, Felix was standing in the hall.

"Eat quickly," Felix said. "I'm going to call back to the station and tell them we have a go op so they can get our nuke team on the plane."

"What about the uncle?" Charlie said. "And Wali. What are we going to do with them?"

Felix looked down at his bare feet and shook his head.

"I guess we have to get them out," he said. "God, I'd love to keep the uncle in place. But I doubt he'd survive a failure like this. You guys take the device in the desert. We can get him to a safe house in the city on his way back to Spin B. Have some of our guys arrest him at a checkpoint. We'll have to get rid of the bodyguards, but that will just please Big Army. They caught some real live Taliban."

Charlie liked the plan.

"And the brother, when do we get him?"

Felix was already thinking about that.

"Between Spin B and Panjwai," Felix said. "We'll ID him at the border, and he just won't make it to the meeting."

Charlie knew what that meant.

CHAPTER 30

Canterbury returned to his desk after meeting Charlie and Felix.

His case was on life support. He needed another smoking gun. A direct link. He pulled up the background investigation audit on his computer. Voss was more interested in it than his Wali investigation. The only solace was he had a date with Anabel in a few hours.

He was almost done with the background audit when his computer pinged. Canterbury checked the new email message. It was from Task Force 2010. The auditors had found something. Canterbury read quickly.

"A deposit for five hundred thousand dollars made 10 August 2010 came from a known al-Qaeda charity," the message said.

The email requested further investigation. The auditors were going to freeze Wali's accounts and put him on the ban list for future contracts. But Task Force 2010 didn't have any power to arrest him.

That was Canterbury's job. But first, the task force needed evidence from his investigation. Canterbury knew Denise's statement wasn't going to be enough. And Jan's statement was the same old song and dance. They needed something more.

Canterbury did a database search and found all of the statements from Jan about Wali. He started to cut and paste the statements' greatest hits into a new document. After an hour, Wali appeared to be a terrorist mastermind. The new document coupled with the auditor's report and the statement from Denise made a damning package. Canterbury was about to head to Captain Voss's office when he stopped.

Where did he get the new statement?

It was still Jan. He needed another source. Denise was gone.

He checked his watch. He had to go meet Anabel. Then it came to him. He printed off a copy of the statement and slid it into a file. He met her at the Boardwalk, and they walked over to the French bistro for an almond croissant. They shared it and sipped coffee.

"I miss her," Anabel said. "I can't believe he fired her."

Canterbury chewed his pastry. He didn't give a fuck about Denise.

"I know," he said. "Harsh. She was doing good work."

"Wellll..." Anabel said, waving her fork around whimsically. "She was kind of a bitch. She acted like the boss. Like it was her money, you know?"

Canterbury shrugged.

"It was Uncle Sam's money."

Anabel didn't get it.

"No, it was Wali's money."

Canterbury put down his fork. He looked around to see if the other soldiers and contractors were listening. No one cared. He leaned in closer to Anabel.

"He stole that money," Canterbury said. "It was all a fraud. He is Taliban."

Anabel reeled back.

"*Noooo!*"

She leaned back in, content to be part of the secret.

"Are you sure?"

"Look, I shouldn't say anything, so don't pass this around, but his uncle is a Taliban commander. He's been funneling American money to the Taliban for years. He just got half a mil from al-Qaeda."

Anabel took a bite of croissant. Canterbury took a sip of his coffee and let the reality sink in for her. She worked for a terrorist.

"What are you going to do?" she asked.

"Arrest him."

Anabel smiled and nodded. She liked the idea. Her boyfriend was going to catch a terrorist!

"But I need your help first," he said.

Canterbury pulled out the statement and slid it over to her.

"I need you to sign this."

She picked up the paper and read it. She let out a few gasps and even whistled as she set it down on the table.

"I didn't know any of that," she said. "I just worked at the store. I had no idea. He seemed to really like Americans."

"That's why we need to arrest him," Canterbury said. "His deception cost American lives."

Canterbury handed her a pen. She took it but hesitated.

"Are you sure this is legal? I never said these things. I didn't know any of this before you told me. It doesn't feel right."

Canterbury checked again to make sure no one was watching.

"It's fine," he said. "It's all fact. You're not lying if it's all true. And no one will ever ask you to testify. You're a confidential source."

Anabel thought for a second and then signed the paper. Canterbury took the statement and the pen back. He slid it back in his cargo pocket and stood up.

"You just saved some lives," he said. "You want to go back to my room and watch a movie?"

She gave him a knowing look.

CHAPTER 31

Wali went to bed thinking about America.

He'd spent the last five years building his companies and helping the Americans win the war in Afghanistan—but now that was over. In four days, it wouldn't be safe for him. He'd be in America, a place he always wanted to go, but not in the way he wanted. If he was being honest, he would soon be a refugee. A very wealthy refugee, but a man without a country.

Wali loved Afghanistan. It was his home. He didn't really want to leave it, but he also didn't want al-Qaeda to have a nuclear weapon.

Wali was just fading into a fitful sleep when a knock on the bedroom door jolted him awake. He rubbed his eyes and checked his phone. It was 2:30 a.m.

Someone tried the door handle. It was locked. None of his employees would do that. Wali climbed out of bed. The door handle shook again.

Slowly, Wali cracked the door.

"Step away from the door," he said.

Wali glimpsed a male form in the dark hallway before the man shined a flashlight into his face, blinding him.

"Come out, you son of a bitch," the man said in Pashto.

Wali hesitated.

I'm dead, he thought. Al-Qaeda was at his door. They'd found out about his uncle and the plot. He tried to shut the door, but the man's rough hands pulled him into the hallway. The man was wearing Western clothes and a scarf covering his head. The black shadow of a pistol passed through the flashlight's beam. Wali's legs buckled as the gunman shoved him forward. He felt his heart hammering in his chest as he staggered down the hall toward the courtyard. The gunman grumbled and swore at Wali to keep moving.

Outside in the courtyard, Wali saw American soldiers positioned against the wall ready to enter his house. It reminded Wali of the raids he'd witnessed while working for the Special Forces as an interpreter. The soldiers seemed ready for a fight.

Among them was Canterbury, who saw one of Jan's men pushing a frightened Afghan out the door.

"Wali!" he called out.

Wali looked around.

"Wali!"

Canterbury, dressed in body armor, came over and rested a hand on the captive's shoulder.

"Don't worry," he said. "Charlie says hi. It's dangerous for you here. We want to take you to a safe place."

Wali didn't know what to say. Was this part of the plan? Did Charlie send these men to come and arrest him?

Was this a prank?

Wali couldn't make sense of what he was seeing. American soldiers were raiding his compound like he was a terrorist. Before Wali could say anything, Canterbury grabbed his arm and led him toward a white Chevrolet Suburban. As they walked, the American keyed his radio.

"We got him."

Canterbury helped him into the back seat of the Suburban. Wali's hands were bound, and his eyes were covered by goggles blacked out with spray paint. All he heard was the transmission engage and the engine roar as they drove into the darkness. Everything was silent around him except for the crunch of gravel under the tires and the rumble of the engine.

Wali seethed in the back but said nothing. He'd worked in good faith with the Special Forces providing support and other services. Now he was being treated like a terrorist.

Finally, the Suburban stopped. Two men helped Wali out and guided him inside a building. The tile floor felt cold on his bare feet. When they took off the goggles, he saw he was in a plain room. Across from him sat an American soldier. She took his name and inventoried his belongings—a T-shirt, pajama pants. She handed him some plastic sandals and took Wali to a Conex, where he was fingerprinted.

"Why am I here?" he asked.

The female guard taking his fingerprints barely looked up.

"I don't know."

She hung a plastic bag with his paperwork around his neck before he was blindfolded again by two soldiers in full body armor. Wali heard the roar of aircraft engines as they led him outside and helped him into a truck. When the door to the truck opened again a few minutes later, Wali was hit by a blast of cold air and the roar of turboprops. A guard's hands pulled him out of the back seat and led him toward the engine noise. With each step, the roar got louder and louder.

"Pick up your leg," one of the guards said.

Wali stepped up onto the steel of the plane's loading ramp and was led aboard.

"Sit."

Wali sat down on the deck. He heard the pitch of the engines change as it taxied and then barreled down the runway. His stomach flipped as the plane started to climb into the dark sky. Hands thumped Wali in the chest, and he felt terror well up.

His mind shot to a story he'd heard from Razaq about how the Soviets used to take prisoners up in planes and helicopters and throw them out. Were these Americans going to do the same to him?

The panic lasted for only a few seconds. He knew better. But being blindfolded and thrust into the plane was disorienting.

The flight lasted only a couple of hours, he estimated. It was impossible to be sure because of the blindfold. Wali shivered against the cold. Sitting on the deck, his legs were sore and his back ached. He was trying his best not to move because he didn't want to break any rules. The plane finally touched down, and Wali was relieved to be on his feet again.

He was no longer in Kandahar, he thought, but he had no idea where he was. It was colder, so he figured somewhere up north. He still heard plane engines, which meant an air base. The engines were loud. Jets. As an interpreter, he'd been to many such bases, and if he had to guess, he was at Bagram, home to a massive American base north of Kabul. He'd only been there once, when the Special Forces team he was with took part in a massive operation in a valley near Kabul.

When the goggles came off, he found himself in another room facing a new batch of guards. He heard the buzz of clippers and felt his hair fall down to his shoulders. He watched as the clumps fell into a trash bin at his feet.

Wali wasn't going home.

He was now inmate 5566.

Wali put on a greenish-gray uniform and a white skull cap. The guards thrust a prayer rug and a Koran into his hands. Then they chained his hands and ankles, put the goggles back on, and sat him in a wheelchair. Wali felt the breeze as he was wheeled outside and then back into a building. He heard some Americans, who he assumed were guards, talking about him.

"HIG or Taliban?" they called.

Wali heard he was Taliban, not Hezb-e-Islami Gulbuddin, a fierce militant group.

When the wheelchair stopped, Wali was ordered to stand up. Once on his feet, the goggles were removed. He was in a cell with concrete walls and a heavy metal door. Wali heard the door slam shut and several locks on the outside snap into place. A camera was mounted above the door. Inside the cell there were a bed with a blanket, a Koran, and a prayer rug. A small latrine about the size of an airplane bathroom occupied one corner.

"That's your water and that's your latrine," an interpreter said. "This is your everything. You eat, you drink, you sleep, you pray, and you go to toilet in here."

Later that night, Wali prayed for the second time in the past few days. This time he didn't do it to calm himself. Instead, he asked for salvation.

CHAPTER 32

Frank's call jolted Charlie awake. It was around 5:00 a.m. This wasn't good.

"Hey, what's up?" Charlie said, his voice raspy.

"Just got a call from Bagram," Frank said. "Shit ain't good. Get over to my office."

Charlie pulled on a uniform and hustled over. Frank was behind his desk, which was covered by an army of empty Red Bull cans. He hadn't been to bed in at least a day. With teams spread out all over southern Afghanistan, he didn't have enough hours in the day to get everything done.

"Got a call from a buddy," Frank said. "They arrested Wali."

The news hit Charlie like a sniper's bullet. Questions started to cascade out of his mouth.

"Who arrested him?"

"What did they arrest him for?"

"Where is he?"

Frank held up his hand, and Charlie stopped talking.

"Task Force 2010 got him," Frank said. "With your boy Canterbury. They processed him this morning."

"Shit," Charlie said. "We're launching in forty-eight hours."

Frank shook his head.

"That ain't the worst of it," he said. "Anyone associated with Wali is a target. Task Force 2010 is going to get a fish they can fry no matter who it is. This is the kind of case that makes people's careers."

Charlie was puzzled. What the hell was Task Force 2010? Frank didn't really know either. All he could confirm was it was tasked with rooting out corruption. It was a new initiative looking to stem the flow of money to bad actors. The task force started poking around when Canterbury sent it Wali's name. This was how it was going to justify its work, Frank said.

"Each question they ask is an affront to the blood and sweat we spill trying to win this thing," he said. "The old man is pissed. I told him they don't understand the battlefield or combat."

Charlie was silent.

"You know what he said?"

"I don't really care, Frank," Charlie said.

He was already heading back to the office and didn't have time to listen to Lieutenant Colonel Kyle's wisdom.

"He said that with billions of dollars flowing into Afghanistan, the auditors had a duty to at least ask how it was spent," Frank said. "And they think it was spent like drunken frat boys in a strip club. Do you believe he said that?"

Charlie did.

"Look, thanks for telling me, but I've got to go unfuck this situation," he said.

ℬℬℬ

It took Charlie the better part of an hour to find Felix's Containerized Housing Unit in a small field of similar units.

The Containerized Housing Unit, or CHU, was basically a shipping container with a small bedroom, desk, and bathroom inside. It was like living in a drawer. The containers were stacked, creating mini apartment buildings. Felix lived in a unit at the end on the bottom floor.

Only after he'd asked several civilians did he run across someone who knew where Felix laid his head.

Felix didn't live near the other agency staff. He had a room in among the other contractors that serviced the base. Most people think of Blackwater and gun-toting mercenaries when they hear the term "military contractors," but the reality is the term also includes everyone from the Green Beans coffee shop clerk to the plumber tasked with unclogging the barracks toilet. There is no plumber military specialty. That shit is up to civilians.

Felix had a shit-eating grin on his face when he opened the door.

"How did you find me?"

He was holding a microwave macaroni-and-cheese cup with a white plastic fork sticking out of the top.

"I asked around," Charlie said. "What are you doing living here?"

Felix finished his bite of mac-n-cheese.

"I like hanging with the folks here," he said, waving Charlie into the room. "If you haven't noticed, agency folk can be a little dry."

"We need to talk," Charlie said.

"Sure. I saw you called, but I've been jumping through my ass getting this op set up. The team just landed. They're sleeping off the jet lag now."

Felix nodded to an empty chair at a small desk. His computer was open, and he was watching reruns of *Jeopardy!* Felix closed the door and sat down on the single bed.

"They arrested Wali," Charlie said. "We're trying to get him released and clear this up before permanent damage is done."

The grin was gone.

"Shit," Felix said. "What the hell did they get him for?"

"Working with the Taliban."

"Was it that little Air Force turd?" Felix asked, tossing the half-eaten macaroni cheese cup in the small trash can near the door.

"Yeah," Charlie said. "I got the call this morning. I guess they grabbed him early this morning. He's already at Bagram."

Felix rubbed his eyes.

"That's fast," he said.

Charlie massaged the bridge of his nose and closed his eyes. His headache had started when the phone rang.

"This thing happens in three days," Felix said. "Let me see what I can do."

He slipped his foot out of his flip-flop and stretched his toes.

"What do I tell Church?" Felix asked.

"How about get our guy out?" Charlie said.

"He isn't going to like that. He wasn't crazy about this mission as is. How about the colonel?"

Charlie only had to look at Felix.

"Well shit, we're proper fucked now," Felix said. "Let me think. If you can, keep your CO out of this. Give me until lunch. I'll meet you over at Brown."

Charlie walked out of the CHU less confident than when he had entered it. His only hope was Felix pulling some strings.

He was almost at Camp Brown when he saw Canterbury driving toward him. Charlie didn't think. He jerked the wheel and cut Canterbury off. Brakes squealed. Canterbury swerved to avoid Charlie's truck and skidded to a halt, inches from crashing into a parked Humvee. Charlie was out of his truck before Canterbury knew what happened.

"You little fucker," Charlie said, coming around to the driver's side of Canterbury's truck and banging on the glass. "You have any idea what the fuck you've done?"

Canterbury was in shock. He recoiled from the glass when Charlie yanked open the door. Charlie's first punch landed with a crack on Canterbury's cheek.

"You're fucking up everything," he yelled, landing another blow that glanced off Canterbury's chin.

Canterbury couldn't answer between blows. He tried to close the door, but Charlie blocked it. He tried to worm his way into the passenger seat, but Charlie grabbed him and dragged him back into the driver's seat. Another blow landed on Canterbury's chin. Hands grabbed Charlie and pulled him off.

"Fuck you, man," Charlie said. "We're losing this war because of pussies like you. I hope you're happy when they fucking nuke New York."

Charlie shoved some Eighty-Second Airborne Division private away from him and climbed back into his truck. He put the transmission in reverse and jammed the accelerator. The tires kicked up gravel at the growing crowd. He spit at Canterbury as he drove past.

"Asshole!"

Charlie's knuckles hurt as he typed on his computer. He'd gone straight to the office and tried to lose himself in his work. It was the only way to keep his mind off Wali. He didn't want to think about where the Afghan was. Or what he was enduring. Every few minutes he looked at the phone on his desk.

Ring, motherfucker.

Charlie willed Felix to call. He wanted the CIA to tell him everything was five by five. All cool, cuz. No worries. I've got you. Wali's on his way home now.

Charlie looked up from his computer. Lieutenant Colonel Kyle was standing in the door leading to the intelligence cell.

"Hey, Chief," Kyle said. "Need to see you for a second."

"Yeah, sir," Charlie said as he got out of his chair. "What's up?"

"Come over to my office," Kyle said.

"If it's about the Air Force guy..."

Charlie didn't get a chance to finish his sentence.

"Get your ass in my office *now*, Chief Book."

Charlie followed his commander into the TOC. Everyone was quiet. It was like getting called to the principal's office. There was a slim chance Canterbury would take his beating like a man. Looked like the chance was too slim.

When Charlie got to the commander's office, Canterbury was standing in front of Kyle's desk with the Special Forces Task Force's

JAG officer. An Army lawyer. He wasn't Special Forces, but he was on the staff to keep Kyle out of trouble. Canterbury's face was bruised. A black ring was forming around his left eye. His upper lip looked like an obese worm. Charlie was taken aback. He'd really beaten the guy's ass! He had no idea.

Charlie followed Kyle inside. The colonel sat down behind his desk.

"Special Agent Canterbury has a warrant for you," Kyle said. "JAG reviewed it. They're going to take your computers."

"They're *what?*" Charlie said, looking at Kyle and then Canterbury.

"We're taking custody of your computers," Canterbury said. "It's all in the warrant. We believe you've been inflating Wali's importance in your intelligence reports. These reports were created to cover your illegal activity."

Charlie looked at his commander.

"Sir," Charlie said. "We can't talk about it here, but you know this is bullshit. You understand the importance of Wali to our ongoing operations."

Kyle glared at Charlie.

"Enough," Kyle said. "Sit down, Chief. Special Agent, you're free to go with the JAG and take the computer."

"Thank you, sir," Canterbury said, looking at Charlie through his good eye.

"Just get the computer and get the hell off my base," Kyle said.

Canterbury didn't know what to say. He stuttered for a second and then walked out of the office. The JAG shut the door behind them. Kyle took off his glasses and then smashed his fist onto the top of his desk.

"What the hell are you doing? Your head has been so far up your ass you need a snorkel," Kyle said. "First you convince me to get in bed with this Wali kid and OGA. Now, we find out he's a bad guy and you're lying to cover him."

Charlie felt the rage boil back up, but he choked it down.

"Come on, sir, you know Wali is working Corona for us," Charlie said. "Of course he's meeting with the Taliban and al-Qaeda. We asked him to. This fuckwad has a hard-on for him because he's in Jan's pocket."

A knock on the door broke the conversation. Frank walked into the room.

"Sorry, sir," Frank said. "This is urgent. Felix is outside. He needs to speak to you."

Charlie looked at Frank hoping to get a read on what was going on. Frank just shook his head and looked away. Charlie knew the look. It was defeat.

"Bring him in," Kyle said. "He can tell Charlie."

"Tell me what?" Charlie said.

Felix walked into the room. He stayed by the door.

"Yes, sir," he said. "Church asked me to give you an update. Operation Corona is on hold."

Charlie stood up when Felix finished. He wanted to smash something.

"What are you talking about? They're going to get a *nuke!*"

Felix took a seat by Charlie.

"Sit down, Chief," Kyle said.

Charlie sat. He felt his heart beating through his chest. His breath came in pants. Maybe having a heart attack might be better than letting terrorists have a weapon of mass destruction, he thought. What made it worse was Felix. He seemed unmoved.

"Yeah, sir, the agency doesn't think Corona is legit. Langley thinks it's a ruse by the Taliban to raise money. Since the Dubai part of the op, we've been able to pinpoint some of the group's network. We're happy to continue to pursue those leads. As for the device, you guys have a green light to take it. I have a team here who can take possession once you secure it."

Charlie sat in silence. He didn't know what to say as Felix talked. The operation might be over, but no one was talking about the most important part.

"What about Wali?" Charlie asked. "We're just going to leave him in prison?"

Kyle sat back in his chair.

"Yeah," he said. "Unless the CIA wants to get him out."

Kyle and Charlie looked at Felix.

"He's a CJSOTF asset," Felix said. "You guys insisted on that. We can't help. He isn't one of ours."

Kyle let Felix's words sink in for a second.

"Thanks, Felix," he said. "I'll have Frank check in with you about your team. We'll send over slides once the op is up."

Felix left without even looking at Charlie. President John F. Kennedy's quote rolled into his head: *Victory has a hundred fathers and defeat is an orphan.*

"Hey, Charlie," Kyle said. "I know this is hard on you. But I need you to stay out of this now. With the investigation and everything, it's better if you stay out of the TOC and your office."

"Do I need a lawyer?"

Kyle stood. It was the signal for Charlie to leave.

"Not yet."

CHAPTER 33

Anabel kissed Canterbury's black eye. He winced. She laughed. They were sitting on the Boardwalk eating ice cream and watching the parade of soldiers and contractors.

"You're such a baby," she said, brushing some hair away from her mouth.

Canterbury didn't take his eyes off her. He watched as she paused to survey her ice cream cone. She rotated it in her hand, looking for the best place to lick it. She flicked her tongue out once. Twice. The third time she gave the cone a dog's lick.

"Ice cream. A surprise visit. What's going on?" she asked.

Her eyes were bright. Canterbury just wanted to sit and look into those eyes.

"I had a good day," he said.

She giggled.

"Your face tells another story."

Another flick of the tongue.

"Yeah," he said. "Besides the assault."

Anabel giggled and reached out for Canterbury's hand. She smiled when he took hers.

"We got Wali. I got the green light to dig into this Special Forces asshole."

Anabel turned to face Canterbury. Her smile was gone.

"I can't believe I worked for a terrorist," she said. "No one knew. I mean, for years this guy was driving around the base. It's amazing."

Canterbury nodded. It took him and his courage to fight against the tide to bring Wali to justice.

"Do you know what's going to happen to his store?" Canterbury said.

Anabel turned away. Wali's arrest put her out of a job. Canterbury wanted to feel bad, but he didn't.

"I don't know," she said. "Our checks are late. With Denise gone, I just open the store every day, but I have no idea what is going to happen. I guess it's for the better. I'm ready to leave."

If she was ready to leave, he knew where he wanted her to go.

"I'm leaving in six weeks," Canterbury said. "I just got orders today. Nellis Air Force Base in Vegas."

"Vegas!" Anabel said. That got her attention. "I've always wanted to go."

"Do you want to go with me?" Canterbury asked.

"Seriously?"

"Yeah," he said. "You just said the store is going to close. You want to leave. Let's go to Vegas. You and me."

Anabel tossed her cone into the moon dust. She threw her arms around Canterbury's neck and kissed him. He winced in pain but kept his lips pressed against hers. It was easy to forget the pain as she pressed against his body.

"Can we go to a casino?" she asked.

"Of course," he said. "They have casinos all over the place."

Anabel sat for a second.

"What am I going to tell my parents? Vegas is a long way from Oakland."

"So is Afghanistan," Canterbury said. "But you're here. I don't want to leave here without you."

Anabel turned to look at him. He took her hands in his. They sat for a minute. Neither said a word. Finally, Canterbury broke the silence.

"I want to meet your parents," he said. "I want you to meet mine. I don't have a ring or anything, but I don't want to be without you."

Tears welled up in Anabel's eyes.

"I don't want to be without you either," she said.

"So it's done," Canterbury said. "We're moving to Vegas, with a stop in Maryland."

Anabel stood up and took Canterbury's hand.

Canterbury caught a glimpse of the CIA man as they walked down the Boardwalk. He was sipping a Diet Coke near the PX. He didn't seem to be watching them. Hell, it was a big base and everybody came to the Boardwalk. He was probably just picking up some drinks. Canterbury started to wave but thought better of it.

"Let's go watch a movie," Anabel said with a wink.

Canterbury forgot about Felix that instant.

CHAPTER 34

Razaq let the phone ring until it reached voice mail.

"This is Wali. Leave a message."

He hung up and called again. Same result. Razaq slid the mobile phone into his pocket and paced under the trees near his compound.

It had been several days since he'd heard from this nephew. The trip to Dubai had been a success. The Quetta Shura was anxious to make the sale. They were already planning how to spend the money.

Guns. Rockets. ammunition.

They saw this bomb as a gift. A chance to energize their coffers. Like the Americans, the Taliban thought they could shoot their way to victory. But Razaq knew violence was no way to win people over, unless you wanted them to live in fear.

It was no path to victory.

And there would be no peace when the camels used the bomb. Blow up New York? Maybe. But his money was on Washington, DC. He hoped the Americans wouldn't trace it back to Afghanistan.

What did he care? If the plan worked, he'd be gone.

To DC.

Maybe he would ask for a new place to live.

His phone rang. He snatched it from his pocket and checked the caller ID. It was the Quetta Shura. Razaq hit the button to answer the call.

"Yes, brother?" Razaq said, one eye toward the sky.

They both knew the Americans listened to their calls. The elder spoke quickly.

"The shipment of pomegranates made it," the voice on the other line said.

"Good," Razaq said.

The al-Qaeda buyer was in Pakistan.

"What of the washer parts?"

Wali.

"I am arranging shipment now," Razaq said. "We've had a slight delay, but nothing that will interrupt our schedule."

Razaq heard an exhale on the other end of the phone.

"I will remind you these parts are essential. Make sure we keep the schedule," the elder said and hung up.

Neither man wanted to be on the phone any longer than necessary.

Razaq found a shady spot just to make sure he was under cover and pulled out his other phone. He searched for the number. If he couldn't reach Wali, maybe Charlie was around. He would know where his nephew was. The call went through and the phone rang before going to voice mail. The mailbox wasn't set up, so Razaq redialed. Same result. He hit redial just as Zahir came outside.

"Commander," Zahir said. "The brothers are back from their mission."

Some of Razaq's men had just returned from delivering night letters to a local village. Packaged warnings not to help the Americans. Empty threats. He'd already told the elder his village was safe. He was just following orders. Razaq smiled and waved to Zahir. He pointed at the phone in his hand.

"One more call," Razaq said. "Then I'll be in. Tell them to get some tea."

What of Zahir? He liked the boy. He was a good man. Always loyal. Attentive. He cared for Razaq like he would his own father. But could he take him to America too? Razaq shook his head. Of course not. Zahir was from the country. Kandahar intimidated him. He didn't even like being in the small villages. What would he do in America? But was he better off in Afghanistan? He would just fall in with another commander. He would likely lose his life, and for what? Another young man killed by an old man's plans.

The call to Charlie went to voice mail again. Razaq stood up and felt his knees pop. His body was sending him a message: Stop, I've given up on this war. He tried Wali one more time. Voice mail. Razaq killed the line and slid the phone back in his pocket when it started to ring.

He answered.

"Hello?"

"No," an American voice said.

Razaq didn't recognize the speaker.

"Charlie?" he asked. "Charlie, please."

The American's voice was muffled. It sounded like he was talking to other Americans in a room.

"He isn't here," the American said. "I'll have him call you back."

The line went dead before Razaq could ask for Charlie again. He glanced over and saw the pile of dirt. Underneath was the bomb. Where was his nephew? He thought about calling back when he spotted Zahir waving him over for tea.

❦❦❦

Back at Camp Brown, Blake powered down Charlie's phone and slid it into his pocket.

"Fucking thing's been ringing for hours," he said.

Blake returned to the operation slides. A team was going to hit a target and recover some bomb-making materials. Charlie was supposed to quarterback this one, but now it fell to Blake. He was in charge until the investigation was over.

After the mission review, Blake followed Frank to the chow hall for dinner. The place was deserted. The remnants of Mexican night sat in hotel pans. Frank and Blake silently spooned chicken, beans, and rice onto plates. Neither took much care in what he was eating.

It was fuel.

Frank spotted Charlie first. He was sitting alone at a table near the exit in front of an untouched plate. Frank nodded toward Charlie. Blake just shrugged. Both men walked over and sat down with him.

"What's up, pimp?" Frank asked, trying to keep it light.

Charlie looked up at his friends.

"Hey, boys," he said.

Frank piled rice, beans, and chicken into a tortilla. Blake grabbed the bottle of hot sauce on the table and shook it onto everything.

"Living hard was easy when I was bulletproof," Charlie said. "It didn't matter what price I had to pay as long as I was right. As long as the mission was done. But what the fuck happened?"

Frank swallowed.

"Big Army took over," Frank said. "The accountants followed us onto the battlefield."

Charlie started to raise his fork, but that was too much effort. He let it fall back onto the plate.

"But the stakes on this one were high," he said. "What are they going to do?"

Frank looked around and then at Blake. The intelligence sergeant kept his eyes on his plate. He didn't want to be sitting at that table. He didn't want to talk about anything. He wanted to get back to work.

"We're going to get it tomorrow," Frank said. "The op is teed up. Corona hasn't moved. We wanted to put ISR [Intelligence, Surveillance, and Reconnaissance] over it, but we didn't want to spook them."

Charlie shook his head in agreement. He was glad the mission was on, yet he knew his career was done. But he still wanted a place to go home to. If AQ had Corona, then he might not have a home when he got back.

"Good," Charlie said. "Good move. What about Wali?"

Charlie caught Blake's scowl.

"What?" Charlie said.

Frank kept his eyes on his plate.

"Nothing," Blake said. "Wali is in Bagram. They say he cheated us. There isn't anything to be done. He's a crook."

Charlie pushed his plate away.

"If Wali is guilty, I would throw him under the bus and watch his eyes get squished out of his head and not think twice about it and still sleep like a little baby," Charlie said. "I haven't slept in days."

Blake stood up and gathered his trash.

"Tell it to the judge," he said. "Look, man, I don't want to get into this with you. You're the second chief I've gone through on this deployment. We're all trying to do what's right. With you out of the office, I've got a shitload to do."

Charlie stood up with Blake.

"I'm sorry, man," he said. "I hate that you're pulling my load too."

Blake nodded to Charlie and started toward the door. He stopped after a few steps. He put his tray down and took Charlie's phone out of his pocket.

"This thing has been ringing all day," he said.

He tossed Charlie the phone.

"Thanks," Charlie said.

Frank followed Blake out of the chow hall.

"Hey," Frank said. "Felix called. He's looking for you."

CHAPTER 35

The next time the guards pulled off the goggles, Wali was in an eight-foot room with two chairs and a desktop computer on a small table. A guard released his leg shackles, then took his hands from behind his back and bound them in front.

As Wali waited, he noticed some photos on the wall. The mountains of Afghanistan. A market in Kabul. The last one was of Bowe Bergdahl, the only missing American soldier in Afghanistan.

When the door opened, a man dressed in civilian clothes walked into the room. He had shaggy brown hair and a goatee with flecks of gray near the creases of his mouth. Wali estimated the man was about forty. He was wearing the "civilian" uniform—cargo/utility pants in tan or brown made by 5.11 or North Face and a plaid shirt. To Wali, he looked like one of his Special Forces friends.

"Hi," the man said. "I'm Norman. What's your name?"

Wali told him. Norman sat down at the table so he could see the computer monitor. Wali was on the other side of the table.

"They took everything from me and handed over your case to me," Norman said. "What have you done wrong?"

Wali shook his head.

"I don't know," he said. "If you tell me what I've done, then I can explain to you this misunderstanding."

Norman nodded. But first, he explained the rules to Wali.

Don't talk to other prisoners.

Don't talk back to guards.

Don't knock on the door.

Don't shout.

Don't try to escape.

Wali nodded that he understood.

"So, according to this report, you're a financial supporter of the Taliban, especially the Quetta Shura," Norman said. "And you bribed soldiers to get logistics contracts."

Wali shook his head and was about to talk, but Norman held up his hand.

"Don't," he said. "We're not talking today. I just wanted to see you and talk to you. We'll start tomorrow. You'll have plenty of time to talk about all this."

The next day, Norman spent hours asking Wali about his family. What was his full name? How many brothers did he have? Sisters? The second day, he wanted to know about Wali's company. All day Wali told the man about how the trucking contract worked. At the end of the day, Wali still had no idea why he was in prison. No one would tell him what he was accused of doing. The third day started the same as the other two. He was back in the spartan interrogation room sitting opposite Norman. This time the American wanted to talk about Wali's former employees and the procedures for executing the convoys.

The next day, Norman started asking questions about Taliban meetings. Each time Wali denied the meetings, Norman would shake his head. Finally, the interrogator slammed his hand on the table.

"We have reports that say the Taliban come to your compound," he said. "And you're paying them."

Wali shook his head.

"You have all the documents," he said. "Check. Everything is documented."

Back in his cell, Wali felt hopeless. He never saw what they'd claimed and didn't know what they wanted to hear. He prayed to Allah asking for guidance. That night, he called out to Charlie hoping his friend would hear him. He heard the other prisoners and hoped they would carry his message, but the only response came from the guards. They told him to be quiet and took away his pillow and mattress for a couple of hours.

The interrogations continued. Norman wanted to know how the money was spent. Wali told him how he used to travel to the bank in Kandahar to pick up cash for payroll and expenses. He said there were about 350 employees—drivers, mechanics, guards, office workers—and about a dozen supervisors.

"No, tell me about the Special Forces you're paying money to," Norman said.

"I never paid them," Wali said.

The same questions. The same answers. It was one long conversation.

"Think about your family," Norman said. "If you cooperate, you'll be set free. If not, you're looking at being gone for years."

After an avalanche of threats, the interrogator shoved a piece of paper in front of Wali. He wanted him to admit to working with the Taliban.

Wali refused.

That night, Wali said a quiet prayer to Allah asking for his freedom. The next morning, he said nothing to the interrogator.

CHAPTER 36

Charlie met Felix at the Boardwalk.

He was still pissed about the cancelled operation and refused the meeting at first, hanging up on the CIA officer. But Felix wouldn't give up. He called right back and guaranteed Charlie would want to hear what he had to say. They met in front of Wali's old store. Seeing the store closed made Charlie a little sad.

Wali had fallen fast.

Felix sat on a wooden bench. He used the tail of his T-shirt to clean the dust off of his sunglasses. Charlie—coffee from Green Beans in hand—sat down. Felix produced a can of Diet Coke and popped the top.

"Sorry about our last meeting," Felix said. "Not a lot of choices. Langley wasn't happy with me when I told them about Wali."

Charlie took a sip of his coffee and scratched his head.

"Yeah," Charlie said. "Well, my command isn't so happy with me either."

"Have you heard anything about Wali?" Felix asked.

Charlie just shook his head no and looked away, ashamed.

"I've got some of our folks keeping an eye on him," Felix said. "He hasn't said anything about Corona."

Charlie nodded. He figured Wali wasn't going to break. He'd done nothing wrong. What was he going to tell them?

"You tracking our op?" Charlie asked. "I guess Kyle wants to snag Corona. He isn't calling it that. But he is sending a team to go get it."

"First I've heard of it," Felix said. "He isn't using our guys."

"Your intel," Charlie said.

Felix chuckled.

"We shut down that tracker days ago," he said. "If they're using our data, it's old as shit."

"They don't know it, then," Charlie said. "I just talked to Blake and Frank. I can't believe we set all this up, only to sit on the sideline."

Felix stood up.

"Come on," he said. "Walk with me."

They walked over to some B-huts where guest workers lived. These were the civilians that ran the shops on the Boardwalk.

"What are we doing here?"

Felix checked his watch.

"Wait a minute," he said.

Charlie and Felix watched as a woman came out of a B-hut. He recognized her as Anabel, one of Wali's shopkeepers. With her was Canterbury, and the two walked hand in hand toward the Boardwalk, laughing.

"You're shitting me," Charlie said.

"Nope," Felix said, turning to make sure Canterbury didn't see his face. "I've been watching them for days."

Charlie looked at Felix sideways.

"What for?" he asked.

"I'm not done with Corona," Felix said. "I've got a chance to roll up an AQ cell. All of them."

Charlie stopped staring at Anabel and Canterbury. The rage started to rumble in his stomach so that he could taste it in the back of his throat.

"This guy is playing house while Wali rots," Charlie said.

Felix folded his arms and leaned against the sandbags surrounding the B-hut.

"I have an idea," he said, his voice dropping to a whisper. "But it means playing fast and loose with the rules. I know you guys are comfortable in the gray, but this is on the edge of black."

Charlie watched as Canterbury and Anabel stopped and kissed. It was a short peck. Charlie wanted to puke.

"I'm in."

❧❧❧

Charlie watched as Blake left the headquarters building for the night. It was well after midnight, and most of the camp was asleep. Once Blake was out of sight, he slipped into the building and punched in the code for the TOC.

It was a few hours after he'd met Felix. They'd gone over the plan. Charlie knew that as soon as he punched in the code, his career was over. The night shift didn't pay attention to him as he walked across the back of the room toward the intelligence cell. The battle captain, a new guy who'd arrived just a few weeks ago, waved to Charlie as he passed.

Charlie glanced at the video screens at the front of the room. A mud hut filled the main screen. The other showed some brush and a dried wadi. No movement. No fighters.

"Anything going on?" Charlie asked.

"Quiet night," the battle captain said. "We had an op, but it was a dry hole."

Charlie just nodded and kept walking toward the intelligence cell.

"Roger," he said. "Just need to get something out of the office."

The battle captain didn't respond. His eyes were fixed on his computer, the conversation a distant memory in a night of forgettable events.

The intelligence cell was dark. Blake's computer was still warm when Charlie sat down. He logged into the laptop and opened up the future ops folder. The Corona mission slides were at the top of the file list. Double click. The first slide filled the screen. A few punches on the keyboard and Charlie had the slide he was looking for. A map of the target area. He checked the grid coordinates on the map and then deleted them. Taking a slip of paper from his cargo pocket, he updated the coordinates with the ones provided by Felix. Charlie saved the changes and forwarded the new slide to the commander using Blake's email. He then opened the source database and found Wali's file. Ten minutes later, he called Felix.

"You get the request?"

He heard Felix typing on his computer.

"Yup," Felix said. "Your boy is ours now."

Charlie saw Wali's status change. He was now a CIA asset.

"OK, I'll make the call. When are you going to pick her up?"

"Once I get off with Bagram."

Charlie hung up the phone. He signed off Blake's computer and left the office. This time the battle captain didn't even lift his head. Outside, Charlie took out his cell phone.

Razaq picked up on the first ring.

"Hello," he said in a thick accent. "Wali?"

"No, it's Charlie."

Charlie heard Pashto being spoken in the background. There was a rustle as Razaq walked out of the room. The background noise disappeared.

"Where is my nephew?"

"He's fine," Charlie said. "The plan is moving forward."

"But I haven't heard anything from him for a week."

Charlie didn't have time to babysit this guy. Execute the plan.

"I know," he said. "That was part of the plan. Everything is set on our end. But you need to move the device tonight."

Charlie heard Razaq sigh loudly.

"No," the Afghan said. "We can't leave tonight. Too dangerous. Tomorrow."

It was Charlie's turn to sigh.

"Not tomorrow," Charlie said. "If you don't move tonight, you will be dead. They are coming for it."

That got Razaq's attention.

"Who is coming?"

"My people," Charlie said. "We need you out of there before the drones start watching your compound."

The mention of drones must have sent a chill through Razaq. Charlie could picture him searching the night sky for a sign of them. "Razaq?"

Charlie's voice pulled Razaq back to the present.

"We will leave tonight," Razaq said.

"Good," Charlie said. "You know where to take it?"

"Panjwai. To a compound owned by Wali."

"Right," Charlie said. "Be safe. See you there."

Charlie called Felix. He picked up after the first ring.

"You talk to him?" Felix asked.

"It's moving," Charlie said.

"Good. Stand by."

CHAPTER 37

Felix hung up his phone and slid it into his pocket. He was standing across the gravel field from Anabel's B-hut.

He held the door so it wouldn't slam shut as he entered the B-hut. The hallway down the left side was dark. Felix made out three wooden doors running down the right side. Each one led to rooms just large enough for a bed and a small desk. Only the third room had a light on. Felix saw its glow under the crack of the door.

He didn't want to knock on all the doors looking for Anabel. This had to be quiet. He took out his phone and used the faint glow of the screen to guide him.

The first door had a combination lock on the outside. No way anyone was in there. The middle door was open, but the room was dark.

It was fifty-fifty. Felix knocked on the door with the light on. He heard someone moving in the room. The door opened just a crack.

"Hello?" a blonde woman with a thick Eastern European accent said.

Felix recognized her as the manager of the German store on the Boardwalk.

"Sorry," he said. "Wrong door."

The woman closed the door. Felix knocked on the last door. Nothing. He knocked a second time. Silence. Felix tried the door and it swung open. The room was pitch-black. He turned on his phone again and used it as a flashlight. The screen sent out a small cone of light. He surveyed the room. It was deserted. The wooden desk in the corner was clean. The mattress was pushed flush against the wall.

Felix was turning to leave when the front door of the B-hut opened. He heard the squish of shower shoes as the person walked inside. He peeked out and saw Anabel. Her hair was still wet. A robe covered her body. A towel was draped over one arm. She held a shower bag in her left hand. Her right hand worked the combination lock on the first door. She didn't notice Felix until he walked out into the hall.

"Men aren't allowed in here," she said.

Felix couldn't see her face in the shadows, but her posture changed. She retreated a half step.

"Anabel Sarwani?" Felix said.

Anabel pulled her towel close to her body.

"Can I help you?"

"Yes," Felix said. "I think you can. Come with me."

Felix took a step toward her.

"Who are you?" Anabel said, digging in her toilet bag.

Felix got to her just as she leveled the pepper spray. A cloud of gas rose between them. Felix turned to shield his face. The spray dripped off his hand. Anabel coughed and staggered out the door. Felix followed. Outside, he took a gulp of air. Anabel was retching at the side of the building. A stream of snot and vomit.

"What the fuck?" Felix said.

He grabbed her towel and wrapped his hand in it. Anabel was crying. Pleading.

She tried to yell. The snot and vomit prevented it.

"Don't rape me," she said between retches. "Please."

"Rape you?" Felix said. "I'm here on official business. We need to talk with you about a statement you made about your boss."

Anabel stopped crying and stared at Felix.

"Who are you?"

Felix grabbed her by the arm and started to lead her toward his truck.

"I'm an interested party," he said. "Let's go find a place to talk."

Anabel turned to look back at her toilet bag lying in front of the B-hut. Felix kept a firm hold on her arm.

"This is going to be easier if you don't fight," Felix said.

Anabel shuffled toward the truck.

"Do you work with Neil?" she said.

Felix looked at her. She was scared.

"Yes, in a manner of speaking," he said. "There is a bit of an emergency, and I should have properly identified myself. I'm going to get him next."

Anabel relaxed slightly.

"But first, I need to know more about Wali and how you got some of your information."

Felix felt Anabel flinch. He pretended not to notice.

CHAPTER 38

The next morning Felix drove over to the AFOSI office. Canterbury was sitting at his desk. He stood when Felix walked into the office.

"What do you want?" he asked.

Canterbury looked frazzled. Felix knew he'd been calling around looking for Anabel. Someone had found her toilet bag outside the hut. Now she was a missing person.

"We need to talk," Felix said. "Let's take a walk."

Canterbury's coworkers stopped what they were doing. Canterbury froze.

"We don't have anything to talk about," he said. "I told you that before. It's up to the system now."

Felix scratched his head. He made eye contact with one of the other investigators, who looked away immediately.

"I know you've been looking for your girlfriend," Felix said. "I think I can help."

"What did you do?"

Felix spread his arms and took a step back.

"I didn't do anything," he said. "But I have some information I'd like to share. That's my business. Can we talk in private?"

Canterbury looked around the room and then nodded toward a conference room.

"Yeah," he said. "Fine. We can talk in there."

Felix turned toward the door.

"Let's take a ride."

Canterbury hesitated for a beat but followed Felix and got into his 4x4 Hilux.

"Where is she?" Canterbury said as Felix put the truck in gear. "Did you kidnap her?"

Felix just looked at Canterbury like he had a dick on his forehead.

"Is she OK?" Canterbury asked.

Felix turned up the radio. Rage Against the Machine. They rode the rest of the way with Zack de la Rocha providing the soundtrack.

"Fuck you, I won't do what you tell me!"

Felix badged his way into the OGA compound. He parked the truck and led Canterbury into an office. On the computer monitor was a live feed from a holding cell. Anabel sat at the table. She was still in her robe.

"What have you done?"

Canterbury's voice came out in a shriek.

"I'd ask you the same question," Felix said.

He slid Anabel's statement toward Canterbury. It was covered in colored highlights.

"We had a long talk about this," Felix said. "I must not be as good as you are, because she didn't have the same recall with me."

Canterbury didn't pick up the paper.

"I stand by that statement," he said. "My investigation saved lives. You guys were working with a sleeper."

Felix walked over to the monitor. He stared at Anabel. She was shivering and fidgety.

"Those rooms are freezing," he said. "I'm glad to be out of there."

Canterbury's gaze was fixed on the monitor.

"I was lucky, though," Felix said. "I had a sweatshirt."

Canterbury followed Felix's gaze to a hoodie draped over an office chair.

"You know the deal," Felix said. "You guys probably do the same thing. You don't want your suspect comfortable. It helped that her hair was still wet when we brought her in. It was cold, and my hair was dry."

Felix crossed his arms.

"Are we done fucking around?"

Canterbury looked at Anabel and then back at Felix.

Felix watched as Canterbury tried to process what he was seeing. In his mind, the CIA had kidnapped his girlfriend in order to free a Taliban spy. He picked up Anabel's statement and started to read from it. After each sentence, he stopped.

"That was from Jan's intelligence report from 13 June," Felix said.

Each time Felix quoted from the report used to build Anabel's statement, Canterbury shuddered. A lie, built brick by brick. His righteousness fading.

"It appears the only thing Anabel gave you was her name," Felix said, putting the sheet of paper on the table. "Everything else came from Jan, right?"

Canterbury closed his eyes and slumped into a chair.

"Now what?"

Felix crumpled up the statement and tossed it into the garbage. He opened the office door and handed the hoodie to one of his men. Canterbury watched as it was delivered to Anabel.

"Let's start with your arrest order," Felix said.

❧❧❧

A few hours later, a guard knocked on the door to the interrogation booth at Bagram. Wali looked up. He was haggard and tired of answering the same questions. It was insanity. His story would never change because it was the truth.

"Send him back to his cell," the guard told the interrogator. "He's heading back to KAF."

A few hours later, the guards came for Wali. He was shackled and blindfolded. Wali couldn't see through the goggles, but he heard the jet noise again.

"You can take off the blindfold and cuffs."

When the goggles came off, Wali blinked away the sunlight. Felix came into focus.

"I've got it from here," Felix said.

He reached out and led Wali to a waiting Learjet.

"You ready to get to work?"

CHAPTER 39

As Zahir drove, Razaq tried to sleep in the back of the truck. The rhythm of the tires on Highway 1—one of the few paved roads in Afghanistan—was luring him into slumber after a long night of work. He'd just faded into a deep sleep when he felt the truck slow.

Zahir shook him awake.

"Commander," he said. "A checkpoint."

Razaq looked through the windshield. The road was blocked by two Afghan Army Humvees. One mounted a machine gun. The other a grenade launcher. Parked nearby was a green Ford Ranger truck. Jan's men. One signaled for Zahir to stop.

"Don't worry," Razaq said. "We'll just pay them."

As soon as the truck stopped, Basir got out of the Ranger and walked over to Zahir's window.

"Get out," he said.

Zahir started to protest, but Razaq put a hand on his shoulder.

"That isn't necessary," Razaq said. "Here. Take this."

Razaq started to hand Basir a roll of Pakistani rupees. Basir pushed it away.

"You're under arrest."

Afghan soldiers surrounded the truck. The bolt of an AK-47 racked back. Any second Razaq expected to hear shots. He popped the rear door open. Everyone froze. Razaq kept his eyes locked on Basir.

"Put down your gun," Razaq said quietly.

Zahir stared at his commander. Basir took Razaq by the arm and led him to the waiting Ranger. Razaq looked over his shoulder and watched as Zahir was forced to his knees while Jan's men bound his hands with a plastic zip tie.

Basir led Razaq to the back of the Ranger. He stopped at the passenger-side window. Jan rolled it down.

"I told you to talk to your nephew."

Jan rolled the window up before Razaq could say anything. The guard hustled Razaq away from the truck. The crunch of gravel under their feet masked the slight buzzing sound in his pocket.

Razaq's phone was ringing.

❧❧❧

The automated voice mail came on just as Wali hung up. It was the fifth time he'd called his uncle. He was about to try again when his other phone rang.

Felix looked at the screen.

"It's him," he said.

Charlie handed Wali the phone. He recognized Samir's voice from Dubai. The al-Qaeda fixer sounded concerned.

"*As salem alheiuk*, brother," Samir said.

Wali exhaled and greeted the caller.

"What happened to you?" Samir asked. "You were supposed to signal two days ago. The brothers are worried."

"Don't be worried," Wali said. "It took longer to get things together on my end. But we are set here."

Wali heard Samir talking to someone in Arabic. He only picked up a few words. Something about the plan and everything going fine.

"Our brother is coming," Samir said. "He will leave tonight. He will be in a white Hilux with three men. Is your truck ready?"

Wali looked at Charlie. Both Charlie and Felix were listening to the call. Charlie gave Wali a thumbs-up.

"The truck is ready," he said. "The shipment will be on time."

"*Inshallah*, by tomorrow this business will be done," Samir said. "And our brothers will finally have a weapon worthy of the struggle."

"*Inshallah*," Wali said. "Tell our brother safe travels."

Wali broke the connection and slumped in his chair. Felix smiled at him.

"It's a go," he said. "Let me get my guys spun up."

Felix picked up his phone and took it outside to make a call. Charlie brought Wali a bottle of water.

"You OK, kid?"

Wali took a sip.

"I just wish my uncle would call back."

Charlie went back to his computer. He saw Razaq's phone moving along the road in Panjawai. Wali joined him in front of the screen.

"Where is he going?"

Charlie looked at the blip on the map again.

"Isn't this where you told him to take Corona?"

Wali zoomed in on the screen.

"No," he said. "He isn't going to the right compound."

"Call him," Charlie said.

Wali dialed the number. Someone picked up after three rings.

"Hello? Uncle?" Wali said.

"No," a voice replied.

Wali heard hushed voices, as if whoever answered the phone was carrying it through a room. The phone was passed off to another person, and then a familiar voice came on the line.

"I thought you were in jail."

It was Jan.

Wali turned on the speaker so Charlie could hear.

"I'm surprised to hear your voice," Jan said. "I figured you'd be in Gitmo by now."

"How did you get my uncle's phone?"

"Your uncle is with me," Jan said. "And so is his delivery for you. Now that I have your attention, I need to remind you how difficult and dangerous it is to transport supplies around Kandahar. Unless you have the right protection."

Charlie hung his head.

"How much?" Wali asked.

Jan paused for dramatic effect.

"Fifty thousand dollars," he said. "Every month to start, plus I want fifty percent of your business. You have plenty of money. You need to share it with the rest of us."

Wali looked at Charlie. Charlie shook his head no.

"I'm not allowed to do this," Wali said. "That's not the way we do business. You have your own business. You don't go after anybody but me, and this is not what Afghans should be doing to each other."

"I guess we'll have to see what happens to you," Jan said. "And to your uncle."

Wali looked at Charlie, who stood up. The American looked at Wali and mouthed "OK."

"We have a deal," Wali said.

Charlie got out a pen and started to write a script for Wali to read. Wali nodded and followed along.

"Wise choice," Jan said. "Your business will be safe now that we're partners."

"If we're partners," Wali said, "I need your help."

Just saying the words made him sick. But that was what Charlie wanted him to say.

"I have people coming to pick up my uncle's crate."

"When?" Jan asked. "Where are they coming?"

Wali looked at Charlie. Charlie wrote down Wali's next line.

"Twelve hours. Have my uncle take you to the clinic near the edge of the Red Desert. I will come to you."

Wali heard Jan put his hand over the phone and say something to someone nearby, likely Basir.

"Come alone," Jan said. "None of your Special Forces friends."

"Of course," Wali told him. "This has nothing to do with them."

He killed the line and handed the phone to Charlie. Wali slumped back into his chair. He was spent. Charlie let out a low growl and threw the phone hard against the wall.

It shattered, like their plan.

CHAPTER 40

Charlie stood on the tarmac waiting for the helicopter to touch down. He shifted his weight from one foot to the other. He was nervous because if he failed, the plan was dead in the water.

The green Chinook settled on the runway and taxied to a stop off the flight line. The back ramp opened and Jerry's Special Forces team—the one Charlie had gone with to get Pacman—and about two dozen Afghan commandos walked off. No one appeared happy. The mission was a failure. They'd been sent out to get the bomb and had come back empty-handed.

Charlie knew that, because he'd made sure the mission was a failure. But now he was going to make it up to them.

The Afghan commandos started heading for a truck that would take them back to Camp Hero, their base. The Special Forces team followed. Stooped shoulders. Tired. Failure weighed heavy. There was no greater sin.

Charlie approached Jerry, the team's captain, who was talking with Red about making sure the commandos refitted before they racked out.

"Hey, Cap," Charlie said. "I need to talk with you guys."

Jerry and the team sergeant stopped talking.

"I'm heading to the TOC once we're done loading up," Jerry said. "We can talk there."

"Roger, sir," Charlie said. "But we've gotten some new intel, and I need you guys to stand pat. We're looking to spin this up again ASAP."

Jerry tightened his lips.

"Look, Chief," Jerry said. "Why do I feel like we're getting jerked around?"

"Because you are," Charlie said. "You hit a dry hole because I wanted you to."

Jerry didn't know how to react. He was stunned, not mad.

"Why would you send us to the wrong place when we're going after a nuke? You fucking nuts?"

"Because this is all part of a bigger operation," Charlie said. "I couldn't have you spook them. I have the exact location now. But I need your help convincing the boss to spin this up again."

Jerry looked at Red. They had a short hand. It was unspoken, but both men were weighing the risk, the mission, the fucking staff guy. It came down to trust, and Charlie had already let them down.

"You've got balls admitting you fucked us," Jerry said. "Especially since we're both holding our weapons."

Charlie smiled.

"I wanted to clear the bullshit," he said. "But we're on the clock. I can brief you on the way to the TOC. We need to convince the boss this is a good idea."

Jerry looked back at Red.

"We're already dressed to go out," Red said.

Jerry took off his helmet and scratched his scruffy hair.

"Fuck it," he said. "You're right."

Jerry took off his kit and handed it to Bobby, keeping only his long gun with him.

"I'll get the guys ready," Bobby said. "You go untangle this nut roll."

Jerry pulled on a ball cap and followed Charlie to the truck.

"I'll brief you on the target while we drive," Charlie said.

When the two men marched into the commander's office, Lieutenant Colonel Kyle wasn't happy to see Charlie.

"Aren't you confined to quarters?" Kyle asked.

"Yes, sir."

"So why are you standing in front of me?"

"Because I know where the bomb is."

Kyle folded his hands and looked at Jerry.

"Didn't you just get off mission?"

Jerry looked at Charlie and then back at Kyle.

"Yes, sir."

Kyle's expression showed he wasn't sure what was going on, but the last person he wanted to see was Charlie. "It was a dry hole, right? I'm not sure if this bomb even exists. It seems to be just at our fingertips all the time, and then when we think we have it, poof, it disappears."

No one spoke. What the hell was Kyle talking about? Charlie snuck a look at his watch. Time was ticking away. Kyle saw Charlie's gesture and his face went from contemplative to a scowl.

"Why are you here with him?" Kyle said, looking at Jerry.

Jerry looked at Charlie as if searching for an answer.

"I brought him," Charlie said. "His team is poised to launch again. I have updated intel on the location of Corona."

Kyle's eyes narrowed.

"Chief, you've been in the military for two decades," he said. "So you know how a mission comes together. This isn't like playing with your G.I. Joe figures in the back-fucking-yard. We just don't shit out helicopters to send willy-nilly on wild goose chases."

"I know, sir, but—"

Kyle stood up.

"*But?* I tried to spare you by confining you to quarters. But you couldn't stay out of it. Now you're back in my office trying to get me to launch another mission, one you know I can't do on my own.

There is a way to do things, and Chief, you know better than to think this is the way."

Jerry took a step away from Charlie. He recoiled as if Charlie had an infectious disease. Just being near him was terminal cancer for his career.

"As for you, Captain," Kyle said. "I'm not sure why you're here in my office, but I am going to assume Chief tricked you into believing this was sanctioned. Let's pretend this didn't happen. I'm sure you can find a ride back to your team."

Jerry started toward the door.

"Thank you, sir."

Charlie started to follow him.

"Oh no, Chief," Kyle said. "*You* don't get to walk out. I'm calling JAG, and then I suspect the MPs. Your days in the Army are *over!*"

Jerry opened the door only to find Frank about to knock. Frank saw Charlie and smiled.

"Hey, sir," he said to Kyle. "You might want Jerry to stick around. Just got off with OGA. They've got a tasking. Seems Corona is back on."

Kyle just looked at Charlie.

"Don't worry, sir," Charlie said. "I dropped my retirement papers. This is it for me."

CHAPTER 41

The wall-mounted air-conditioner whirred as Felix walked inside the metal prefab building that housed the Joint Special Operations Air Detachment.

The small AC unit strained to keep up with the stifling temperature outside. The computers, servers, and the six fifty-inch plasma screens that lined the walls around the commander's podium needed to stay cool. Each screen showed the video feed from the various Predators and Reapers flying around the region.

Some were in Afghanistan.

Some were in Pakistan.

The commander was a lanky Marine in cargo pants and a polo shirt. He stood on a dais at the center of the room, with the six monitors arrayed in front of him.

"That him?" Felix asked, pointing to a monitor showing video from one of the Reapers. "Not sure," the Marine said. "We confirmed he was active about five hours ago."

The Marine didn't look away from the monitor showing the Reaper's video feed.

"We're still looking to get eyes on him right now."

Not having "eyes on" meant they were tracking the target via signals intelligence. In this case, they were monitoring the target's mobile phone.

The target was Hamza, Samir's brother.

A few minutes before, Felix had confirmed Samir had been arrested in the United Arab Emirates. He was on his way to Jordan and eventually either Bagram or Gitmo. Now Felix was going to take care of his brother. His plan was to capture Hamza en route.

On the monitor, Felix saw a mix of mud-brick and cinder-block houses haphazardly thrown together. The black-and-white Reaper feed on the plasma screen was locked onto a battered van. But until they confirmed that Hamza was in the van and no civilian noncombatants were nearby, they couldn't shoot.

"Want me to call him?"

The Marine glared at him.

"Not kidding," Felix said. "I have his number. If I get him to answer, is that enough?"

The Marine looked at his JAG. The JAG nodded.

"Call him up."

Felix took out Wali's phone and dialed the number. It rang several times and then went to voice mail. Felix dialed the number again. This time, a man answered. Felix muted the phone but kept the line open.

"That's him," someone in operations said.

The officer gave the coordinates of Hamza's mobile phone signal. The Marine checked the feed. It was the same spot where the van was parked. Suddenly, five men spilled out of a nearby house and hurriedly climbed inside the van. They wore garb traditional to the area. Long shirts, baggy pants, and headscarves. One wore all white and climbed into the back. The doors had barely shut before the van took off, trailing a plume of dust and exhaust.

"Stay on them," the Marine said.

Felix watched on a monitor as the strike order was transmitted through a secure internet chat to the Reaper crews in Nevada. Seconds later, the sensor operator of the Reaper observing the van shifted the drone's crosshairs onto the vehicle.

"Sir," one of the staff officers said. "Hamza just announced he was moving."

"Agreed, sir," another staff officer said. "Call came from the van. He mentioned our crank call as well."

The Marine nodded.

"I want all eyes on."

Within seconds, two other Reaper feeds shifted to the van picking its way through the village's market. Vendors and shoppers clogged the road in the evening, making final purchases before returning home to cook. The crowd slowed the van's progress as the driver darted through breaks in the sea of people.

The goal was to hit Hamza while he was in transit. An isolated strike meant no witnesses. It also kept civilians out of harm's way. Hamza simply wouldn't show up to pick up the device.

But the Reapers couldn't shoot until he cleared the village. A Hellfire missile would obliterate the van but also send deadly shrapnel into the surrounding buildings. A miss in the village would be catastrophic.

"Running ROE now," the Marine said, meaning they were going over the rules of engagement before final approval. "Have the crews spin up their missiles."

The Marine put on a headset to talk to the Reaper pilot. A secure internet chat documented coordinates and clearances.

"Spade," the Marine said. "This is Hammer One Four. You've got the lead. Acknowledge."

A clear voice, tinged with only a hint of static, responded.

"Copy. Spade's got lead," the pilot said. "Checklist complete in two mikes."

The driver took his time in the village knowing the civilians protected them. The van made it through the market and picked up the pace as it neared the edge of the town. Speed was its only cover now. The van wound its way through the outskirts of town and sped into the open, following a curvy track that passed through smaller villages and open desert.

"Target's clear. Any word?" Spade said.

The Marine looked at one of his staffers. He shook his head no.

"Negative, Spade," the Marine said. "Still awaiting word."

Felix knew "awaiting word" was a euphemism for slow decision making.

"Copy," Spade said.

"Try to maintain position so we can get a shot off quickly," the Marine said.

"The road is leveling out," Spade said. "Looks like we're about to hit a straightaway."

"Copy," the Marine said.

The straightaway was the most logical place to take the shot. The van would maintain a constant speed on a predictable course. There were few ridgelines to block the missile or the targeting laser.

Hamza's van hit the straightaway and accelerated. Twin rooster tails of dust kicked up behind the rear tires as the vehicle raced through sand deposited on the road by a recent windstorm.

"Ten minutes," the Marine said.

They had ten minutes until Hamza was scheduled to make a proof-of-life call. The call would take less than a minute. It was just a check-in with AQ leadership. Felix didn't want to risk it. What if they knew about his brother's arrest? Unlikely, but it wasn't worth the risk. If the Reaper was going to shoot, it needed to do so on this road before the call.

Felix watched the monitor as Spade maneuvered into position. Flying faster than the van, he executed S-turns to keep from passing it. If Hamza knew a Reaper was above him, he wasn't acting like it. The van sped straight down the highway and then slowed.

"Spade, say status," the Marine said.

"Checklist complete, awaiting clearance," Spade said.

"Copy," the Marine said.

"Five minutes and the window closes," Spade said. "Say status."

The van stopped on the side of the road. Someone threw open the cargo door and climbed out. It was one of Hamza's guards. He had a satellite phone.

Felix watched as the Marine hung up his phone.

"It's time," he said. "Pass the Nine Line."

The liaison officer pushed Enter on his keyboard. He'd already typed the 9 Line, which spelled out the order to shoot in scripted lines. Each line passed specific information to the pilot.

"Spade, this is Hammer One Four," the Marine said. "Nine Line is in chat. Call in with direction."

The video feed remained fixed on the van. Occasionally, the picture would tilt and rotate as the camera adjusted to the Reaper's maneuvers. Spade didn't respond. The pilot was briefing his sensor operator, the second man in this crew, on the shot. Felix was impatient. He watched the guard talk on the phone. There was no sign of Hamza. He was still inside the van.

"Spade's in from the south," the Reaper pilot said. "One minute."

"Spade, you're cleared hot."

The guard wandered to the front of the van, the phone still pressed to his ear. His face filled the screen in front of Felix. The pixels on the screen sharpened. Felix saw the folds in the man's clothes. The guard gave no indication that he heard the drone. The feed shifted to the van's open cargo door.

"Thirty seconds," the Marine said.

The open door showed large in the screen now.

"Twenty seconds."

Clouds flashed across the image.

"Ten seconds."

The sensor kept the crosshairs locked on the open cargo door.

"Three, two, one..."

The Reaper pilot pulled the trigger. Twin white-hot flashes erupted in the video feed as a pair of Hellfire missiles left their rails and raced toward the target.

"Rifle," Spade said, indicating he'd fired the missiles. The Hellfires' trails went into the clouds following the sensor's laser marker.

"Five, four..."

The guard heard the twin sonic booms of the missiles. On the video screen, it seemed as if he were staring right at Felix.

The guard froze.

A split second later, Felix saw the missiles slam into the cargo door of the van and detonate. A blinding flash whited out the plasma screen. It took a few seconds for the screen to clear as the heat of the explosions subsided. Smoke hung in the air. All that was left of the van was a scorched chassis and engine block. The missiles had vaporized the rest. Debris radiated outward from the impact crater like compass points. Felix studied the debris field looking for a body.

The video feed pulled out to a wider angle. Felix noticed something dark about thirty yards from the shredded van. The sensor operator saw it too and moved the crosshairs toward the object. It was a human torso. There were no signs of arms or legs.

The remains were completely burnt and unrecognizable.

CHAPTER 42

Wali's red Toyota 4x4 bounced along the dirt road that ran parallel to the Red Desert, a stretch of small, red sand hills and open rocky and clay-covered areas between Helmand and Kandahar provinces in southeastern Afghanistan. In the back of the truck, he had an AK-47 and a tracker so Charlie would know his location.

After about an hour, the truck's lights flashed across the façade of a medical clinic. The clinic was in disrepair. The Taliban had used it as a headquarters before it was liberated by the Afghan military. Wali had tried to refurbish it. Using a crew of workers from Kandahar, they repaired the holes, cleaned up the examination rooms, and restored the power and water. But a night letter from the Taliban scared away the doctors and the NGO providing supplies and money.

It now sat unoccupied.

Wali backed the truck up next to the building and got out. He put his rifle on the hood and slid a Glock pistol into his waistband. In the distance, he saw the headlights of two trucks.

Wali walked into the clinic's lobby and stood his rifle near the door. Next to it he put a gym bag containing $50,000. He returned to the front of the clinic just as the trucks arrived. Zahir sat in the back surrounded by guards. There was no sign of Razaq. An Afghan soldier jumped from the truck bed and unslung his rifle.

"Put your hands up," he said, closing on Wali.

Wali stood firm. His hands remained at his side.

"Where is my uncle?"

The guard raised his rifle.

"Stop," Jan said as he climbed out of the truck.

The guard looked at Jan and then lowered his rifle. Jan opened the back door on the passenger side. Razaq was sitting on the seat. He hung his head when he saw Wali.

"And his cargo?" Wali asked.

Jan smiled.

"Not before the money."

Wali walked back into the clinic and grabbed the gym bag. He left the rifle.

"It is here," Wali said.

The guard took the bag and set it on the ground. He opened and searched it. Confident it didn't contain a bomb, the guard brought it over to Jan.

"Thank you," the general said.

"Release my uncle," Wali said.

Jan walked back to the truck and put the bag in the front seat. He removed Razaq's beads and flicked them absently for a few seconds.

"What is this cargo?" Jan inquired. "I looked at it. It looks old. Is it an antique?"

Wali was growing impatient.

"Yes," he said. "Now where is it? I have people coming to get it."

Jan walked toward Wali, the snap of the beads in his fingers growing louder.

"It is safe," he said. "It is close."

"We're done here. You have your money. Let my uncle and his bodyguard go."

Jan looked at his guards. They dragged Razaq and Zahir from the truck and forced them to kneel in the dirt. One guard stood behind Razaq, the other next to Zahir.

"But the deal has changed," Jan said. "I have new terms."

Wali started to drift toward the clinic's open door. He kept his eyes locked on his uncle's bowed head.

"New terms?"

Keep Jan talking. Let him act like the sheik. Wali wasn't sure what he was going to do once he reached his rifle. He couldn't shoot his way out of this situation. But he also wasn't going to watch his uncle get executed.

"Yes," Jan said, walking back toward the truck. "You're going to introduce me to these people buying the antique."

Wali took another step toward the front of the clinic.

"Anything else?"

"I want all your contracts. You're out of the trucking business."

Wali sighed. He tried to appear defeated.

"What happens to my uncle?"

Razaq's head popped up when he heard his name. Wali looked into his eyes. He was broken. But his look told Wali to fight.

"He goes home," Jan said. "Or he becomes a news release for my American friends: 'Local Afghan forces kill Taliban commander.'"

Wali stole a glance at his watch. Where was Charlie?

"My uncle is not going to die tonight," he said. "Take my business. Take my money. But give me my family."

Jan tossed Wali his uncle's beads.

"Deal."

Jan walked over and helped Razaq to his feet.

"But his man is coming with me," he said. "I am General Gul Mohammed Jan. I've killed more Taliban than any other commander. I can't have filth like these men telling stories about me."

Razaq stopped and looked at Zahir and then back at Wali.

"You have your uncle and your health," Jan said, looking at Zahir. "But I am going to execute him."

CHAPTER 43

Charlie tried to keep his boots out of the pool of piss. The flight had been long, and his back teeth were floating by the time the ramp dropped and he and the rest of the Special Forces team and Afghan commandos rushed into the night.

Everyone paused to wait for the helicopters to depart. Charlie took a minute to drain his bladder. With the last drops hitting the dirt, he could finally concentrate. The last couple of hours had been a whirlwind. One second, he was going to jail. If he was being honest, he still might be. But at least he'd go out on one final mission. After Frank and Felix had intervened, Kyle relented and sent Jerry and his commandos back out.

Kyle had balked at first when Charlie asked to go. But he relented when both Jerry and Frank convinced him Charlie was needed to ID Wali and Razaq.

"He's the only guy who knows our Taliban source," had Frank told Kyle, who by then was trying to fight off a headache by squeezing the bridge of his nose.

"Fine," Kyle said, looking at Charlie sitting in the corner of his office trying not to be seen. "He can babysit Felix's team."

Kyle finally turned his attention to Charlie.

"Get your kit. But when you get back, you're going home on the next thing smoking."

Charlie was gone before Kyle could change his mind. Felix drove the CIA team to the staging area. Both he and Charlie were dressed in Army uniforms without patches or rank. They wore body armor and each carried a pistol and an M4 rifle.

Charlie tried to make small talk before they left Kandahar, but it didn't go anywhere. The CIA team was there for one reason, and it wasn't to make friends. They hung out on the edge of the group of soldiers getting ready to go on the mission. It was easier just to leave them alone.

Now on the ground, there wasn't time for small talk. The team had a convoy to stop. Monitoring the signal from the tracker hidden on the device, the Americans and Afghans hustled across the broken dirt and rocks of the high desert. After an hour-long patrol—more run than shuffle step—over the soft sand, the team arrived at the spot. Peering through night-vision goggles, they observed four trucks parked in the open and a group of Afghan soldiers.

Jan's men.

The team set up near a jagged rock outcropping.

Three trucks formed a loose circle. A fourth was parked far away. That one had Corona in it, according to the tracker. Charlie counted ten Afghan soldiers. Most were squatting away from the trucks, cooking tea over a fire. Charlie zeroed in on a guard sitting on the hood of truck one, a Ford Ranger. The soldier had an RPG across his lap. Two rockets poked up over his shoulders. Charlie waited for the order from Jerry to fire.

"Stand by," Charlie heard in his headset. "Watch your background. Corona is in truck four. No one fires near it."

Just before Jerry gave the order to fire, a cell phone rang. The guard in Charlie's sights fished out his phone and pressed it against his ear. The hushed Pashto conversation carried a long way on the wind. The other guards turned toward the guy on the phone.

"Take 'em," Jerry said.

The silence of the Red Desert was shattered. Muzzle flashes from the commandos' AK-47s exploded in Charlie's night-vision goggles.

He turned away for a second before locking back on his sights. The guard with the phone was frozen, trying to decide between flight or fight. Charlie didn't wait for his mind to engage.

The M4 kicked slightly as Charlie pumped a burst into the man's chest. The fighter's arm flung into the air as the rounds slammed into his body. Then he exploded. A whitish-pink mist appeared where he'd been standing and then slowly dissipated. Bits of his torso fell in front of the truck's bumper. Fragments of bone and flesh radiated out in a starlike pattern.

"What the fuck was that?" the captain called over the radio. "Watch your fire!"

One of Charlie's rounds must have caught a rocket. Charlie shifted his fire. He scanned the area for a new target. A pair of fighters stumbled out from behind a truck, dazed by the explosion. Charlie fired two quick bursts. One man dropped like a rag doll. The other turned and sprayed and prayed in Charlie's direction. The Afghan soldier waved the barrel of the rifle back and forth like he was watering grass.

It was more sound than fury.

Charlie started to move to get a better vantage point when Jerry's voice broke through the cacophony of fire.

"We've got an eagle down," Jerry said. "Doc, I need you over by me."

Charlie glimpsed the medic moving past him toward the captain's position. He looked back at the trucks and saw the soldier—no longer firing—racing toward the open desert. On his left flank, some of the commandos and Special Forces soldiers were surrounding the trucks. No one noticed the squirter. Charlie looked back at the CIA techs. They were hiding behind the rocks.

"Head toward the captain's position," Charlie told the CIA team. "I'm going after a squirter."

Charlie squeezed one of the commando's shoulders.

"You're with me," he said.

It was dark, but his night-vision goggles made tracking the Afghan soldier easy. The squirter was about fifty yards ahead. He was staggering, more than running, from the fight. Every few steps the soldier seemed to lose his balance. Charlie and the commando were gaining on him when he fell again and then disappeared.

Charlie stopped.

"What the fuck?"

He looked back to see where the commando was but saw only desert. Charlie took a knee. The fighting near the trucks had stopped. It was quiet again. Maybe the commando was lost. Charlie pulled the Peltor headphones off his ears and listened for the crunch of rocks or gravel.

Nothing. He was on his own.

Instead of following the same path as the squirter, Charlie approached at an angle. If the Afghan soldier was waiting for him, Charlie would hit his flank instead.

There was no reason to run. The squirter was likely lying low hoping no one had seen him escape. Charlie took his time. Each step was measured. He kept his gaze fixed on where the squirter was likely to be hiding. As he crested a small hill, he spotted a wadi. The squirter must have crawled into the dry creek bed and disappeared between its banks.

Charlie picked up his pace and slid down the bank of the wadi behind where he'd last seen the Afghan soldier. Step by step, Charlie closed on his quarry. Up ahead, the wadi made a dogleg turn to the left. Charlie set up on the corner. He slowly scanned ahead, expecting to see the squirter holed up against the bank, but no one was hiding there.

There were scrape marks where the soldier had slid down to the bottom of the wadi. His scarf was lying next to a crushed bottle. Blood was smeared on the plastic.

Charlie's heart rate picked up. The squirter was gone, but he had been hit by the first volley. Charlie flicked on his IR flashlight and looked for the blood trail. He found a few drops leading east toward the clinic and Wali.

"Got you, fucker."

CHAPTER 44

Wali reached for his pistol when he heard AK-47s firing. He ducked, thinking it was Jan's soldiers. It took him a sec ond to realize the sound was too far off to be Jan's men at the clinic. Jan turned to look in the direction of the gunfire. One of his guards ran back to the truck for the radio.

"Are those my men?" Jan asked.

Wali didn't hesitate. He slipped the pistol out of his waistband and opened fire. The sound startled the guards, who froze. A round struck the windshield of Jan's truck, turning the glass into a spiderweb of cracks. Wali didn't wait for the guards to return fire. He sprinted to Razaq and helped the old man to his feet. Razaq was confused. He wasn't sure what was going on.

"We've got to run," Wali told him.

Razaq looked back at Zahir. The bodyguard made eye contact with his commander. Wali caught the glance.

Wali looked over his shoulder as he and Razaq dashed toward the open door. Zahir was wrestling with one of the guards. Both men had their hands on the guard's AK-47. For a second it looked like the guard was going to win, but Zahir wrenched the gun from his hands.

"Zahir!" Wali called. "The clinic!"

Zahir turned the rifle on the trucks and fired. It looked as if it took every ounce of his energy to maintain control. The barrel kicked up and down, sending rounds into the ground and over the top of the trucks. But the fire was enough to force Jan and his men to scramble for cover.

Inside the clinic, Wali chambered a round in his AK-47 and pulled it into his shoulder. He pumped short bursts into the trucks' engines and cabins. Between bursts, he watched Zahir zigzag his way to the clinic. Wali covered him as he dove through the door. Razaq greeted Zahir with a hug and a kiss.

Zahir pushed the old man away and joined Wali at the door.

"You have to leave," Zahir said. "Take your uncle and head into the desert before they surround the building."

Wali saw Jan's guards fanning out. He fired a burst at a group moving along the right flank. The rounds dissuaded them, for now.

"What about you?"

Zahir smiled.

"I'm mujahedeen," he said. "You're a businessman. You fight with a pen. This isn't your kind of fight."

"OK," Wali said. "But you follow right behind us."

Zahir nodded.

Razaq was sitting in the corner. He was breathing heavily. The strain of the run and being under fire was too much. He was showing his age.

"We need to go, Uncle."

Razaq waved his nephew away.

"I'm tired," he said. "No more running for me."

Zahir opened fire again. The sound echoed through the clinic. Razaq cowered from the roar.

"Get up," Wali urged, grabbing the old man by his shirt and hauling him to his feet. "You can't stay here."

Wali led Razaq toward the back of the clinic. A thin film of dust coated everything. The examination rooms were dark. Wali tried the back door, but it was jammed. He kicked the lock with his boot. Nothing. He kicked again. The door bent but didn't break.

He cursed himself for demanding the contractors install new doors and locks.

Outside, he heard AK-47 fire. Each burst was answered by the other side. Zahir only had a few magazines. He couldn't keep returning fire for long.

"Stay here," Wali told Razaq.

Wali ran back down the hallway. He ducked into one of the examination rooms. The beds were piled in a heap in the corner. The glass of the medicine cabinet was smashed. Wali scanned the room quickly with his flashlight. Nothing. He went to the next room. This one had been cleared out. A rug covered the center of the room. Wali never put a rug there.

Using his boot, he slid the rug back and uncovered a wooden board. He shined his flashlight on it. It was smooth and concealed a hole that had been dug beneath the floor. Wali pried the board away, exposing a hole about three feet deep. Wali shined his light inside and spotted a PKM machine gun with a few belts of ammunition. And an AK-47 with a dozen magazines. He took the rifle and slipped a spare magazine into his pocket.

Outside there was a lull in the fighting. Both sides repositioning. Wali took the PKM and ammunition up to Zahir.

"Where did you get that?" Zahir asked.

"Does it matter?" Wali said.

Wali handed Zahir the other AK-47 magazines and headed back toward Razaq and their escape route.

"We're going out the back," Wali told Zahir. "Cover us."

Zahir quickly loaded the PKM and fired a short burst. The loud, guttural gunfire followed Wali as he ran down the hall. Razaq was sitting on the ground with his hands over his ears.

Wali unslung the AK-47 and fired into the door lock. The rounds punched holes all around the mechanism. Wali's boot finished the job. Razaq was up now and started to bolt out the door. Wali caught him by the shirt before he crossed the threshold.

"Wait."

Wali looked out into the dusty courtyard. A generator under a roof was in the left corner. A hole was punched in the back wall near the right corner. That was their exit...until he spotted two of Jan's men kneeling near the generator. He raised his rifle just as the PKM stopped firing.

Zahir came up behind them with the machine gun.

"We've got to go," he said.

Razaq pointed to where Jan's men were hiding.

"Two guards," he said. "They'll kill us before we get ten steps."

Wali looked at Zahir.

"Covering fire," he said.

Zahir set the PKM just inside the door.

"When I start firing, go, Commander."

Zahir turned to Wali.

"You go with him."

Wali looked at Zahir and then Razaq. These were his enemies. The men outside were fighting for his country. Everything was turned upside down. Once again, Wali understood he didn't have a country. It didn't matter what he tried to do in Kandahar. Afghanistan was fractured. The sides were too fluid to create a rigid system of good guys and bad guys. That designation changed by the day.

The PKM fire blasted him back to reality. Wali bolted from the door. He heard Razaq behind him as he cleared the corner. Wali squeezed through the hole in the wall and waited for his uncle.

The Red Desert was spread out in front of him. Razaq slipped through the opening. There was only blackness. Wali paused for a second to allow his uncle to catch his breath, his hands on his knees.

"You OK?" he asked.

Razaq looked at his nephew.

"Thank you for coming for me."

Wali helped the old man up.

"We're family," he said. "You're going to America."

Razaq reached out and grabbed Wali's arm.

"I am going to America because you didn't abandon me."

Wali nodded. But they weren't going to America unless he could get their asses to safety.

The clinic sat on a hill overlooking the desert. There was a path that ran downhill a few feet from the opening. It was their only way out. The firing died down again.

"You ready?"

Razaq straightened up. Wali led as they hustled along the wall. Movement up ahead. Wali stopped and knelt. Razaq squatted behind him. Men were moving toward them. It looked like two men. The point man had a rifle and a uniform. It wasn't Zahir.

Razaq put his hand on Wali's back. Wali felt the old man's nervous energy as he raised his rifle and focused on the front sight post. The point man started to fill his sight picture. The sight post rolled like a boat in a storm. He was having a hard time maintaining his sight picture under all the stress. Wali held his breath and squeezed the trigger.

Wali watched the muzzle flash as the point man disappeared in the darkness. The second man opened fire and ran back down the path. Wali heard bullets crack over his head. Behind him, he heard his uncle cry out.

Wali let the gunman go and turned to Razaq. The old man was sitting in the dust clutching his arm. Wali ran his hand over his uncle's arm. A chunk of flesh under Razaq's right shoulder was gone, and Wali felt shards of bone in the wound.

"Uncle!"

Razaq reached for Wali.

"We've got to go," he said, groaning in pain as Wali helped him to his feet.

Wali led the way, racing down the path away from the compound and into a nearby wadi. There was no waiting. They barreled headlong into the darkness hoping to escape.

For a split second, Wali relaxed. The next second, he was on his back and his head was on fire. He felt the knot growing on his forehead. Nearby, he heard the groan of another man. They'd collided in the dark. Wali felt hands grab under his arms.

"Hurry," Razaq said. "We've got to keep running."

Wali staggered a little as he regained his footing. He recognized the man he'd run into on the path.

It was Jan.

The general had been coming up the path and Wali missed him in the dark. Wali looked for his rifle. He'd dropped it when he fell but couldn't find it. He didn't dare turn on his flashlight. He felt a tug on his sleeve. It was Razaq.

"Leave him," Razaq said. "Come on."

Jan was dazed. He tried to stand but could only get to one knee. Wali took one more look around for the rifle and then followed his uncle.

But not before he kicked sand in Jan's face.

CHAPTER 45

Charlie followed the blood trail for fifty yards before he lost it. He took a knee in the wadi and looked back toward the trucks. The firing had stopped. He knew the CIA team was taking possession of Corona because of the radio updates.

He keyed his mic.

"Hey Cap," he said. "This is Chief. I'm about one hundred meters south of your position. I've got a squirter."

"Roger, Chief," the captain said. "Who are you with?"

"Solo," Charlie said. "I tapped a 'Ghan to follow up but lost him."

"Stay put," the captain said. "I'll send a posse."

Charlie keyed the radio just as AK-47 rounds cracked overhead. He pressed himself against the wall of the wadi. Another burst. The fire wasn't close, but it was still aimed at him. Charlie found a crease in the wadi's wall and settled behind his rifle sight. He knew the squirter was nearby. Each burst gave up his position.

Another burst and Charlie had him. The squirter's head popped up like a groundhog. Charlie started to fire, but the head disappeared.

Charlie exhaled. It was a waiting game. He'd pop up again. *Be patient. No need to run to your death.* Charlie slowly moved his M4 into position.

Movement. Charlie shifted the barrel to the right a few degrees. The squirter's bare head filled his sight. The man had his AK-47 pointed in Charlie's direction.

Exhale. Fire.

Charlie's first shot shattered the AK-47. The squirter's head disappeared in a cloud of dust. Charlie slid out of his hiding spot and worked his way down the wadi, his rifle up and ready. Charlie paused at a bend. He reckoned the squirter was just around the corner. If he wasn't dead, he was wounded. Charlie climbed up the opposite side of the wadi and worked his way behind the squirter's last position.

From the top of the wadi, Charlie spotted movement and took a knee. Farther down the creek bed he saw another man. A soldier. He was cradling an AK-47. It was hard to make out if he was friend or foe. Charlie wasn't sure if the captain had sent help. He didn't dare call back now. The man slid down the side of the wadi and disappeared.

Charlie didn't have time to wait for the mystery man. He kept moving toward the squirter's position. Lying prone, he crawled the last few meters to the lip of the wadi. He waited a full minute before peering over the edge. The squirter's body was lying in a heap, blood pooling under him. Charlie hopped down and kicked the shattered AK-47 away.

The squirter's legs were split apart like he was running in the air. Hair and bits of bone created a ragged edge where his face used to be. Blood was splattered across his chest.

Charlie knelt next to the body and rifled through its pockets. He found a handful of Pakistani rupees and an ID. A police ID.

"Chief," the captain said over the radio. "We're finished up here. Time to take it back to the house. Where are you?"

Charlie keyed his radio.

"Doing SSE on the squirter," Charlie said.

"Fuck that," the captain said. "Beat feet back here. We're moving to exfil. Helos are inbound."

"Roger," Charlie said.

Charlie started to climb out of the wadi when he heard the crunch of dirt nearby. It was probably his mystery man. But Charlie had a helicopter to catch.

CHAPTER 46

Wali held Razaq's arm as they scrambled down the wadi. They'd heard the shots. Wali wasn't going to wait and see if they were the targets.

"I need a break," Razaq said.

His voice was a wheeze. He was struggling to keep up. Razaq pulled his arm away from Wali.

"Leave me," he said. "I'm an old man. I will only slow you down."

Wali stopped. He pressed his back into the wadi's dirt wall. He still had his empty pistol in his hand. It was useless. But it gave him comfort.

"I'm not leaving you," he said. "You're my only family."

"I left you before," Razaq said. "We've fought on opposite sides for most of your life. We might be family, but only by blood."

"But you brought us the device," Wali said. "You did the right thing."

"I don't trust the camels," Razaq said. "But I don't trust the Americans either."

Wali hooked his hand under his uncle's arm.

"Maybe not," he said. "But you don't have a lot of choice."

Razaq grunted as Wali pulled him to his feet.

"We're going to miss our ride if we don't hurry."

Wali had taken a few steps down the wadi when rocks and dirt exploded around him. He threw his arm over his face and dove backward. Shards of rock and clumps of dirt peppered his face and arm. Behind him, Wali heard Razaq yell.

"My leg," Razaq moaned, gripping his right thigh just above the knee.

Wali crawled over to his uncle. He saw the blood staining Razaq's pants.

"Keep pressure on it," Wali said, turning to see if the shooter was coming.

Another burst.

The bullets slammed into the dirt wall, kicking up a dust cloud. Wali covered his head. Jan was standing over him when he looked up.

They were dead.

The distant thump-thump-thump of a helicopter's rotor echoed across the desert.

"They're coming," Wali said. "They have the device. Your guards, at least the ones that lived, are going to talk. You're done. You might as well run."

"Stay down," Jan said.

He was disheveled and no longer looked like the polished general who'd used his power to create a mini empire. He was desperate. His plan to extort Wali's business had turned into a life-or-death situation.

Jan took a step back.

"I'm not the one helping the Taliban," he said. "When the Americans get here, they will only see your bodies. And they will know you were a traitor."

Jan leveled the AK-47 at Wali.

CHAPTER 47

Charlie heard the first burst of gunfire and hit the deck.

There was no way he was going to run across the open desert now. Charlie was only a few feet from the wadi. He rolled until he reached the edge and then disappeared over the side.

The second burst rang out just as he hit the bottom of the wadi. It was AK-47 fire. The sound was unmistakable. The shooter was nearby.

"Cap, Chief. I've made contact. Going to need a minute."

Jerry keyed his mic.

"Stand by," he said. "Where are you? I'll resend the posse."

But Charlie was already moving. The helicopter would have to wait. This mystery man was a threat.

He'd worked his way down the wadi away from Corona and his ride home when he heard moaning. He climbed up to the lip of the wadi. Just beyond the bend were three men. Two were on the ground. The other, pointing an AK-47, was standing over them. He was wearing an Afghan uniform. Charlie recognized him immediately.

General Gul Mohammed Jan.

Charlie zeroed in on the two men on the ground. One had a pistol. The other was holding his leg and trying to crawl away. Jan was blocking the men's faces until he stepped back. Wali's face filled Charlie's sights.

"Shit," Charlie said.

Jan was staring down the barrel of Wali's pistol.

"Stop!" Wali said. "Back up."

Jan took a step back.

Charlie hesitated. He couldn't shoot an Afghan general. Jan had fucked up the operation, but he didn't do it on purpose.

"Chief, Cap. where the fuck are you?" the captain said over the radio. "We've got to move."

Charlie keyed his radio but said nothing. For the first time in his career, he didn't know what to do.

Charlie heard the thump of helicopter rotors getting louder, but it didn't matter. He put his laser slight on Jan's back when Wali started dry-firing his Glock. The click of the empty pistol made Jan jump for a second, his body preparing for the bullets.

Wali charged. The barrel of Jan's AK-47 leveled, and a burst from the rifle shattered the silence. Wali flinched at the boom.

"Charlie, the helos are circling," Jerry said. "We're gone in five mikes. Where are you? I'm sending help."

Charlie didn't answer. He just ran toward Wali.

CHAPTER 48

Wali heard the gunfire and expected to feel the pain of bullets slicing into his chest. Instead, Jan crashed to the ground next to him. Wali looked down. Jan's body lay in a heap, his legs apart. Blood leaked into the dirt beneath him.

Wali crawled away as another burst tore into the general's back, ripping his uniform shirt open. Wali curled his legs into the fetal position and covered his head as bullets impacted around him.

The gunshots made his ears ring. The shooter was close. Wali stayed still for several seconds waiting to get shot. Then, as the sound of gunfire faded, he heard a familiar voice.

"Commander, are you OK?"

Wali uncovered his head. He propped himself up on one elbow and looked back toward his uncle. Zahir was kneeling next to Razaq.

"I'm hurt," Razaq said. "I need a doctor."

Wali joined Zahir. He started to fashion a tourniquet from his belt. Razaq yelled when Wali slid the belt over his thigh.

"Stop," Zahir said, putting his hand on Wali's. "You're not a doctor."

"I was trained by the Americans," Wali said. "This is the only way to stop the bleeding."

Zahir removed his hand.

Wali tore strips of cloth from his shirt and packed them into the bullet wound. He covered them with strips from Razaq's shirt. While Wali worked, Zahir crawled to the top of wadi.

"They're coming," he said.

"Who?"

"Americans," Zahir said. "Come on, Commander. We have to go."

"You go," Wali said. "He is better off here. The Americans will get him a doctor."

Zahir grabbed Razaq's arm and started to help him up.

"And then they will send him to Gitmo. Come on, Commander. I have a truck nearby."

Wali and Razaq's eyes met. His uncle was fighting the pain as he stood up. There was a sadness in his eyes. Zahir had risked his life to come back for his commander. He easily could have escaped and left Razaq to die.

A tear ran down Razaq's face. Wali saw something change in his uncle's face. The old man who just wanted to live in peace was gone. The Taliban commander was back.

"Take me to the truck," Razaq said.

Zahir put Razaq's arm over his shoulder. The pair hobbled down the wadi away from the thump of the helicopter rotors. Just before they disappeared into the blackness, Razaq looked back at Wali.

Wali heard someone coming up behind him. He turned just as Charlie grabbed him and shoved him out of the way.

"Stay down," he said, his chest heaving.

Wali was shocked to see his old friend again. Charlie kicked Jan's AK-47 away from the general's body. Then he turned, leveled his rifle, and put his laser on the fighter's back.

"Let them go," Wali said.

Charlie took his eye off the target.

"What?"

"Let my uncle and his bodyguard go," Wali said. "He doesn't want to come to America anymore."

"Why?"

Wali really didn't know why. He just knew Razaq, like all of his family, would die in Afghanistan. For what, he wasn't sure. The only thing that was certain of was that Allah wanted him to fight.

"His place is here," Wali said.

CHAPTER 49

Felix stood with Lieutenant Colonel Kyle as the helicopter's rotors came to a lazy stop.

As the crew chief lowered the ramp, Felix climbed into a pickup truck and backed it up to the rear of the helicopter. The CIA team came off with Corona. Felix watched as they loaded it into the pickup's bed. He handed the men cold bottles of water as they climbed into the crew cab.

"Congrats on a good mission," he said as he climbed behind the wheel.

"Easy day," the tech said. "I had a chance to do a preliminary check while we waited for your friend to come back to the LZ."

"And?"

The tech took a sip of water.

"Inconclusive," he said. "But I still have my doubts."

Felix nodded.

"Got a cable from Langley," he said. "They want you to check it for safety and then load it up tonight. The plane is gassed and ready to go. You can do a better analysis back in the States."

The tech took another sip of water.

"You got our stuff?"

"It's all loaded up. You'll be home tomorrow."

"Cool," the tech said. "My kid has a baseball tournament this weekend."

Felix smiled. He'd been in Afghanistan too long. The idea of a baseball tournament felt alien. The idea of going to watch kids play baseball felt far away.

"What position does your kid play?"

"Pitcher," the tech said. "He's pitching this weekend. The wife will kill me if I miss another start."

"I hear you," Felix said. "Well, let's make sure you don't."

The tech stared out the window of the truck as the airfield passed by. Even this late at night it was busy. Cargo planes—military and contract—were parked on the tarmac. Supplies were loaded or unloaded. The steady pace of war.

Felix drove the truck into a hangar. The ground crew closed the door behind them.

Back on the tarmac, Kyle stood by the ramp shaking hands with the Afghans and Special Forces soldiers as they filed off the helicopter. Charlie was the last one.

"Chief," Kyle said, shaking his hand. "Congratulations on a good mission."

"Thank you, sir," Charlie said.

"Not bad for a final mission."

"No, sir, it's not."

"I spoke to JAG," Kyle said. "When you get back to Bragg, drop your packet. Take terminal leave and retire and no hard feelings. You tracking?"

Charlie smiled.

"Yes, sir."

Kyle shook his hand one more time.

"Air got you a flight on a bird leaving tonight," Kyle said. "We'll pack up your room and send it back on the next rotator."

Charlie didn't say anything. Kyle patted Charlie on the shoulder and headed to his truck. Charlie walked over to Wali and motioned toward a waiting truck that would take them to Camp Brown. Wali hadn't said anything since they left the wadi. The whole ride back,

Charlie kept playing the mission over in his head. They'd gotten the bomb. They'd brought Wali back. Razaq had made his own decision. It was a victory. But something felt hollow. The elation of a job well done wasn't there. Charlie wasn't done taking a gun to work. He'd be back, this time working for a defense contractor.

"Thanks for letting me tag along," Charlie said, shaking Jerry's hand. "You've got a great team. Be safe."

"Roger, Chief," Jerry said. "You boys need a ride?"

ೲೲೲ

The captain dropped Charlie and Wali off at Camp Brown. Charlie waved to the guard as the two men walked through the gate. Felix came out of the headquarters building just as they passed.

"Hey, boys," Felix said. "Just giving your boss an update."

"Ex-boss," Charlie said. "I'm headed out. My war is over."

Felix shook Charlie's hand.

"I heard. Safe travels home. You did good here."

Felix shook Wali's hand next.

"Sorry to hear about your uncle," he said.

Wali looked away.

"I am too," he said.

Felix patted him on the back.

"You did a good thing tonight," he said. "I know it sometimes doesn't feel that way. But not only did we get Corona, we got an AQ leader and captured a financier. My guys in Dubai say he's talking. We're getting good stuff."

Wali just nodded.

"The asylum offer is still on the table for you," Felix said. "Just let me know what you want to do."

Wali kept his gaze on his feet.

"Thank you," he said. "But I am going to stay. This is my country. My home."

"I can respect that," Felix said. "I'll keep that visa paperwork, just in case. Be safe. You have my number if you need anything."

Felix started to leave. Charlie stopped him.

"Hey, can I talk to you a minute?" Charlie asked.

"Sure," Felix said.

They walked over by the latrine. Charlie put his helmet on the ground and leaned his rifle against the wall. He needed to know whether his career had been sacrificed for a worthy cause.

"Is it real?"

Felix looked around. No one was paying attention to them. He leaned in closer to Charlie.

"We're not sure."

Charlie felt a flush of anger.

"Save the OGA bullshit. Just tell me I sacrificed my career for something."

Felix patted him on the shoulder.

"You did."

Charlie recoiled from Felix's touch.

"The fuck I did. Was it real? Did we stop them from getting a nuke?"

Felix watched a soldier walk past. The soldier didn't acknowledge them.

"We don't know," Felix said. "We only checked it for safety. It left twenty minutes ago for further tests."

"What the fuck does all that mean?"

"It means we're being careful. It means we're making sure we don't fuck it up."

Charlie had no patience for this. The whole war had become overly cautious. Just open the fucker up and see if it was a real bomb or not. His rage started to boil up. He never used to mind just being part of the machine. Now being a cog grated on him.

"I just have to know," Charlie said.

Felix let out a long sigh.

"Does it matter? It's not like we could let it go either way. We had to get it off the battlefield. Your op did that."

Charlie wasn't following.

"If it wasn't a bomb, we failed," Charlie said. "We sacrificed a lot to get a fake."

"I don't see it that way at all," Felix said. "Think back to the Soviets. We went all in to bleed them here in the eighties. When it was over, we left. We didn't act when bin Laden came here. We didn't act when the Taliban started rolling up the Northern Alliance. We didn't act until al-Qaeda killed thousands on 9/11.

"After that, we got up to our necks in it over here. We chased out the Taliban. Hunted down every AQ shitbird we found. We had a victory in sight, and then we went to Iraq. Now, we're trying to find that victory again here and there, and you and me both know it's getting damn hard. To me, the bomb was Afghanistan after 9/11. We had to go and get it. Fake or not, it doesn't matter. It had to be done. Now go home. Find some peace. Your war is over."

Charlie hung his head, resigned to his fate but still unhappy.

"I know," Charlie said. "But I'm not ready to stop fighting."

Felix thrust his hands into his pockets and took a few steps toward his truck.

"Hey, you get to spike the football," Felix said over his shoulder. "This was a victory, you know. When this is all through and we leave, most of us won't be able to say that."